Infinity.

Layne Harper

Cover Design: Michelle Preast
Edited by: Lauren McKellar
Formatting: Polgarus Studio

Other Books by Layne Harper:

Infinity Series Reading Order
Falling Into Infinity
From Now Until Infinity
Finding Infinity
Aiden's Broken Heart (Infinity Series Short Story)

Coming Soon …
The World: According to Rachael

Acknowledgements

Oh my! I feel like a celebrity who has just won an award. I'm going to forget to thank someone. So before I even begin, let me apologize to whomever I'm ignoring.

First of all, I need to thank my husband for his support. Wow! The man cooks (hot dogs and barbacoa), cleans, and can teach spelling words like a professional. He tolerates my lack of sleeping, doesn't complain when I beg for just five more minutes of peace in my office, and has the ability to calm me down when I'm freaking out about something inconsequential.

To you, my kids. The greatest honor of my life is being your mom. Seriously. I'm not sure what I did to deserve you, but I'm sure glad I did it. One day, when you're adults, I'll share these books with you. I hope you'll see that relationships are never a fifty/fifty deal. They're one hundred percent from both of you all the time. Sometimes, you'll have to give more than your partner. It's okay. Because if they're the right person for you, they'll return the favor the next time. Also, I hope you learn from Charlie and Colin that falling in love is the easy part. It's the staying together and making it work through the years that takes the commitment to do whatever is necessary. I love you with all of my heart.

To my beta readers, there aren't adequate words. You take what I think is good and make it so much better by challenging me. I love your snarky comments and eye rolls. I especially love your praise. You girls are the absolute best. Thank you for reading the same story three and four times and still contributing ways to make it better. I owe you much more than a few sentences at the beginning of the book. Thank you. Thank you. Thank you.

Finally, to the bloggers who've shared Colin and Charlie with their followers. Oh my gosh! I owe you all dessert first and an expensive bottle of wine. You took my bucket list item to publish their story and turned it into a career. Wow! There isn't a day that goes by that I don't feel overwhelmed by your generosity. Thank you from the bottom of my heart.

One last thing before I go … A year ago, I stood before my bathroom mirror and took inventory of my life. I acknowledged that I was a mom, wife, volunteer, and friend. I spent all day, every day, being something to everyone else, but asked the question, "What do I do for me?" The answer was nothing. My dream has always been to share my stories with you. I decided to hit publish on my first book. You connected with my characters and fell in love with them, faults and all, as much as I have. Thank you for supporting me. I now add author to the list of adjectives that describes who I am. That's really cool and all because of you.

Dedication:

Once upon a time, there was a girl with a dream. One day, she dared to speak the dream out loud, and her husband overheard. Since that moment, he's stood by her side, and hasn't let her quit – even when the going has gotten tough. This book is for him …

CONTENTS

Chapter One

Charlie

"Dammit, Brad. We're going to be late." I throw my head back against the tan leather headrest and look up through the glass of the moon roof in complete frustration.

"What would you like me to do? Even I don't have the power to part the sea of cars in front of us," Brad replies while he tap, tap, taps, his thumbs on the black leather steering wheel. My fingernails dig into my palms as I try to keep my temper under control. This's one of the habits that he's picked up driving the freeways of Dallas.

Leaning forward, I fumble through the radio stations, hoping for a traffic report. I've already checked Google Maps, which indicates that we should be going fifty miles per hour. Not so much. A turtle just lapped us.

Brad's driving is maddening, but there was no point in taking two cars so I'm stuck. Colin left in Big Bertha, his awesomely horrible truck that's painted Dallas Cowboy colors, two hours ago. However, I've quit complaining about Bertha. She earned Colin an endorsement deal with Ford. And he's fully clothed in the commercials. Score one for me.

Stuck in the car with Brad and his annoying habit. Stuck in traffic on one of the most important days of my life. Stuck behind a semi-truck so I can't even see why we're stuck.

I pull out my phone and text my oldest sister Chelsea.

Me: *Are you there yet?*

Chelsea: *Been here for 20.*

Me: *Stuck in traffic. We'll be there shortly. Freaking out. Don't want to miss the party.*

Chelsea: *How are you feeling?*

Me: *Fine. Anxious. Nervous we're going to miss it.*

Chelsea: *K. Be careful.*

I had been so stubborn last night and refused to stay at the hotel. Colin, or should I say, Jenny, has had the hotel rooms booked since December. If I'm honest with myself, and really admit it, I was feeling needy. Colin's schedule has been so crazy this season that we've been more like nomadic roommates than lovers. Last night was the first time in almost two weeks that we were both in our house.

In our bedroom.

Together.

Alone.

I chose to walk through the living room and into the kitchen nude, because I could. It was liberating.

You would have thought that we would've had a house full of people, but luckily Jenny, Colin's best assistant in the world, booked enough rooms so everyone could stay at the hotel. Chelsea is on a long-term assignment for work in downtown Dallas, so she just decided to stay at her apartment.

Finally, we inch by a fender bender that's been moved to the shoulder of the freeway. *Seriously, all of that traffic for nothing.* Damn rubberneckers!

"Floor it, Jeeves!" I instruct Brad as my knee bounces up and down.

Even though he's looking ahead, I can see him roll his eyes out of my peripheral vision. "Colin will kick my sorry behind if I let something happen to you. No. I'll drive the speed limit, thank you very much Doctor Collins."

Brad's Range Rover - compliments of Colin - was part of his negotiations for moving to Dallas. I told Colin that Brad was just being a brat, and he'd move here without a car thrown in to sweeten the pot. Colin insisted on buying Brad the car. I know it's because he wants me riding in what he believes is the safest car on the road, and not my cute, little two-seater Mercedes. There are times that I fight him, and there are times that I just let Colin be Colin. Brad getting a new car was one of those times.

Brad uses the steering wheel radio controls to change the music. "Let's listen to some Fall Out Boy, shall we?"

"I don't care," I reply, trying to stay calm.

The clock on the dashboard is mocking me. As I watch the red numbers change, I want to scream, "I get it. I know that I'm freaking late!"

Finally, Brad takes the exit for downtown Dallas. I want to kiss him in a very platonic, thank you way.

"Alright, missy. I'm going to drop you off in the parking garage of the hotel. Carter and Miguel should be waiting for you. I'll see you up in the room."

Sure enough, I see my two gigantic, no-necked bodyguards waiting for me. Carter smiles bashfully and waves at Brad as we pull up to the garage elevators. Carter is still one of the most gorgeous men I've seen. He looks like he's been carved out of dark chocolate.

Brad and Carter are an interesting couple. Physically, they couldn't be more different, yet they have so many similar interests. I love how cute they are together.

Miguel gives me a courtesy nod. I've made it my life's goal to loosen him up a bit. I've tried getting him drunk. He doesn't drink. I've tried forcing Miguel to watch a funny movie with me. He never relaxed. I've decided to table my efforts until after this is over. I bet I can get Colin to help me think of a way to make him laugh.

Carter moves around to Brad's trunk and unloads my bags. It's not a lot, but God forbid that I might carry something heavier than my purse. Carter's the pack mule, and Miguel flanks me on my right side. I'm quickly whisked into the hotel's service elevator and taken to the third floor.

I'm not sure if they're attempting to keep me hidden, or if they're actually concerned for my safety. I've really quit caring. As Colin would say,

"I've added it to my list of stuff that I don't give a fuck about." Apparently, security is now a part of my life. At least, I'm comfortable with these guys.

We quickly walk down the beige-striped hotel hallway with green-fern-print carpet. I've always wondered if there's a hotel-decorating store, maybe Hotels 'R Us, where they sell crazy hotel hallway carpet. I've never been into a carpet store and seen the wild prints on a display sample. Now, I'm super curious. I make a mental note to Google hotel carpet when I have a free moment.

Miguel stops in front of a door that's about midway down the hall. He knocks twice and then slides his key-card into the lock. When the green light shines he opens the door, allowing me to enter first.

There they are: my girls! I squeal with excitement. Janis is the first to greet me. She throws her arms around my neck, and gives me a big kiss on my cheek. "You look gorgeous, Caroline. You're simply glowing."

Giggling because I do feel beautiful, and now that we're here I also feel more relaxed. "Thanks. You're too kind. Where's Clay and company?"

"They're two rooms over. You know Colin rented out the whole floor," she says with an exaggerated headshake. Janis South is an exotic beauty. How the woman has had four kids and looks this good is beyond me. She has her coal-black hair pulled back in a simple bun with two gold chopsticks crisscrossed through the center. I'm not even sure that she wears makeup. She doesn't need to. Janis has got to be in her late thirties or early forties, but she still looks like she could rock a high-fashion runway. On top of her beauty, she's one of the nicest people I know. Her friendship became precious to me as she helped mentor me through the perils of living with one of the most famous athletes on the planet. I've learned that there aren't too many of us in this elite club. Janis could write a best-selling tell-all on what it's like to live with one of the world's most famous men. Her marriage to Clay is a great example of making it work.

"Hey, Miss Marley," I say. She runs to me and throws her arms around my thighs. That child may wind up better looking than her mother. With her large brown eyes and killer smile, Colin and Clay are going to have to scare some sense into the boys who want to date her.

"Auntie Charlie, my daddy says that I have to go easy on Uncle Colin because he's gettin' old." Kids kill me. Just when you think you know what's going to come out of their mouths, you get something like that.

Janis flashes Marley a look, and Marley gets the picture. She gives me another squeeze and then skips off to rejoin her tea party on one of the full-sized beds with her Just Like Me American Girl Doll. That really does look just like her. Marley could care less about today's festivities.

Carter steps past me and places my bags on the other full-sized bed in the room. Jenny darts over to his side and begins unpacking their contents. We've developed a comfortable truce. We both agree that we adore Colin and will protect him above all else, but our relationship has not always been that simple. Colin's fortyish, multi-colored-haired assistant can be a bit to take in. No one will argue that Jenny's a master at her job. The woman knows when to drip honey and when to spew vinegar to achieve her goals. She doesn't mince words, and missed the whole southern etiquette class.

Soon after I moved in with Colin, it became apparent that Jenny needed an office somewhere other than our home. She was used to being in charge of all aspects of Colin's life. I was willing to let her run his professional life and keep his work calendar, but our private life was ours. That meant that if Colin and I wanted to sleep in until ten o'clock, I didn't want Jenny sitting at my kitchen table when I strolled in to fix a cup of coffee. It also irritated me that Jenny knew my house and my man's life better than I did.

After some heartfelt tears and reasoning with Colin, he got the message. Colin rented office space about half a mile from our home. It's in a professional building. He has his own office and private bathroom. There's a conference room for meetings and, most importantly, there's enough wall space to hang Colin's football memorabilia, as well as a super-deep storage closet. We're both much happier.

"Caroline, you forgot to bring Colin's champagne," Jenny says in her brusque manner.

"No I didn't. It must still be in Brad's car."

Then, like the ninja that Jenny is, she whips out her smart phone and expertly hits Brad's number, which is saved in her favorites list. "Bring up

Colin's champagne." One sentence only, and she doesn't wait for his response. Brad and I will have a field day making fun of her the next time we're alone.

Chelsea and Liza are on the balcony drinking what look to be mimosas. Checking my watch—which matches Colin's—I note that it's 10:30. I guess my girls are starting early.

The parade is supposed to pass by our hotel in fifteen minutes. I rush over to my bag and grab the camera that Colin bought me for Christmas and quickly snap a picture of Marley playing dolls. Colin will get a kick out of it. Then I point my lens at Chelsea, Liza, and Janis (who now has a drink in her hand) and yell for them to cheers while I take a couple of shots. Even Jenny plays along, flashing me a forced grin, when I aim my camera at her. Her hair is a lovely shade of Dallas Cowboy's blue right now. It's fabulous.

Next, I catch Brad as he walks into the hotel room, holding two bottles of sparkling cider. Brad's embraced the glasses trend, and is sporting a rather attractive pair of fake lenses. He stops when he sees my camera and strikes a male model pose straight out of a high-end fashion magazine.

Then, he grabs my camera and turns it on me. I throw my arms up in the air in a very silly dance move. He snaps away while I make funny faces.

When he realizes I'm still in my street clothes, he cocks an eyebrow and drops his chin to his chest as he hands me back my camera. "Do you plan on staying in faded jeans and a sweater?" He checks his watch. "You know the festivities are about to begin."

"Nope. I'm just about to change. You know me. I like making you sweat," I reply with a wink. He rolls his eyes and mutters that I'll be the death of him.

My camera goes back into its protective case, and I place it carefully in the tote that I brought with me. As I'm slipping into the hotel's bathroom Chelsea yells, "Let me know if you need some help."

Brad quickly admonishes Chelsea. "That's my job, sister friend."

I close the door to block out their bickering. Brad's truly become the brother that we all missed out on. He's the best kind of brother, though.

One day we'll be lucky enough to get a brother-in-law instead of a sister-in-law that will just have to fit in with the Collins' ladies.

I unzip the dress bag and stare at the garment inside. How did I let Brad talk me into this? It's really hideous. All I want to do is stay in my comfy jeans, but Brad convinced me that Colin would love it. Sometimes, I need to trust my gut instincts instead of listening to my flamboyantly gay assistant.

I slip off my rose-colored wool sweater and faded jeans, and then haphazardly stuff them in my black tote bag. Next, I remove my chocolate-brown Ugg boots that have been my uniform for the last couple of months and replace them with my cowboy boots. They're literally Cowboy boots. Some famous boot designer made them just for me. The tops are Dallas Cowboy blue with a white star, and Colin's football number—eight—displayed artistically. The bottoms are cinnamon-brown leather. It was a very kind gesture, but they're just not my style. Brad pointed out that this is the perfect occasion for me to wear them. He's right, as usual.

Finally, I slide the dress on over my head and shimmy it down, making sure that my backside is covered. There are women that would kill for this dress. Unfortunately, I'm not one of them. Turning to look in the full-length mirror, I roll my eyes. I'm the picture of a fangirl.

I can almost hear out loud the music that's playing in my head. Wonk … wonk … wonk …

Cautiously, I make my way towards the balcony where everyone has congregated—even Marley. She spots me first. "Ohhhhhh Auntie Charlie. You look silly." Out of the mouths of babes …

Then, the rest of the girls and Brad turn around and inspect me. "It could be worse," Liza offers. My stylist friend, Liza, created this work of art for me.

I spin around on my boot heels and head back towards the bathroom. "I'm changing," I announce to the group.

Lots of "no's" and "don't do it" and "you look great" fill the air.

Then, I hear Jenny's voice above the rest, "Colin will love it."

That stops me. For some reason, hearing Jenny's opinion means more to me than the rest of the gangs'. Sometimes her constant honesty is refreshing.

I turn back around and step out on the balcony. *I'm doing this for Colin. I'm doing this for Colin.* Janis pulls me into a sideways hug. "I have to say, Caroline, that this is one bet that I'm sure you don't mind losing."

She's right. Colin told me once that he'd walk through fire for me. Apparently, I love him enough to wear Dallas Cowboy boots and his jersey made into a dress on one of the most important days of his life.

The streets of Downtown are packed with people. I mean, packed like sardines in a can. It's been about thirty-six hours since Colin and the boys brought the Vince Lombardi Trophy home to Dallas, and the metroplex is buzzing with excitement. I'm sure that some of these people are still drunk from Sunday.

Chelsea chimes in, "Can you believe the mayor declared today a holiday?"

Jenny adds, "I've heard they're expecting over a million people to either watch the parade on TV or line the streets. It's not like any work has gotten done in the last couple of days anyway."

The parade will pass under our balcony and end at a ginormous stage that's been set up near our hotel. Some famous local bands will play music. Then the team owner, head coach, Colin, and a few of the other players will address the crowd.

Because Big Bertha has become the unofficial mascot for the team, Colin will be riding in the bed of the truck, showing off his MVP trophy. Some poor police officer has been tasked to drive her. Colin worried last night that she might break down, which is a very legitimate concern. He seems to be the only one that the old girl will start for these days. We laughed about her stalling in the middle of the parade, and him having to jump out of the bed of the truck to lay his magic hands on her. He reassured me that the two of them would have a nice chat on the way into town this morning. As a precaution, his mechanic will be riding shotgun.

Colin winning the Super Bowl was the culmination of his Hall of Fame career. I was thrilled that I could be there and share the moment with him. Realizing my own goals has been such a sense of personal accomplishment. Having the opportunity to watch the man that I'm madly in love with make his dream come true had been one of the greatest moments of my life.

Liza leans over and pretend-whispers, "The dress wouldn't look nearly as bad if you didn't have that gigantic belly in the way."

I look down at my stomach. It's been a long time since I've seen my feet without leaning over. I tease her back. "I don't think that it has anything to do with my stomach, and everything to do with the dress designer."

She gently pushes me and laughs. "You look good. I stand by my statement. You're simply a snake that swallowed a basketball."

Janis chimes in and agrees. "I gained almost seventy-five pounds with Marley. Beached whales were cuter than me. And trust me, I let Clay know every single day just how miserable I was." She laughs at the memory. "You look awesome, Caroline."

"Auntie Charlie, I think you should name the baby Marley. It's the perfect name for a boy or a girl." She's beaming.

"Well, sweet pea, we're going to have to discuss that with Uncle Colin. He still wants Bertha for a girl and Bert for a boy," I tease. Colin and I are not finding out the sex of our baby, which has led to many spirited arguments over names. As of right now, we aren't even in the same baby-naming book, let alone agreed on anything.

"She's naming the baby Brad if it's a boy, and Brandy if it's a girl. Everyone knows this." Brad offers his two cents with his know-it-all wink and a raised champagne glass.

Then out of nowhere, Jenny says, "Fuck off, Brad. If it's a boy, it can be Brad. If it's a girl, it's Jennifer." Jenny cares about the baby's name? That's a new one. Colin's assistant is full of surprises.

"Geez, Jenny," I reprimand. "Not in front of Marley." Fortunately, Clay has a mouth that makes sailors blush, so it's nothing that she hasn't heard before. But still, I don't want Jenny teaching my child dirty words. That's, at the very least, her daddy's job.

"Argue later, kids. We've still got at least two weeks before he or she is here." I laugh at my crew. If you'd have told me a couple of years ago that Liza, who was angry I wasn't Sasha the first time I met her, Janis, who only knew that I broke Colin's heart, Chelsea, the most selfish self-centered person in the universe, Brad my overly gay assistant, and Jenny, who's a hornet's nest would be my support system and the ones that I chose to share in this moment with Colin and I, I would've said you were mental. Yet, here we are. One big dysfunctional family.

Brad goes inside to find a chair for me so I can sit down. I'm still performing surgeries which requires I stand for sometimes up to five hours straight, but it's become very obvious in the last couple of days that I'm going to have to take leave. I can feel my feet swelling in these boots. I say a silent prayer in hope that I can get them off after Colin has seen me.

I glance down the row of balconies on the front of the hotel and see a lot of people that I know. Colin invited the players' wives, girlfriends, and families to watch the parade from our hotel rooms. Colin's parents are on the balcony next to us with a group of their friends from Colin's hometown. I catch his mom's eye and wave. I'm still not her favorite person.

She hated Colin and I living together, but there was much more to it, I've since found out. Susan blames me for Colin's first marriage, and the disaster that it was. If she only knew about the prescription pills and overdose. Not even her first grandchild would get me back in her good graces.

Colin's dad is much friendlier, and smiles. I walk over to the edge of the balcony and lean across the railing to give him a hug.

"How's my grandkid?"

"Growing and moving like his daddy," I reply with a smile as I stroke my hand over my taut stomach.

"It's got to be boy. Colin was so active. Susan would have to push him back to remind him to be gentle," John says, getting a little glassy-eyed as he reminisces about his only child.

As if on cue, Baby McKinney gives me a firm kick to the ribs. I wince, and rub my side. Then, I feel a tightness spreading across my abdomen— one of the many Braxton Hicks contractions that have plagued me for the last month. I almost didn't make it to Miami for the Super Bowl. I thought these were labor contractions, and spent a night in the hospital before I was assured that everything was fine and sent home.

Poor Colin was beside himself. He was already in Miami doing all the pregame press. I wouldn't let him fly home until we knew if this was indeed show time. Brad was my rock, holding my hand and keeping Colin updated. Fortunately, Doctor Starr got on the phone with Colin and explained that Braxton Hicks contractions are nature's way of preparing the body for labor, and I was perfectly fine. Just to be on the safe side, she chose me an obstetrician in Miami and forwarded him a copy of my medical file.

Colin rented me a private plane to travel to Miami so I could stay lying down, and so our family could travel together. Between my overzealous assistant, who's also an RN, and Colin's mother, I thought that I might toss them or myself out of it. She kept telling me about her pregnancy with Colin, and Brad tried to time contractions that weren't really contractions. I love them both—dearly, but I wanted to scream *Have you all forgotten that I'm a doctor?*

On the other balcony to my left is Colin's management team. After Colin fired Mark, he hired Aiden to be his business attorney and manager. So far, it's worked out well, with Colin just using Mark on a case-by-case basis, like the whole walking out of the ESPY-Awards fiasco. We haven't needed a full-time public relations person because Jenny can reply, "Mr. McKinney and Doctor Collins do not comment on their private life" just fine. Colin has gone so far as to refuse to confirm the pregnancy, or that we're even married. After many discussions and bamboozlement— according to Colin—he finally agreed that me keeping my maiden name in the professional world was a great idea. Okay. Maybe not a great idea, but it was an idea that we could both live with.

One reporter asked him after a game how I was feeling. His reply was, "I don't comment on my private life." The reporter pushed on and said, "I saw your wife. She looks ready to pop." What was Colin's answer? "I'm sure Doctor Collins will be amused to know that the media thinks that she looks fat in her pants." I felt sorry for the reporter. Even though I was about seven months and clearly looked pregnant, the guy had a horrified expression on his face.

Aiden's balcony is filled with other clients that his firm represents, and some junior attorneys. Mark notices me and gives me a slight wave.

Rachael is off doing what Rachael does best; becoming the ruler of the known world. My best friend is a piece of work who's only gotten more awesome as the years have gone by.

Aiden motions for me to come over so I walk to the other end of our balcony. "How ya doin'?"

I smile. "I'm hanging in there. I just wish the kid would quit kicking me, and these damn contractions would stop."

Aiden's eyes grow wide with worry. "I'm okay. They're just pretend contractions, but damn they hurt." I smile reassuringly at him trying to communicate that I am okay.

It must work, because he changes the subject. "How was the douchebag this morning?"

Their terms of endearment for each other no longer faze me. "Quiet. Reflective. He's ready for the parade to be over, and everyone to leave town. He begged me to stay in bed all day with him tomorrow."

"Are you?"

"Yes. But, I told him I had to go to the hospital to check on patients," I say with a wink. "I can't let him have his way that easily."

Aiden laughs and shakes his head.

God. Another Braxton Hicks contraction hits me, and it takes all of my strength to not double over. I wince, grab on to the balcony railing, and clench my jaw, waiting for it to pass.

"You okay, Caroline?" Aiden asks.

"Yeah. I just need to sit down," I reply as I gingerly walk to the chair that Brad brought out for me.

The crowd erupts in loud cheers as the first of the police cars, with sirens blaring, come into sight, announcing that the parade will be here shortly.

Marley claps her hands and excitedly rushes to the balcony railing for a better view. Janis put her hair in two ponytails that look like pompoms. She's wearing Colin's jersey. Cute is an understatement. She's precious!

Colin and Big Bertha are at the rear of the parade so I settle in knowing that it's going to be awhile. Brad brings me a glass of water that I slowly begin sipping.

As the first fire truck passes us, an odd feeling washes over me. Not bad. Just odd. There's no better way to explain it. I take another sip of water, hoping that it'll help settle me. I reach up and touch my infinity necklace that Colin gave me the day after we reconciled in Los Angeles. The infinity symbol is an eight, which is Colin's football number, turned on its side. The necklace has remained on my neck without being removed since that day. It's my talisman, and brings me unbelievable reassurance. I need that right now.

Then, another Braxton Hicks contraction hits me. It literally takes my breath away. I grasp my stomach, saying a silent prayer that my muscles will relax quickly. I try to mask how intense it is, but Janis catches the grimace on my face. "You okay?"

"These practice contractions," I say putting air parenthesis around practice, "are killing me today."

"You sure they're practice?"

"Yeah. I was examined yesterday when we arrived home from Miami. I'm not even dilated," I reply through my grimace.

Our conversation is cut short when a high school marching-band drowns out our voices. Next, the first float of players pass under us, and confetti rains from the sky. Our balconies go crazy, yelling and waving at the boys. When they spot so many friendly faces in one place they begin acting extra silly. There are huge smiles, and lots of whoops and cheers and

13

waves. A couple of the players spot me in my promised garb, and point and smile. It makes this ridiculous get-up worth it.

This is so amazing. The roar of the crowd is deafening. Colin and the boys have made this crowd—hell, this city—go this crazy. I love it. My heart floods with pride for my man.

Almost simultaneously, another contraction hits me, and makes it impossible for my lungs to expand. I put my head between my knees and beg the pain to let up.

Then it dawns on me. I know what this is. My previous Braxton Hicks contractions never felt like this. This is the early stage of labor. *Oh, God! I can't have this baby yet. Its daddy is in the bed of his truck in the middle of a parade.* I have a mental talk with my body and this baby. I'm not leaving the parade early. My husband will see me in this ugly-ass number-eight Dallas Cowboy's jersey dress that I promised to wear as part of our marriage vows. He will see me clapping and cheering for him. He'll know I'm here, and I'm fine, because he's not leaving his victory parade early for me or for this baby.

I also reason that I'm a first-time mom, and our labor will take a notoriously long time. I'm fine.

I stand up when I see Big Bertha in the distance, and mentally say a thank-you prayer to God for not letting her break down. She's still chugging along, polluting the environment with everything that she's got.

The crowd noise reaches a deafening pitch, making my ears ring as Colin and the old girl pass by them. I can barely see my husband through all the confetti, turning and waving to his adoring public. I know exactly when he spots the hotel though, because he begins to ignore the crowd and search for me. He holds a hand up to his forehead, blocking out the sun as he scans the balconies. I watch his gorgeous wavy dark-blonde hair catch the light. He takes my breath away. *See, baby? That's your daddy. The one that everyone is yelling for.* I make it easy on him, and stand up waving both of my arms like a raving lunatic.

When his sparkling green eyes spot me, he points in my direction, or should I say at my dress, and gives me a thumbs up. His gorgeous half-smile, which is all mine, cocks his right cheek up. Wearing the dress and boots were worth it. Seeing the happiness on his face floods me with love. I touch my infinity necklace hoping that he gets my hidden message that I love him.

He places his left hand over his heart showing me the engagement/wedding ring with our secret meaning.

I want to scream to the world, "See that man right there? He loves me. Colin fucking McKinney is in love with me." What an amazing feeling.

Just then, another contraction hits me. It takes everything in my power to not double over, but I don't. By God, I'll give him no reason to question if I'm okay.

I force a smile on my face and cup my belly, which makes his smile even larger, if that's possible. Next he points and waves at his parents, and then he finds Aiden and very discreetly flips him off while he pretends to scratch his nose.

Once Big Bertha has passed us, I sit back down, so grateful for the chair. I decide to time my contractions and see how far apart they are. The bands are going to play while the players get unloaded from the floats and make their way to the stage. Colin is going to be one of the last to speak. He hasn't let me read his speech, and I'm dying to hear it.

Another contraction hits me as I suck in a huge gulp of air and squint my eyes. My muscles begin to relax as the tightness in my abdomen loosens up.

Chelsea stares at me with wide eyes. "What's up? You look green."

"Thanks," I reply tartly. "You need to pluck your eyebrows." Fortunately, my sister's vain enough to worry about her unibrow and forget about me for a few minutes.

I settle back in my chair and note the time. Just when I've convinced myself that I was wrong and these are just Braxton Hicks contractions, it hits me—a contraction mixed with the worse stomach cramp that I've ever felt. I stand up and make my way towards the hotel room's bathroom. I need a moment of privacy, because there is definitely something going on that's making me feel funny.

I'm waddling as fast as I can when I feel a pop. Seconds later, a huge gush of water begins flowing out of me, soaking the carpet, my boots, and well, everything. There's no sticking my head in the sand any longer. My bag of amniotic fluid just broke. I'm having our baby in the next twenty-four hours, celebration party or not.

I stand there like a moron.

In residency, I had to do a rotation in labor and delivery. I've watched women's water break, and I've had to break the bag of fluid myself. I know scientifically what's going on. However, that doesn't diminish my panic one bit.

"Brad," I scream, but he can't hear me over the crowd noise. I'm paralyzed, and scared to death. I keep staring down at my soaked dress, boots, and the green-fern carpet. I want Colin. He'd have picked me up and carried me to the car by now. We'd be on the way to the hospital while I was yelling at him to slow down. Then, I'd be repeating my mantra: first-time mother's babies are notoriously slow. It'll probably be tomorrow before the child comes.

Instead, another contraction hits me, and I reach out for the chest of drawers next to me to steady myself. Once I can breathe again, I yell louder for Brad. When his auburn hair turns, and I see his face, I want to cry. I instantly know that he'll take care of me. He'll know what to do.

Brad comes rushing to me with his eyes bugging out of his head. When he's close enough to hear me, I burst into tears. "My water broke."

Brad immediately goes into nurse mode. He grabs his phone and calls my doctor who Colin made him put in his favorite's list. While the phone is ringing he yells for Jenny, which causes everyone to turn around.

Jenny and the rest of the gang immediately recognize what has just happened. Janis ushers Marley past me and out of the room while she keeps asking what's wrong with Auntie Charlie. Liza takes my hand, unparalyzing me, and leads me to the bathroom. "It's okay, Caroline," she says over and over as she helps me walk. "You're going to be just fine."

Jenny rushes ahead of us and grabs some towels out of the bathroom to throw over my mess, while Chelsea claps and squeals, "We're having a baby."

I put the lid down on the toilet seat and begin removing my soiled clothes while my dear friend Liza helps me out of my soaked boots. I can't believe this is happening. My friend is touching my amniotic-soaked clothing. This is so humiliating.

She must read my face because she says, "I've removed puke and come-drenched jeans from rockers. I've had to cut clients out of leather pants that they've worn eight days straight without even bothering to take a shower. It's a hazard of my profession." She shrugs. "At least this is sanitary." And just for that fantastic answer, if this baby is a girl, she'll be named after Liza.

I'm sitting on the toilet lid in only my skin-colored maternity bra that supports my now huge hormone-induced triple Ds when Jenny, Brad, Chelsea, and Janis join us. Fortunately my giant protruding stomach hides my girl parts, so there's really nothing to see other than a semi-nude pregnant chick, but I still lean forward just to give myself an ounce more dignity, and grab for an unused hand towel nearby. Now, at least I feel like I'm attempting to be modest.

Liza pulls out the clothes that I had stuffed into my tote. I wish that I had folded them nicely. She hands me my creased sweater first. I slip it over my head, so grateful for something soft against my hyperaware skin.

"Doctor Starr's going to meet us at the hospital. I've called Carter and Miguel. They're bringing the car into the parking garage. She said that there's no need to rush because first-time mother's babies are notoriously slow," Brad informs me. Somehow, hearing him say the words that I've been saying in my head out loud gives me much more reassurance. I also like that he said the word *notorious*. Yes. They're notoriously slow.

Jenny looks at me and says, "You want to call him, or you want me to do it?"

"No one's calling Colin, yet. As a medical doctor and Doctor Starr just confirmed, first-time mother's babies are notoriously slow." I reinforce *notoriously.* "After Colin makes his speech, then you can tell him." I say looking all of them in their eyes—especially Jenny.

In the almost two years that I've known her, I didn't think that it was possible to shock her. However, I just did. "You're not telling Colin, Caroline?" she says, shaking her Cowboy-blue hair as her eyes grow wide. She reaches out and grabs the doorjamb as if she needs the support.

"That's what I said." I really wish that I could stand so I could be in more of a position of power, but my unwaxed bits might cause Brad to pass out. "Colin will make it in plenty of time. We're fine."

Jenny bends so we're on eye level, and begins talking to me as if I'm an errant child. "If you have that baby and Colin's not there, he'll never forgive you, Caroline. I mean, like, resent you his whole life. All that man's wanted since I started working for him was to be a dad. Don't deny him his moment."

Talk about a knife to the heart. "Fine. Let me clean myself up. In private," I add, "and I'll think about it."

Another contraction hits as the last person shuts the bathroom door. The pain is so intense that it makes me nauseous. I fly to my feet quicker than I thought possible, and turn around just in time to throw open the toilet lid. There's a part of me that believes that my upset stomach has more to do with my decision not to tell Colin than my labor contraction. My nerves are shot. I don't want to pull Colin away from one of the most important events in his life to sit at my bedside for another eighteen hours while I'm in labor. On the other hand, Jenny's right. If Colin's not there for the birth of his child, it'll kill him.

After the contraction releases, I stand up, bracing myself against the sink counter while I rinse my mouth out. I take a long stare at myself in the mirror. This was not part of our perfect birth plan. The perfect birth plan states that I should go into labor after all the hoopla of the Super Bowl has settled down. Colin and I'll drive to the hospital together while we listen to George Strait, and other music that we mutually can agree on. My hospital bag, which is at home, has been packed since last week. It's got a beautiful pair of pajamas for me to put on after the baby's born, and both a blue and pink blanket. There's also a coming-home outfit in both colors. I'm going to attempt natural, drug-free childbirth until Colin can't take my agony any longer and then, and only then, will I allow drugs. It dawns on me. I don't even have a baby car-seat, for God's sake.

Yet, here I stand, wetting a towel to wipe amniotic fluid off my legs while my mouth tastes like ass because I vomited up my breakfast while trying to decide if I tell the baby-daddy that he's about to be a father.

I look down at my stomach and have a heart-to-heart with Baby McKinney. "Look, kid. I know that your mom and dad have passed on the unconventional, warp-speed relationship genes. It was a risk we took when we conceived you, but there's not been a baby on this earth as wanted as you. You've got to stay put for a little while longer, because your daddy will murder your mommy if you're born before he gets there." In middle of my little speech I have another contraction. It's almost as if this kid already has my personality.

Once it's passed, I continue to give this baby a pep talk. "You can do it, kid. Make me as miserable as you want, but you're not coming until your daddy's in the room."

I know Rachael would tell me to, "put your big girl panties on." I would, except my only pair is sopping wet. My contractions are far enough apart to wait to tell Colin. That's my decision and I'm sure of it.

Maybe.

When I step out of the bathroom, now completely dressed in my wrinkled clothing, everyone is staring at me like I'm going to break. "I'm fine. I've timed my contractions and this baby isn't coming anytime soon. Jenny, please let me know as soon as Colin's done speaking. I'll call him, and tell him that I'm in labor. Don't let him drive Bertha. In fact, don't let him drive at all. You bring him to the hospital. The last thing that I need is for him to get in a car accident trying to reach me." Everyone gives me a nervous giggle, but the dilated eyes and gaping mouths say that I am crazed pregnant lady.

Jenny chimes in first. "You're seriously asking me to drive that fucking maniac when he finds out you're in labor to the hospital?" She throws her hands up in the air and backs away from me, shaking her head. "Ask Aiden."

I roll my eyes, but I can't reply just yet as another contraction doubles me over. Thank God I don't vomit. I really can't take listening to Brad fret about me getting sick in his precious car.

Once the contraction has passed, I look at Jenny and state, "When he's out-of-control angry, remind him it was my call. I'll stay on the phone with him the whole drive. He'll be fine." I cross my fingers behind my back, because we all know that he's going to lose his mind when I tell him. But this is for the best. Colin gets to have his cake, and eat it too. He'll have his moment in front of his fans, and arrive in time to meet his child. He'll just miss the boring waiting part of labor.

Brad has my purse, phone, and tote bag, the latter of which is slung over his shoulder. "All right, best doctor-friend. Let's go meet Baby McKinney."

With that, I give everyone a hug and listen to the *congratulations* and *good lucks*. As I'm walking out the hotel door, I turn around and address the group, remembering I forgot the most important part. "Look, guys. You can't tell anyone about what's going on. That means don't breathe a word to Colin's parents, Aiden, or anyone else. He deserves to hear this news from me first. Okay?"

The group nods their heads in a collective understanding. I pray that they'll keep their word, or the State of Texas might be raising Baby McKinney.

Carter is waiting for us in Brad's Range Rover. Miguel sits in the passenger seat while Brad and I crawl into the back. We take the back exit out of the hotel's parking garage. Traffic is at a standstill. I let out a frustrated sigh. I forgot that Downtown had been closed for the victory parade.

Just as I'm about to panic in epic fashion, another contraction doubles me over. I grip the door handle and clutch my stomach. This is excruciating. There's no way on God's green earth that I'm doing natural childbirth. As soon as I get to the hospital, I want an epidural—STAT!

"Brad, call Doctor Starr and tell her that I want an epidural waiting for me. Tell her we're stuck in Downtown traffic, and my contractions are regular and seven minutes apart. Get her opinion on not telling Colin," I bark.

Brad quickly does as I ask, and I listen to a lot of his one-word answers or agreements. When he hangs up, he says, "She thinks that you're fine waiting to tell Colin. You can get an epidural as long as you're far enough along. She's at the hospital, and is waiting for you."

I look outside the windows of the car, and see nothing but people. We're not moving. This might as well be Armageddon.

Chapter Two

Charlie

Seven months earlier…

"Bartender, another round," Rachael slurs.

Juan Carlo's beautiful, full lips spread into a sexy little smirk. "*Mis Amores,* do you really think another round is a good idea?" he asks in his broken English. He shakes his head, and begins mixing us our drinks before he hears the answer to his question.

Rachael laughs. "It's our last day in Cabo. We're not giving in until the sun comes up."

Rachael and I've been in Cabo for the last three days. She happened to call when I'd started my period—again. She and Aiden were having issues, and on top of that, she'd been worked to her breaking point. We decided that we needed a girl's trip, just some time to decompress, relax, and reconnect again. Two days later, I met her at the airport in Cabo.

It's almost embarrassing to admit, but this has been the longest that I've been away from Colin since the week we spent separated between our reunion in Los Angeles and him coming to stay with me in Houston. I've missed him terribly, but Rachael and I needed this vacation together.

We've grown apart since Colin and I married. I think that I depend on him now for things that I used to only need from Rachael. Also, our fertility problems have been like an albatross around our necks. No one knows. Colin feels like this is a very personal issue, and not something that we should broadcast to our family. I believe there is something in his head that makes him feel like less of a man because I'm not pregnant. It's not like he can help having Celiac Disease. Not sharing such a huge part of our lives has been difficult; however, I've respected Colin's wishes to keep it just between us.

This trip has been a chance for Rachael and me to find our groove again. The first two days we were here, Rachael was still in work mode. Her phone was glued to her ear, putting out mini fires. Finally, this morning, she turned it off. "Today's our last day in paradise, and I'm off the clock."

We carry our drinks to the sun-loungers near the pool. The more I drink, the looser my lips become. I think they're finally nimble enough to ask the million-dollar question. "So, Rach, what happened between you and Aiden?"

She looks around to ensure that there are no prying ears. Juan Carlo is on the other side of the bar and we have no else around us so Rachael asks, "You really want to know?"

I sit up and turn towards her, adjusting the back of my sun-lounger so I'm more upright and wiggle backwards getting comfortable. I have a feeling that I might finally be getting the story. "I do. I've tried to stay out of your relationship. Colin tells me nothing that Aiden says. I'm truly in the dark."

The scene in front of us is picturesque. The blue of the infinity pool is matched only by the clear, azure ocean-water, lapping up on the almost powder-white sand. There aren't many guests sunbathing or even swimming, for that matter. Colin booked us at a very exclusive hotel in their more private section of rooms. I get the feeling that this block of rooms and pool is reserved for honeymooners and rich people stepping out on their spouse, not a best-friend vacation. Still, neither one of us were complaining. Picking up men was the last thing that we wanted to do on this trip.

Rachael's face turns into a violent, twisted sea of emotions. I reach over and grab her hand giving it a reassuring squeeze. "Talk to me, Rach. I'm your best friend."

She picks up her drink from the plastic table between us and slams it down her throat. "If we're getting into touchy subjects, we need tequila." She motions toward our bartender and calls, "Juan Carlo, bring us a bottle of Don Julio, stat."

Poor Juan Carlo raises his eyebrows at my tiny friend. I smile at him. *It's okay, we're staying in tonight*, I mouth. "A bottle and two shot glasses please," I reply out loud.

Rachael and I've done this many times before. I think our tequila tradition started when I was at Harvard and her at Wharton. Although, it's our first bottle on this trip, the tequila has been a long time coming. My clean living for the past year is out the window this vacation. I must admit that it feels awesome to just let loose, and eat and drink whatever I want. Tomorrow, I know that my fun is over. I have an appointment with Doctor Starr next week to begin the infertility journey. I'm living it up for my last twenty-four hours of dietary freedom.

I turn to the waiter who has been hanging out near the bar. "Can we get a bowl of guacamole, chips, and some salsa?" He nods his head, and looks very relieved that I ordered food.

Once we're two shots of tequila in, Rachael rolls to her side and says, "Aiden asked me to marry him." Her face is blank, so I can't read what my response should be. But, I'm shocked; I really have been clueless about the two of them.

She pauses and lets her news settle in. I can feel my jaw dropping. This was not the revelation that I was expecting.

"Not once, but multiple times. I've told him no each time, and now he will not take my calls."

"Wh … Why …?" I stammer, sounding like a complete loser. "Why did you tell him no?" What I really want to ask is if it is because he's black. This was Aiden's big revelation around Christmas time. He thought the reason that Rachael wouldn't marry him was because her future constituents wouldn't approve of her mixed-race relationship.

Rachael lets out a sigh, and takes a big, heaping bite of guacamole on a chip. "He wants a relationship. I just want a friend with benefits. He wants kids. I think a dog is too much responsibility. He wants me to move to LA. I've informed him that our nation's government is in D.C."

I nod my head. I understand where she's coming from. It was hard as hell to walk away from my practice in Houston and join Colin in Dallas. It was worth it, though. I certainly don't regret the decision, but if anyone understands the balancing act between relationships and careers, it's me.

"Well, Rach …" I start.

She sits up board-straight, and her body coils tightly with tension. "Stop it. This is why I haven't discussed this with you," she cuts me off. "Just because you and Colin have gotten your happily-ever-after doesn't mean that Aiden and I will have ours. I'm not judging, but your career plays second fiddle to Colin's. I'm not willing to sidetrack everything that I've worked so tirelessly to achieve for Aiden. Call me selfish. Call me a bitch. Call me whatever you want, but I've worked too damn hard and spent too much time shoveling shit to give it up for any man."

She pours us each another shot without looking at me. Alcohol has never been so desperately needed than after that diatribe. She hands me my glass, finally meeting my eyes. I can read hurt, sadness, resolve, and determination in them. We clink glasses, and down the amber courage.

The alcohol lights fire to my throat like Rachael's words should to my soul, but I know that they're true. Yes. I'm still a surgeon, but I wouldn't be working at a charity hospital if it weren't for Colin. I'd be, probably at this point, seeing elite athletes as my patients. That was the goal that I was working toward before I chose the path less traveled, labeled Colin Fucking McKinney.

Rachael continues. "I'm happy for you and Colin. I know that your year anniversary is coming up. I'm assuming that in the next year or so you'll get pregnant. I'm happy that you're happy, but that's not the life that I want for myself, and I can't make Aiden understand that."

I skip over the "having a baby" comment. "Have you told Aiden all of this?" I ask, feeling the burn of the tequila in my stomach, and grabbing a chip to help soothe it.

"Caroline, I've come right out and said, 'I just want to fuck you and that's it.' He doesn't listen to me. He thinks that he can convince me to change my mind." I've known Rachael for most of my life. There's no changing her mind once she knows what she wants. "He even had the audacity to tell me that he thinks that it's because he's black."

She takes off her oversized Chanel sunglasses and rolls her eyes. Her white-blonde hair falls over her shoulder, and her light-blue eyes cloud over in anger. "I almost lost my damn mind on him. It was just further proof that he doesn't listen. I'm not sure how putting my career first equates to the shade of his skin."

I laugh, so relieved that she brought it up. "Do you think that you'll ever want a relationship that's more than just sexual?" I ask as I finger the edge of the hotel-issued towel.

She slips her sunglasses over her eyes. Rach has absolutely no breasts, so her over-padded bikini top gapes open as she lies back down. I teased her earlier that we could use her top to store our sunscreen and room keys. Fortunately, she takes her size in stride. Her hair stays to the side in a fan-like shape framing her snow-white skin. "I don't know. Maybe one day. Maybe not. He just keeps pushing me, so I told him that I can't see him anymore. I didn't know that by not agreeing to marry him that I was also losing a friend. I meant that we shouldn't have sex anymore, not that we shouldn't talk on the phone."

My stomach drops for poor Aiden. He's such a good friend to Colin and me. I hate that Rachael ended it with him. "He needs to move on. Aiden needs a good girl. Someone who can accept the love that he so freely gives. That isn't me, and I can't keep feeling like I'm a bad guy for not wanting what he keeps trying to give me."

I roll over on my side, and see the pained look on my best friend's face. She's hurting also. "I'm really sorry, Rach. I'm sorry that you can't make it work. Hopefully, in time, you guys will find what you're looking for, and maybe become friends again."

We drink another round of tequila shots, toasting to our friendship. I settle back in my sun-lounger and pull out my e-reader. I've been engrossed in a great book our whole trip. I have about two chapters left, and am looking forward to the ending. When I've read the same page five times, I realize that I've had too much to drink.

I put my e-reader back in my beach bag, and look at my friend. She's passed out, with a dribble of drool collected on the side of her mouth. I shake my head and laugh. She's something else. I can't help myself. I grab my phone and snap a picture. Who knows? I might need blackmail material one day.

I pour myself another shot of tequila and slam it while I snack on the chips and salsa. The sun is sinking below the ocean, and the sky is painted with the most breathtaking jewel tones. I miss my boys so much that my chest aches. I want my husband lying next to me while our dog bites at his hand, attempting to entice him into an epic wrestling-match.

I reach for my phone to call him, but I admonish myself before I hit dial. I'll be home tomorrow, and back to the grind. I need to enjoy this time for myself, because Rachael is right: since Colin stormed into my life, there've been very few minutes of peace. I spin my very plain, but beautiful wedding band on my finger as I think about the last year with Colin. Between drama with my dad, me moving to Dallas, allegations of him being a prescription pain-pill abuser, walking out of the ESPY Awards, our wedding, not being able to get pregnant, and his broken leg ... we've had a year. His limp is almost gone. It's much more pronounced when he gets out of bed in the morning and after a hard practice, but he's running very well. His mobility is back, along with his spirits.

Yes. Tomorrow, I'll have my boys back. They're picking me up at the airport in Dallas. Now, I'm going to spend one more night pretending that Colin and I can have a baby whenever we wish, and that the football season isn't looming on the horizon. That I don't have the ESPY Awards in a week, and that the media hasn't already begun reminding the world of us walking out during the comedian's monologue. One more night of being in my fairytale bubble.

After the sun has completed its journey, I wake up Rachael. We grab our bottle of tequila, shot glasses, the basket of chips, beach bag, and stumble to our suite to change for an evening in the clubs in downtown Cabo—or so Rachael thinks.

The next morning, I wake up with a pounding headache, achy body, and rolling stomach. I don't remember anything after we decided that we were too drunk to leave our hotel room. I stare up at the ceiling, chastising myself for drinking way too much, but anxiously counting down the hours until my plane leaves to bring me home.

****

"For the love of God, dog, if you don't stop yanking on your leash, you're never going running with me again," I admonish Pancho. I've become as bad as Colin about talking to the dog as if he speaks English.

Pancho runs to the end of his leash, forcing my arm to jerk him back. He's grown into quite the big boy at fifty-two pounds. I keep reminding Colin that if we don't get his behavior under control, he's going to be more of a problem at full size. Colin has blinders on when it comes to him, and says that he's just being a puppy.

I jerk his leash one more time, and resolve myself to the inevitable conclusion—my run is over. I slow down to a walk and remove my ear buds. I'm not far from the house, still inside the gilded cage. It's a muggy, hot July morning. Colin and I leave in a couple of days, headed to Los Angeles for the ESPY Awards.

I'm in a horrible mood. I've felt off since I got back from Cabo. At first, I thought I was still hung over, but this would be one hell of a drunk-ache if that were the case. My latest working theory is that I picked up a bug in Mexico.

Today is the first appointment with Doctor Starr regarding what fertility procedure she wants to try. I plan on asking her to run some additional blood work. I don't want to put my body through the fertility process if I'm not feeling one-hundred percent.

To make matters worse, I gained enough weight in Cabo that the sample-size dress that I planned on wearing to the ESPY Awards, that the designer was just going to have to let out a little now no longer fits. I wanted to cry when I slipped the beautiful beaded, white gown over my head, and it wouldn't zip over my breasts. I looked at Brad, whose eyes had grown as wide as saucers. He'd immediately starting asking the questions that I couldn't formulate. Could we let it out more? Would other undergarments help the fit? How much did I need to lose before Wednesday?

It seemed the majority of the weight had been gained in my breasts. I'd noticed my bras fitting a little more snuggly. The designer, stylist, and Brad opted instead for a backless dress that would give my boobs some more wiggle room, in case I couldn't lose those extra pounds. Hence, why I really need this run. Now, I just feel more annoyed.

Pancho and I have a routine. When we're two houses from home, I release him from his leash, and he runs the rest of the way. We get to the point where it always happens and his body shakes with excitement, as he looks back at me with pleading dark-brown eyes. I smirk at him. *What a spoiled boy he is.* I undo the red leash from his Dallas Cowboy's dog collar, and he takes off for home without a second glance back at me.

I have trained my good boy to wait for me patiently at the back gate, and when I catch up to him I open the gate, and give him the command, "Go find Daddy." He takes off like a bullet, checking the garage for Colin's cars, and then once he confirms that Colin's still home, I let him in the house. He runs from room to room looking for him, and when he finds him, he barks like crazy until I give him a head pat. I also might be a tad obnoxious over the dog.

I stop by the kitchen when we enter the house. Pancho starts his searching routine while I grab a bowl for cereal. I pour the bran flakes into a bowl and get the milk out of the refrigerator. Opening the container, the smell of the milk makes me gag. *Great! The damn milk is bad.* I quickly close the lid, and place it in a plastic garbage bag and take it to our outside trash bin.

I pick up my pathetic bowl of dried cereal and pick at the flakes until Pancho barks. It sounds like Colin is in the master bathroom. I remind myself that I have to walk the red carpet in two days and toss out my cereal. I'll starve myself for the next forty-eight hours. Maybe then my boobs will deflate.

Pancho found Colin right in the nick of time. I turn the corner and walk into the bathroom glimpsing my naked, gorgeous, husband stepping out of the shower. Leaning against the doorjamb, I take a moment to drink in the sight. Water droplets cling to his muscular back, chest, and arms, making me jealous. He puts his leg up on the side of the tub and runs a towel over his finely sculpted legs. I note that both legs now seem to be the same width. For a while after the "break seen around the world" his right calf muscle and thigh had noticeably atrophied.

He doesn't realize I'm behind him, watching. Pancho lets out another yelp as if to tell him to turn around. Colin misinterprets it and says to him as he scratches his ears, "Don't worry, boy. She'll be in here in a second."

Colin brings the towel up, and moves it back and forth over his dark-blonde hair, making his curls a tussled mess. When he's done, he hangs up the towel and does his signature dog-shake move. Him and Pancho—no matter how dry they get, they both still have to wiggle their bodies, as if to release the last bit of water droplets hanging on for dear life.

I stroll in the bathroom and Colin, sensing my presence, looks at me with those piercing green eyes. They skim over me, head to toe, and make me smile. "Like what you see?"

"Like it much better when it's naked, wet, and underneath me," he says flashing me his sexy half-smile.

I shake my head and giggle. "What am I going to do with you?" I head for my closet to strip off my sweaty running gear.

He follows behind me. "I've got ten minutes before I have to leave," he says suggestively wiggling his eyebrows.

He watches me with his mischievous half-smile plastered on his face as I remove my sweat-drenched sports bra. "I've got my appointment with Doctor Starr today, and I don't want to smell like fuck-musk, so the answer is no. You can have your wicked way with me tonight."

He crosses his arms over his sculpted pecs and says, "Fine. Don't forget, you're coming by the office today for the cologne meeting."

I bat my eyelashes. "How could I?" Colin just signed a new deal with the cologne company to release another scent this year. A group from the company is in town today to let Colin sample the new scents, and talk about packaging. He wants my opinion on the fragrances. I've told him that I don't think that I'll be much help. In reality, I'm not a big fan of cologne. Even though Colin has a signature scent, he rarely wears it. But he asked me to join the meeting, so I plan on being there.

"Maybe after the meeting we can look at some of the 3D renderings the architectural firm did on the Lake Somerville property," Colin says as he walks out of my closet.

I turn and watch his naked behind sway suggestively from side to side. *Maybe a quickie?*

"How do they look?" I ask distracting myself from the rather hot mental-image of him taking me against the bathroom counter.

He has the vision to turn the densely wooded property surrounding the small tributary lake into a dream vacation compound for us. I'm not seeing it yet.

"They did four drawings for us. Two I think we can easily eliminate. The other two have some great ideas. Maybe we can mix and match," he calls from the depths of his closet. Then, without missing a beat, "Feeling any better?"

I walk through to the bathroom and turn on the shower. "Not really. I just don't have any energy. I constantly feel queasy and achy."

As I'm stepping in the shower, he approaches the glass with a very serious look on his face. "Could you be pregnant?" he asks so quietly that I can barely hear him over the running water.

I feel my face drop in despair. I shake my head back and forth. "No, baby. I had a period. Remember?"

"I know. I know," he says, running his hand through his still wet hair. The overhead light catches his wedding ring, making it sparkle. "I just thought that I would ask."

****

I pull into the CharCol Inc. office-building parking lot with five minutes to spare. I hope that the cologne people aren't here yet. *Maybe their plane is delayed.* I could use the extra time with my husband. Images of him taking me quickly in his office have kept me bothered all day.

My dress-fitting earlier today was a disaster. Even though I've exercised like a fiend and counted every calorie, my new dress is now snug across my chest. I almost cried. Everyone promises that it will be fine for Wednesday.

The whole time that I stood there, while the designer's assistant, seamstress, and Brad poked and prodded me, I just wanted my husband. Normally, I have a decent sex drive. Today, I almost feel manic for him. Quickie in his office? I hope so. I brought sports wipes in my purse just in case I get lucky. I was serious when I told him this morning that I don't want to smell like sex for my appointment with Doctor Starr, but my mental images have made me not give a damn anymore.

Jenny greets me with a warm hello and we exchange pleasantries, although she never takes her eyes from her computer screen. Her office is what greets visitors when they walk through the doors of CharCol Inc. Today, her hair is a rather tame shade of strawberry-pink. She has on a baby-blue blouse, and yellow skinny jeans. Jenny, with her new hair color, looks like a My Little Pony commercial. "So, I hear you're batting for the other team."

"Stupid paparazzi," I quip. "I greet my best friend at the airport with a big hug and kiss on the cheek, and now I'm cheating on Colin, the media's golden boy, with Rachael. But I guess it could've been worse. The media could have assumed that she's a child, 'cause she's so tiny, and called me a molester." I shiver at the thought that the press gets it wrong so often.

"Yeah, Colin came in the other morning and threw the magazine on my desk. I believe his exact words were: 'Frame this bitch. It's hanging in my office.'" Finally, she looks away from the screen and rolls her eyes.

We both agree that men are pigs.

Jenny shows me into the conference room, which is already filled with the cologne company representatives, much to my dismay.

Colin rises to his feet and glides towards me with the grace of an athlete. He pulls me into a tight embrace, giving me a chaste kiss on the cheek. He announces to the room, "Everyone, this is Doctor Collins. She's going to be sharing her expert opinion with me on the new scents."

He then proceeds to introduce two men and three women, all with French names that I'll never remember. Colin motions for me to take an empty chair next to him. I do, feeling rather uncomfortable because of the intense heat in my stomach. Being in his presence makes me want him even more if that's possible. I lean in, attempting to wrap his aura around me. I can't seem to keep my hands to myself, and reach under the table to touch his thigh. *What's wrong with me?*

His eyes cut sideways as he gives me a questioning look. Colin and I are never overly affectionate in public, let alone at a business meeting. I get that my hand on his thigh is probably inappropriate, but it has a mind of its own, and refuses to be removed.

He mouths, *You okay?*

I dip my chin and look up at through my eyelashes. *I love you*, I mouth back.

He flashes me his half-smile, and I melt into a puddle right there in the CharCol Inc. conference room.

Before I can proposition him for a quickie in his office, Jenny gets his attention. They begin a quiet discussion amongst themselves, turning away from me. The cologne people speak in French to each other while I pull out my phone and pretend to be busy checking my email, feeling lost that his attention is no longer focused on me. There's just junk and shopping offers. They remind me that I'm too fat for my dress I must wear in two days. I want to cry again.

Jenny excuses herself, leaving the conference room. Before I can make my move, Colin steps outside to return a phone call. I'm half tempted to follow him out and offer some sexual suggestions, but he's standing in front of the conference room windows, pacing back and forth. He looks so hot in his dress slacks and linen button-up shirt. My mind races with thoughts about ripping the shirt off and watching the buttons fly across his office while I lick, bite, and mark his chest with my teeth. My impure thoughts make my face flush, and warmth floods my panties. *I've got to get myself under control.* Silently, I admonish myself. *The perfume people will know exactly what we're doing.* Decorum overrides my sexual desires, and I slump deeper into the soft black leather chair, counting the seconds until I can get my husband home.

About five minutes later, Jenny returns, arms loaded down with bags of Italian takeout from the little shop around the corner. As she starts setting it up buffet-style on the granite bar, the smell of marinara sauce hits me, and my stomach does a very uncomfortable flip. I turn away from the smell, and bring my hand up as if to shield my nose from the offending odor.

Colin slips back into the seat next to me. "Are you okay?" Colin leans over and whispers. Worry lines crease his beautiful eyes. "You look funny."

I nod my head, not wanting to open my mouth. I manage to squeak out, "Water." He jumps to his feet and walks over to the bar. He opens the small refrigerator and takes out two bottles of water for us to have with our lunch the chef prepared at home.

He unscrews the cap, and sits my water bottle down in front of me. He also removes the foil from my lunch. Thankfully, there are two rice cakes. I pick one up and break off an edge. The bland nothingness of a rice cake never tasted so good. Soon, my stomach settles, and I glance up at Colin, who's still clearly very worried.

"I haven't been eating much trying to get ready for the ESPY Awards. I think that I just got low blood sugar."

He drops his chin and cocks an eyebrow, "And …"

"And, I'll mention it to Doctor Starr, who I'm seeing in two hours." I try to remind him that my time today is limited, so he should get the show on the road.

Once everyone has the lunch plates fixed, a woman in a beautiful black suit stands up and begins the presentation. I listen to her drone on and on about market research, product placement, and other things that I don't care about. It would be snooze-worthy if I didn't find her French accent so alluring to listen to.

She talks about how they plan to go after a different demographic with this new cologne. Instead of targeting the average sportsman, this cologne is more sophisticated. It will be targeted to the man who appreciates luxury, and fine details.

When she's done speaking, she introduces one of the men, who hands out five sheets of paper each to Colin, Jenny, and me. Each one has a number on it. "I'm going to pass a scent, and each of you will evaluate it based on the criteria on the pages in front of you. We'll do this for all five scents. This should give us a better idea as to what you're looking for, Colin, in a fragrance. I suggest you bring the vial right under your nose to block out the scent of lunch." He brings the first tube under his nose to demonstrate.

I want to roll my eyes. *What he's looking for in a fragrance?* Try Ivory soap and dog spit. Mix in the essence of sex, and he's a happy man. Colin reaches under the table and squeezes my knee as if he knows exactly what I'm thinking.

They give the first vial to Colin. It's marked with a number one. I reach down and break off a piece of my rice cake and pop it in my mouth as Colin removes the lid. The musky, earthy scent of the cologne mixes with the aroma of marinara sauces, and then combines with the smell of the half-piece of grilled chicken breast still sitting in front of Colin.

My stomach becomes sloshy, my mouth fills with too much saliva to swallow, and I break out in a cold sweat. I tear off another piece of rice cake, and say a silent prayer that I'll not get sick. Colin dabs a tiny amount of the cologne on the cuff of his shirt, releasing more of the scent in the air, and bile rises from my stomach to my mouth.

I push my chair back, and try to walk calmly out of the room. I know that I'm failing when I feel all seven sets of eyes track me towards the door.

Colin announces to the room, "Excuse me for a moment."

I don't wait for him to catch me. I can't. I walk into his office and open his bathroom door as I begin to lose my stomach. The cold sweat is pouring off of me, and whatever has made me so sick is coming up violently. I can still smell the combination of scents lingering in my nose, which is making me sicker.

Colin rushes to me. "Charlie, dear God, what's wrong with you?" I can't see him, but his baritone voice is cracking in fear.

As he moves closer, so does the smell of the cologne. It makes me wretch even more violently. I try waving my hand back, hoping that he'll leave.

But he keeps coming, probably thinking that I'm just embarrassed that I'm sick in front of him. He's got to get away from me. I can't stop gagging until whatever smell is on him is gone.

Finally, between stomach rolls, I'm able to get out, "Your smell is making me sick."

I've never been this ill before. This is a different kind of sick. It's certainly not food poisoning. It's almost as if I feel better that I'm vomiting, which makes absolutely no sense.

I hear the rustle of Colin's shirt being removed. He leaves the bathroom with it, and is blissfully gone for a few seconds. Immediately, my stomach begins to settle. I sag against the cold bathroom tiles, strangely feeling so much better.

When he walks back into the tiny bathroom, Colin stares down at me like I have two heads. "Jesus Christ, what was that?" he asks after what feels like minutes of his scrutinizing glare.

I feel weak, but not weak like I just vomited from a stomach bug. It's more that my abs scream like they've gotten a good workout, but I feel the best I've felt since I got home from Cabo.

"I don't know," I say shaking my head. "But I feel so much better. Maybe I got whatever has been plaguing me since Cabo out."

I tear off a piece of toilet paper and wipe my mouth. I flush the toilet, and as soon as Colin realizes that I'm trying to stand he rushes to my side, helping me to my feet. I push him off and take the two steps to the sink to rinse out my mouth. "Seriously, I feel fine. Give me a few minutes in here to freshen up. Go back to your meeting. Make my excuses for me. I'm going to head over to Doctor Starr's a bit early."

"I'm going with you. You can't drive." I brace my hands on either side of the sink and look at his reflection in the mirror. His forehead is etched with worry lines, and his gorgeous full lips are turned down. His arms are crossed over his chest in a determined stance. He looks like a puffed-up bullfrog, and I almost laugh.

"These people flew nine hours for this meeting with you. You aren't going with me. She's just going to do some blood work. That's it. There will be plenty of appointments that you're needed at," I say looking down at his crotch in the mirror. "Besides, you'll just be in the way."

He reaches out for my arm and spins me around, tilting my chin up so I can see into his blazing green eyes. "I don't give a fuck they flew nine hours for this meeting. You're what I care about. I. Want. To. Come," he says.

I place my hand on his chest and playfully push him back. "I'm fine. Now, go earn us some Lake Somerville house money. You know I'm going to want a Viking range."

This has become our joke. Since the architect asked for our wish list, I've been teasing Colin about all the expensive upgrades that I want. We even started a spare-change jar in the bathroom for my marble counters. Yes, Colin has made enough money that he can write a check for whatever we want for the house, but it takes away the fun of dreaming and working for it. I want to know that the marble counters we've saved for, and not from some arbitrary investment that Aiden made on Colin's behalf.

Dreaming of our vacation/getaway home has been a great distraction from our infertility. In fact, it's almost been as good as Pancho.

"We can't afford it without this extra cologne money." He smirks, thankfully allowing me to change the subject from being sick. "Promise you'll call as soon as you're out?"

"Yes, Dad," I reply, letting out a sigh.

"You'll text when you get there?" When he cocks his eyebrow up, it's really not a question. It's more of a forceful reminder.

"Yes, Dad," I say, folding my arms over my chest and rolling my eyes, playing the part of the bratty teenager. I turn back around to the sink to finish freshening up.

He swats my behind as he walks out. "I take it you didn't like number one," he calls over his shoulder.

"You think?" I reply. "Might want to leave the shirt at the office."

I hear his laugh as I turn on the water.

****

This is not how it's supposed to be. Colin and I made a pact that if I thought I was pregnant, we would take the test together. Instead, I'm sitting in a sterile, white examining room in a blue hospital-gown with diamond patterns on it, staring at a white stick.

Doctor Starr must sense my anxiety, because she walks over and pats my back. "This is great news. Let's hope that you're pregnant, and you can just find a fun way to tell him."

I look up at her through blurry tear-filled eyes. "We've just been through so much this year. I wanted Colin to have this moment as validation for all of his hard work."

She smirks. "The hard part starts in nine months when the baby has colic, your nipples are raw and bleeding, and y'all haven't slept in a week. Trust me, Caroline, Colin will have a lot more moments."

She can certainly put things in perspective, like Rachael. I know that she's right, but I feel so guilty for not letting Colin come to this appointment, especially after he asked to attend.

When the timer goes off, she looks at me. "Want me to do the honors?"

"Please," I reply as I wait for the news. I keep telling myself over and over there is no way I'm pregnant. I had a period. *I HAD A PERIOD!* The test is negative, and Colin and I'll begin infertility treatments. You don't have periods if you're pregnant. Break through bleeding sure. But, not a period where you have to use products over multiple days.

I watch her walk to the counter and look down at the stick. She turns back around and her eyes reveal the truth before her mouth does. *I'm pregnant.*

The tears that I've been fighting to keep in check come pouring out. *I must have gotten pregnant in the last couple of weeks.* I can't believe it. The realization hits me. I'm going to be a mom. Colin and I are going to be parents. Colin is going to be a daddy. Pancho will have a baby to play with. My parents and Colin's parents will be grandparents. My sisters will be aunts. I leap to my feet and throw my arms around Doctor Starr. "Thank you. Thank you so much!"

She hugs me back and says, "Honey, I didn't do anything. Seems like you and Colin did all the heavy lifting."

I laugh at her cute joke.

"Now, we need to see how far along you are." I crawl up on the exam table and wait for her questions. "When was your last period?"

"Three weeks ago." I reply.

"That can't be right. It's too early to confirm a pregnancy with one of these sticks. Are you sure that your dates are right?" she says, looking in my chart as if the answer is hiding there.

"Trust me. I know exactly when I had that period," I reply, now a bit concerned.

"Here, let's go do an ultrasound, and see if we can see anything."

I follow her out of the exam room and down the hall to the last door at the end, hoping that this gown is providing at least a degree of modesty. She knocks once, and then opens it. I lie down on the table as she dims the lights. She takes a seat on a bright-blue plastic rolling-stool.

She flips on the monitor and grabs a wand, slipping a condom over it. She places a huge dollop of gel on it that she removed from a warming container.

I put my feet in the stirrups like a good girl, spreading my knees. She slides the wand inside as I feel pressure expanding me.

"Okay, Caroline. We might see your baby. We might not. Please don't panic. This is just to see how far along you are," she reassures me.

"I understand." I nod my head.

I close my eyes, and pray that I'm newly pregnant. My alcohol-infused trip to Cabo cannot have happened with a life inside of me … can it? I finger my wedding ring, hoping for good news.

"Open your eyes," Doctor Starr instructs.

I do as she asks, and roll my head to the side to see the monitor. There's our baby, about the size of a bean. The grainy black and white image is the most beautiful thing I've seen. Tears roll down my cheeks as I clasp my hand over my mouth. "Oh my God, that's my baby," I gasp.

"Do you see that tiny flicker?" Doctor Starr says, pointing to something on the screen that looks almost like a buzzing mosquito. "That's your baby's very strong heartbeat."

She does some measurements while I lay there in awe, staring at what Colin and I made together out of love. It's hard to comprehend the tiny little being on the screen is growing inside of me. I didn't even know that it was there thirty minutes ago, but I love him or her with everything in my soul.

Doctor Starr breaks into my love-fest. "Well, from the size and the heartbeat, I'd say that you're about seven weeks along. So that would put your due date at," she says turning a dial on a circular card, "around February 27."

Panic overwhelms me. "Doctor Starr, I just got back from Cabo, and drank half a bottle of tequila in one night. I had a period, so I didn't think I was pregnant," I begin to explain. The feeling of plain terror is more intense than I've ever experienced before. *What if my drinking has hurt our baby?*

She cuts me off with a raised hand. "You and every other pregnant lady. It's not ideal, but you're fine. The baby's obviously okay. Worry about how you're going to tell Colin that he's going to be a daddy."

"But I don't understand. I had a period. Like, I used tampons," I start again. I can't stop myself. I feel she needs all the facts.

"Some women still have a light period their first month of pregnancy. You saw your healthy baby, Caroline. You're going to be a mom." She smiles down at me while I lie on the table, feeling completely helpless.

I repeat it. "I'm going to be a mom." Saying it out loud seems to make it more real. I repeat it again, feeling a smile that meets my eyes. "I'm going to be a mom."

As I make my way out of Dr. Starr's office, still numb from all that has transpired in the past few minutes, I notice the children's boutique on the first floor of her building, and make a split second decision to enter into the world of everything baby. It's hard to believe that the little bean growing inside of me will one day be wearing one of these newborn, footed sleepers. I choose a neutral color just so I can show Colin how small our baby will be. When I place my purchase on the counter, I spy a pair of Nike newborn-sized tennis shoes displayed by the cash register. A stroke of genius hits me, and I know exactly how I'm going tell Colin that he's going to be a daddy. I almost squeal I'm so excited.

The lady checking me out has a kind, grandmotherly face. She smiles knowingly at me as she hands me my purchases and says, "Congratulations." I can feel my perma-grin cracking my cheeks. This is a new kind of happiness that I've never experienced before. I'll be able to add "mommy" to my list of titles.

On my way home, I send this baby's daddy a text.

Me: *When will you be home?*

Colin: *Whenever you need me. Feeling okay?*

Me: *Okay. Are you working out after your meetings?*

Colin: *Not sure.*

Me: *Do you mind running with me this evening?*

Colin: *Sure. I can probably think of other ways to work you out.*

Me: *Mind out of the gutter.*

Colin: *Never! Be home in an hour.*

When I arrive home, the first order of business is to let Pancho out of his kennel. He's been such a Destructicon, as Colin calls him, lately, that he must be kenneled when no one can watch him. Just last week, he chewed the handle off of Chef's Coach leather messenger bag. That cost us eight-hundred dollars.

Pancho howls when he sees me head toward his kennel that we keep in the laundry room. I open the door and kneel down, bracing myself for his greeting kisses. He wiggles so much that it's surprising his front half doesn't separate from his back. I scratch behind his ears, and kiss his head.

"Guess what, big boy? Mommy has a secret for you. You're the first to know. You're going to be a big brother."

It feels so good to say those words out loud. Pancho says congratulations by bathing my face with licks. I open the back door, depositing Pancho outside so he can take care of his business.

Next, I walk into the kitchen. Thank goodness whatever Chef prepared for dinner doesn't smell disgusting. There's a pile of mail on the granite countertop, but I ignore it. I want to make sure that everything is perfect for telling Colin our great news before I start mundane chores.

Carrying my new purchases into the bathroom, I head straight for Colin's closet. His running shoes are in their usual spot, neatly placed on the floor under his hanging workout shirts. I slip the tiny pair of Nikes out of the boutique shopping bag, and place them next to Colin's custom-made Nike shoes. In some wonderful twist of fate, they actually match. Colin's are only twenty times larger. I take out my phone and snap a picture, for posterity's sake. Then, I clap like a fool so excited at how this turned out. It's the perfect way to share our news.

Next, I remove the ultrasound pictures from my purse and instantly become transfixed. Sinking to the floor of my husband's closet, I take a breath to absorb the enormity of the moment. The positive pregnancy test changes everything about my life. My body has been hijacked by Mother

Nature. I can't control my weight, or the size of my breasts. My abdomen will expand without anyone asking me if it has my permission.

I think back to my earlier nausea. What if I get sick in surgery? What does being pregnant mean to my career? What does a baby mean to my future? Did I go to Harvard to practice medicine for only four short years? Is Rachael right? Have I shoveled shit to get where I am just to give it up for mommy-hood?

I lie back on the soft carpet and close my eyes, blocking out the harsh florescent lighting. Colin's body scent is strongest in his closet, and thankfully, it doesn't make me feel bad, even though there's a hint of his cologne. Smelling my husband tethers me back to reality, and away from the tornado of emotions whipping over me.

Being pregnant is my new normal. Worrying about our little bean thriving inside of me will become a part of my everyday routine, like brushing my teeth. One day, I'll forget what it felt like to only be concerned about me. In that moment, I wish that I could rewind time one month, knowing that I was about to conceive a child. I would spend that last month being so much more carefree. Maybe Colin and I would do something risky, like travel the Amazon River, or go skydiving. I would definitely wear a bikini one more time in public. However, what I think that I would do the most with my borrowed time is just spend hours upon hours basking in Colin's attention, enjoying being the center of his universe.

In about thirty minutes, my life is going to change forever. Once Colin knows about the baby, he's going to be even more neurotic than he usually is about me. There are going to be battles at every corner. He'll probably fight me on running every morning, even though Doctor Starr said it was fine. His anxieties over my safety will go through the roof. Every bite of food that goes in my mouth will be scrutinized. Will he be afraid to make love to me? God, I hope not.

I don't doubt that he's going to shower me with attention and care, but it will be about the baby also. I let out a sigh, and place both hands over my pubic bone. Yes. I would give anything for just one more month not being pregnant, but with the future knowledge that we would conceive soon.

I have my first conversation with this kid. "Your daddy is going to drive Mommy crazy. You'll probably hear some arguing, but it doesn't mean that we don't love each other. It just means that sometimes we love each other a little too loudly. Now, be a good baby, and don't make me sick again. That's the surest way possible to get Daddy riled up. We've got to be a team here," I say, rubbing my hand over my lower abdomen. "And right now, you're on my team. We're calling ourselves Team Collins, but don't tell Daddy."

I make a note to talk to Doctor Benson, my therapist, about these out-of-control feelings. I know from all of my therapy that pregnancy is a big trigger for my disease. Submitting oneself to nature is very hard when control is my weapon of choice in the battle against my eating disorder.

Before my thoughts have fully played out, Pancho comes barreling into Colin's closet, finding me and alerting Colin with a yelp. *Oh no! Daddy's home early.* I scramble to pull myself together, and tuck the pictures into my bra that's still feeling rather constrictive.

Colin comes sauntering into his closet seconds later, raising his eyebrow at finding me sitting on the carpeted floor. Fortunately, he changed shirts, so he doesn't stink like that horrible cologne. He gives me his best "What the fuck?" look. I usually get this look when Brad and I've just come up with the best idea ever. "Any particular reason you're sitting on the floor of my closet?" he asks, cocking his eyebrow.

"Nope." I smile, looking up at him as Pancho lies down beside me, placing his head in my lap.

Colin toes off his brown-leather dress shoes first, and places them in the empty spot on his shoe rack. I hold my breath, hoping that he'll notice my new addition to his closet, but his eyes pass right over them. Next, he slips off his navy slacks, revealing his bare bottom to me.

"Can you ever be troubled to put on underwear?"

He shimmies his behind. "You love it." His voice is full of mirth.

He tosses the pants and cream linen button-up shirt in the dry-clean basket. I'm not sure why. He couldn't have worn the new shirt but for a couple of hours. However, now's not the proper time to question our dry cleaning bill.

Then, he saunters over to his drawer that he keeps his workout shorts in. If the baby shoes were snakes they'd have bitten him by now, but he still doesn't notice.

Look down!

He slides on a pair of his brand of shorts, and tugs a black sleeveless T-shirt—also his brand—from the hanger.

I hold my breath as he joins me on the floor with a plop, tossing his shirt over his shoulder.

"You're sure acting strange," he says as he reaches toward his Nikes.

Time stands still. In mere seconds he's going to know my secret. He's going to know that our life is about to change in ways that we can't even imagine. I hold my breath in anticipation and study his face, craving his reaction as he spots the tiny shoes. A chill drives down my spine, marking this moment.

I know exactly when he spot them. His face shifts from impassive to disbelief in nanoseconds. His head whips around. Eyes, as green as emeralds, blaze at me. His eyebrows meet his hairline as he opens his mouth and closes it, as if he's a guppy. I watch him swallow and try to speak again.

I'm frozen as he leans forward, picking up the baby shoes, holding them in the palm of his hand. They both fit there perfectly. He marvels at them as if they're precious jewels. Then he turns back to me with wet eyes. Wonderment fills his voice. "These are baby shoes."

My face lights up, not needing to confirm the obvious. He turns back and stares at the shoes in his hand. I watch his Adam's apple bob up and down—hard. After a couple of heart beats, he whispers, "They go on a baby."

I gently tease him as I scoot closer and rub my hand on his thigh, feeling his soft leg-hair tickle the tips of my fingers. His body heat is soothing, and an overwhelming feeling of peace washes over me. "I think they're too small for me, and there aren't enough of them for Pancho." My voice is rich with humor and love.

Colin swallows again as he continues to stare at the little Nikes. I can't tell if he's in shock, or simply too overwhelmed to comprehend that we're actually pregnant. "But that means that they'll go on a baby," he says after some time.

I reach up with my thumb and brush a tear that's trickling down his cheek. "Yes. They'll fit the baby."

"Our baby," he whispers as if he's trying out the words for the first time. "Our baby," he repeats a little more loudly with awe in his voice.

He turns and stares at me. "Our baby." His wet eyes glisten, and the corners of his mouth turn up in a beautiful little smile. "You mean that you're pregnant with our baby."

I can't resist, because the air is thick with way too much emotion. "Well, I never said that the baby is yours, but yes. I'm pregnant," I reply trying to hide my smile.

He pulls me onto his lap, and tickles my sides while I scream. Pancho leaps to his feet and barks incessantly at Colin. His tickle-torture only lasts for a few seconds before he captures my mouth in a soul-searing kiss. It starts out as a sweet kiss and turns into a hunger for each other that is palpable.

His mouth leaves my lips, and he begins trailing delicate kisses along my jaw, over to my right ear, and down my neck following my pulse. When he reaches the sweet spot between my neck and my shoulder, he gives it a nip. A small cry escapes my lips, which further fuels him on. He stops just long enough to unbutton my aqua sleeveless blouse. As my top falls open, exposing my swollen breasts, he lets out a gasp. "What the fuck is in your bra?"

"Oh." My cheeks blush. "Those are pictures of the baby."

He reaches into my lingerie and extracts the small, folded sheet of pictures and holds it up, letting them unfold accordion-style. "What? Were these some sort of kinky surprise?" he asks with a smirk.

I begin defending myself, explaining how he came home too soon, and I panicked but he stops my rambling with a wet kiss. "I don't care. Tell me about these."

He repositions himself with his legs spread, and I scoot in between, pressing my back against his chest, nuzzling into his pale chest hair. His chin rests on my shoulder as I walk him through each image. He's entranced with every shot. Asking questions. Pointing at details.

The last picture is the one with our due date. When he sees the date, there's a brief pause, and then his body stiffens. "How far along are you?"

"Seven weeks, she thinks." I lean back, hoping to read his eyes.

Before I can say anything, he shakes his head. "But you had a period. You drank in Cabo like a damn fish. You got so drunk that you've been hung over for days." His chin resting on my shoulder tenses becoming painful as it digs into my collarbone.

I attempt to scoot away, but he grasps my hips securing me against him. "I did have a period, and I did drink. Doctor Starr says that we have a very healthy baby with a great heartbeat. There's no need to worry. And as for my long hangover, it's called morning sickness, baby. We've had a preview of what the next seven weeks will likely be for me."

"But you got shitfaced, Charlie." He leaves the statement dangling out there. There's an accusatory undertone that bothers me more than I care to admit.

Finally, he releases my hips so I'm able to move out of his comforting triangle that now feels hostile, and turn around to look him in the eyes.

"I did get drunk," I say, in the same voice that I use to pacify my mother when she's lecturing me about something or other. "If I had an inkling that I was pregnant, I would not have let anything unhealthy touch my lips. What's done is done, Colin. I can't reverse time." I silently add, *But I sure wish that I could.*

I pause and collect my thoughts to make sure that I say the next part exactly as I mean it. "Honey, I can't spend the next seven months living with a neurotic crazy-man. You can't control this pregnancy. The only thing that I need for you to do to help me through this is be supportive of my needs. Hey! I've already decided to give up coffee." I drop my chin, raising my eyebrow. He knows how much I like my morning coffee. "That's got to mean something, right?"

"If that means that I want pickles and ice cream at four a.m., I need for you to rush to the store and buy it. I need for you to go to my appointments, and watch this baby grow. What I don't need is for you to micromanage my life. I might crave greasy, slimy pizza, and you just have to keep your mouth shut and let me eat it." He grimaces at my food comments, but I watch his face as he processes what I'm saying.

Continuing, I take his hands into mine and run my thumb over his wedding ring. My voice is stronger, and more confident now. "I'm scared to death. My body is no longer mine. It's been hijacked by Mother Nature. I'm growing another organ, for God's sake. Mother Nature has now decided that this little tiny bean growing inside of me is more important than me.

"I need your support. I need for you to listen to my fears, and not freak out and try to fix them. I need you to hold me when I can't sleep. I'll need you to rub my swollen feet and shave my legs when my stomach will be too big for me to reach around it. I need your love. I don't need your obsessive, controlling worrying. Got it?"

The internal war in Colin's head is fascinating to observe. I watch fear at what I'm saying grey his face. I see wonderment at what my body can do fill his eyes. I see the idea of having to shave my legs and rub my feet dance on his beautiful lips. Finally he confirms, "I can do that." Then, without missing a beat, "So when can we tell everybody?"

"We have another appointment in four weeks. As long as everything is still on track, we can share our news with our family and friends."

He face lights up like Christmas morning. "Can we tell them the same way that you told me? Can I show them my shoes compared to the baby's?"

How could I tell him no when he's this cute? "Of course we can."

Colin gently pushes me back on the beige flooring, making quick work of removing my pants, and leans down to rest his head just above my pubic bone. I don't have the heart to tell him that my uterus is not that high up yet. "Hi bean," he says. "This is your daddy's voice. Get used to hearing it, because I'm you and your mommy's biggest fan. You be nice to her and quit making her feel bad. 'Kay?"

I laugh at his silliness, and run my fingers through his wavy locks. He lifts his head and stares down at my panties as if he's found a buried treasure. They're removed, and tossed haphazardly over his left shoulder with the shirt he never put on. Before I can moan "Oh God," Colin's buried in the apex of my thighs.

Apparently, I can cross *Being afraid to make love to me* off of my worry list.

This feels so right. Perfect. Not just the wonderful attention that he's paying to my body, but the whole energy surrounding us. He's happy, which makes me fret less. He still finds my body appetizing. God, my thoughts, are interrupted when he slips one, two, hell, a whole hand's worth of fingers inside me, finding that perfect place that makes me moan his name while he continues to suck and nip at me.

"Colin, that feels so good," I encourage him begging for more. More of what? I'm not sure, but I'm not ready to find my release.

He reaches up with his free hand and gives my nipple a hard pinch. As if I'm Popeye and have just been handed a can of spinach, I become sex crazed and desperate for him. His tongue feels delicious against my clit and his fingers are magic, but I need rough. I need to feel him inside of me. I want him buried balls deep, and pounding my special place over and over again. I feel like it's been days since we've made love instead of less than twenty-four hours. Even though what he is doing to my body feels great, it's not the assurance hard lovemaking brings me. Instead of running my fingers through his hair, I'm grabbing it, and begging him for more.

"Please Colin," I all but sob, "fuck me." I sound pathetic to my own ears, but at least I can use pregnancy now as an excuse.

Before I register what he's doing, I'm positioned on my hands and knees, and he begins feeding his penis into me inch by perfect inch. When he's completely inside, I rock back against his hips, taking all of him. This is the closeness that I need. The connection. Our feeling of oneness. When we're like this, I become unaware of where I stop and he begins.

He grabs my hips. "This how you want it?" He drives in harder, hitting my cervix, which makes me unable to answer him with a coherent word. Instead I just groan.

"God, you feel so perfect. So wet. So tight. Pregnant pussy is perfection." He's jackhammering into me.

No. No, I definitely don't have to worry about him being careful with my pregnant body.

I almost laugh at his alliteration, but at the moment I'm too consumed with making sure that I'm properly fucked. I rotate my hips around his cock and pull forward, slamming back against him. "Oh God," he yells out. "Like that, Charlie."

The longer that I rock back and forth on his erection, the wilder I become. This level of intimacy becomes not enough. I pull off of him and turn around. I'm eye height with his long, thick, gorgeous penis, the same one that was inside of me when we created a new life together. Perfection!

I know what I need. I need him inside of my mouth. Craving this new level of intimacy, I need to taste the essence of my husband.

I tap his thigh indicating that I want him to lie down. He does, but wrinkles his brow in confusion. I kneel over him and bend down taking him into my mouth, and suck as if I'm starving. I cup his heavy balls in my other hand, feeling how warm they are. "Fuck, Charlie, what are you doing to me?" he growls.

I ignore him, taking him deeper down my throat than I ever have before. My cheeks hollow, and my throat swallows around him.

His moans spur me on, making me ache to have him filling me again, but I don't dare quit. My power over him is hedonistic.

He reaches down and grabs my head, trying to make me stop as I feel his balls tighten up against his body. "No," he says, in a voice that says he really doesn't know if he means for me to actually quit.

All the king's horses and all the king's men couldn't get me to remove him from my mouth. I want his come. I want to taste him. I want to swallow it. I'm starving for it. This is definitely the pregnancy hormones talking.

He grips my hair, tugging painfully, and says, "I'm going to come, Charlie." His voice is so authoritative that it almost makes me pause for a second.

That's what I want.

When the first spurt hits the back of my throat, I hollow out my cheeks even more, longing for every drop.

I only stop when he pleads through gritted teeth, and with graveled voice, "You're hurting me baby," he says as he taps my head.

I'm not sated yet. Standing up without looking back at him, I walk through our bathroom and into the bedroom. I open the bottom drawer of my nightstand and pull out my favorite toy. It's my vibrator with a rabbit clit-stimulator. *Yup! It'll do*, I decide.

Colin walks into the bedroom just as I'm turning on my toy and shoving it not so gingerly inside of me. "Care to help?" I ask as he stares at me like I'm an escaped psych-ward patient.

"What is wrong with you?" He's in all his naked glory while his semi-firm penis flops against the inside of his toned thigh. He doesn't say it like he's concerned for my safety. Poor Colin is clearly confused as to what to do with me.

Ignoring him, I close my eyes, concentrating on how good the vibrations feel inside. This is what I need to find my release.

I guess Colin decides if you can't beat 'em, join 'em, because I feel him slip his large hand around the base of the BOB, replacing my grip. "Is this what you need, baby?" he asks with a concern-etched voice.

I moan as I let him take over pleasuring me. Opening my eyes, I check to make sure that he's okay with this. Not that I particularly care at the moment, but I want to see his reaction to using toys on me.

I'm pleased that he seems to be getting into it. His lust-heavy eyes watch the toy sliding in and out of me. "God, Charlie. You're so fucking beautiful, baby. Do you like this?" he asks while he changes the angle of the BOB. "Do you like it when I angle it forwards and then back?"

"Colin …" I moan. I've been a fan of sex toys since I discovered what an orgasm was in high school, but I've never had anyone else use them to pleasure me. It's hot. Maybe beyond hot. There's a new level of intimacy with Colin that I wasn't expecting.

"How about if I squeeze your nipples like this?" He pinches my over-sensitive nipple between his thumb and forefinger, and my eyes roll back in my head.

The jolt of pleasure and pain travels to where the vibrator is working me into a frenzy, making me yell out something incoherent to my own ears.

"Keep doing that," I plead. "Oh, God, please keep doing it just like that." The orgasm that wracks through my body is so overwhelming that I might have temporarily lost consciousness. *Holy hell! That felt amazing.*

Colin slowly begins to turn down the vibrations on my toy until it's off. When I feel him slide it out of me, I open my eyes for the first time since I came to look at my lover's face. When he sees my irises, he shakes his head and smirks. "What has gotten into you, Charlie? I've never seen anything like that, except on a porno."

I tartly reply, "Your baby."

****

We've shared a near perfect evening of dining outside and swimming, until a night chill filled the air. Colin and I showered together, and made love against the cold slate wall. Later in the evening, as I was tucked in tightly against his chest and covered in our summer sheet and blanket, Colin sang to me "I Haven't Even Heard You Cry" by Aaron Lines. The words couldn't have been more perfect to mark our feelings. Pregnancy hormones got the best of me, though when he sang the line, *And I'll make mistakes there's no doubt. But love's one thing you won't live without. 'Cause you own a place in my heart now.*

So true … So very true for both of us.

Colin's been asleep for hours, but I'm too wound up to relax. Tomorrow, we leave for the ESPY Awards. It's the one-year anniversary of the day we shocked the world by Colin grabbing my hand, pulling me to my feet, and escorting me out of the theater while the audience and host of the show watched us in stunned silence.

The media has been reminding everyone what we did. I swear, the clip has been played in a continuous loop, to the point that I haven't turned on the TV in days. All eyes will be on us, and I'm pregnant with boobs so big that the dress barely contains them. I flip over, attempting to find a cool place on the sheets and clear my mind of the anxiety.

Colin has reminded me I don't have to walk the red carpet with him. I didn't last year. However, I feel like he needs my support. We need to show the world that despite the rumors, our relationship is solid. I also need to prove to Colin that I can be his partner in his career. No, I'm not going to hide in the control room like I did last year. I will walk the red carpet with my husband, proudly standing by his side as he answers the media's asinine questions. And our baby will be there with us. Our little secret from the world. The thought makes me smile as I finally relax into my pillow.

Chapter Three

Colin

"You look like a dream," I whisper into Charlie's hair, inhaling the grape scent of her shampoo. It stands out against the plethora of sunflowers covering the ground beneath our feet.

My hand cups her firm abdomen, feeling our son pushing against my callused fingertips as Charlie leans into my embrace.

The sun is shining so brightly it's blinding my vision, and I can't read the emotions on her face but I know that she's happy. How do I know? Because the world is colored in shades of yellows and golds.

I also know that our son will be here soon. The knowledge makes a smile touch my eyes, and my heart warms with anticipation.

Charlie's laugh forces a giggle from me. I didn't know that I could giggle, but with Charlie I can be myself, laughing freely, without worry of what the media might print.

She turns, looking at me over her shoulder, and begins to run in the other direction from where I'm standing. She's obviously teasing me, and I love it. When I capture her, I'll ravage her body and make her yell, "Colin" over and over again while I bring her pleasure. I'm the most content when Charlie is happy.

The field of sunflowers that we've been standing in shifts to a vast wasteland of tangled grey vines right before my eyes. The world is desolate and the earth looks like it's been scorched. As I turn to move toward Charlie, the toe of my shoe catches in a deep crack. I stumble forward, barely regaining my balance.

"When did that happen?" I ask. But she just shrugs her shoulders almost as if she can't hear me.

She turns, and again, she starts running away. "Charlie," I call. "Slow down. You're going to trip and hurt yourself or the baby." My stomach clenches in panic. Why would she run away from me when we're so close to meeting our son?

She doesn't seem to hear me and keeps taunting me, looking over her shoulder. She's still playing with me, throwing her head back, laughing like crazy. Daring me to capture her. I realize that she thinks she's still in the field of sunflowers. She thinks she's safe, but she's not.

I take off in a sprint after her. She must be warned. The vines will take her and the baby.

"Charlie," I scream as I chase her.

The vines start closing in around her, grabbing and dragging her away. They're taking her to some place in the blackness before us.

I can't let her go. If she enters the blackness, I'll never hold her again.

There are no more smells in this world. When I breathe, I inhale the scent of nothingness. The vines wrap around my ankles, anchoring me to the dead earth. I can't get away. The more I grab at them, the more they latch on to me, wrapping their tentacles around my body. Something wet oozes between my fingers. It's my blood, but I can't feel the deep lacerations the vines have made all over my body.

Charlie realizes she's in trouble. I can't see her face, but she screams "Colin" in a high-pitched, terrified voice.

"I'm coming for you. Don't give up, Charlie. I'll save you," I yell back to her, trying but failing to keep my emotions in check.

Then, I watch in horror as Charlie's rounded stomach deflates, and the vines carry her and our son into the dark.

"Oh God," I plead. "Don't take them away from me. They're all I have." The vines are now wrapped around my legs up to my hips. My arms are at a forty-five degree angle from my body held immobile by the sickly grey vines.

Helplessly, I stand pinned to the ground while my wife and child fade away.

"Fuck!" I sit up and swing my legs to the edge of the bed. My heart is pounding so hard, I can't catch my breath. Sweat has drenched where I was sleeping. My hand has to touch Charlie's stomach to reassure my mind that she's still here and the baby is safe.

I drop my head in my hands, trying to calm myself down. *This was just another bad dream.* One of many, but just a dream.

Not wanting to wake Charlie, I finally stand up and cross our bedroom to the door that leads to the backyard. As quiet as can be, I turn the lock and open the door, slipping into the cool night air.

My body is worn out. I feel every bit as fatigued as I normally do after a game. *It was just a dream. She's safe inside the bedroom.*

I slide down the brick façade of our house, allowing my head to fall in between my knees. At some point, I realize that I'm naked and couldn't care less.

These goddamn dreams have got to stop. I've mentioned them to the sports psychologist that Doctor Benson recommended I see. He explained in his typical doctor bullshit that it's normal for men to feel out of control when their wives are expecting. I'd inwardly rolled my eyes. It's not normal to be so obsessed with your wife's safety that fucking dreams make you have panic attacks.

They're always the same. In some sort of twisted, dreamlike way, she and our unborn baby are being taken away from me. Sometimes it's a car accident, or she dies in childbirth. Other times, it's a nameless face that kidnaps or murders her. The hardest yet, though, is the dream where she tells me that her and the baby can do much better than me. I spend too much time playing football, and she and our baby leave me.

Unfolding from the curled-up position I was in, I rise to my feet and begin pacing between the pool and the door.

"The threats are real," I speak out loud to no one. Because somehow trying to justify the nightmares helps to soothe my jagged nerves.

I know that I've become insane about her safety. Okay: *more* insane about her safety. She doesn't know it, but she has her security at the hospital, plus I have her tailed wherever she goes. My guy reports back on her every movement. It's not that I don't trust her, it's that I don't trust all the crazy people in the world with my wife and unborn child.

"Fuck!" I yell, but not too loud. All I need right now is my wife worrying about me, or Jamie rushing out of the pool house to find me naked. I reach up and use my fist to try to work the knot out of my chest.

Finally, I give in to my aching legs and sprawl on one of the sun-loungers by the pool. The night is cloudy, so there isn't a star to be found, but the neighborhood lights reflect off the clouds, creating a glowing night sky. It's actually rather pretty. If Charlie didn't need her sleep so desperately, I'd wake her up so she could admire it with me.

But Charlie needs her rest, because the first trimester of Charlie's pregnancy can be summed up like this: nausea and mind-blowing sex. I mean, Charlie and I never had issues pleasuring each other before, but damn, Charlie getting pregnant equals crazy sex. Wild sex. Sex that makes me feel like I'm being used. Best. Feeling. Ever.

I chuckle at the thought that there have been days that I've had to use her toys on her—which I hate, sort of—because my dick can only come so many times before there's nothing left in my balls but dust. She wakes me up in the middle of the night to ride me. *Awesome!*

I was lectured on the day we found out she was expecting that it's my job to support her. So I've done what any man would do in my situation: have the best sex of my life, since that's what my girl needs. In fact tonight, she was ready and waiting for me when I arrived home with her dinner.

The downside to her first trimester of pregnancy is that when we aren't having sex like bunnies, she's sick. She was so sick on the plane to the ESPY Awards in LA that we took a private jet home.

I have to say, though, my girl handled the red carpet at the ESPY Awards like a pro. She looked damn gorgeous, and kept her smile firmly planted on her lips while the press questioned our relationship status, asked me the same tired questions about the upcoming season, quizzed me about my ankle, and even asked what kind of stunt we were going to pull this year. That question caused her to dig her fingernails into my hand. I agreed. Stupid reporters.

Charlie held her own, though, and didn't, fortunately, feel bad during the awards. What we've discovered is that smells seem to be her trigger. In particular, it's my cologne. I've moved all the bottles to my office building, because she swears that she can smell the oil drop on the tip of the sprayer. I'm not saying that I don't believe her, but it seems like this is a tad mental.

And because my cologne is one of the bestselling male fragrances in the world, the smell is everywhere—especially here in Dallas.

We're hoping that this ends soon because right now, the only foods she can seem to keep in her stomach come from fast-food restaurants.

I roll over on my side, facing away from the pool, feeling the bite of the night air. My sweaty skin is now goose-pimpled. I should probably stand up, walk inside, and curl up with my wife. Her pregnant body radiates heat. But, if I'm honest with myself, I know that I've become terrified to sleep. *I can't have another nightmare tonight.*

Think pleasant thoughts, Colin, I command myself. Charlie's tits … *Dear God, thank you for Charlie's tits.* She pretty much had ant bites when we were in college. When we got back together, they'd grown to a small handful. Now, the Pregnancy Fairy has blessed us with heaping mounds of boobs. They're so big that she looks like she's had enhancement surgery. Her stomach is still flat, but her tits go on for days. *Playboy* models would be envious.

Every morning she stands naked in the mirror, and gripes about how another shirt doesn't cover them. Every morning I measure them with my hands, thanking our baby for the best rack I've ever seen.

Even though I've been in the middle of training camp and all that entails, I've been able to be around for Charlie. She's needed my help this first trimester. Besides the food runs, I've loved this time between the two of us, although watching her be sick every evening makes me crazy. I didn't think it was possible to love her more than I did before.

I do.

She's doing this for us, and I'm in awe of her pregnant body. Our baby is growing inside of her—so fucking cool. Her attitude is amazing. Even when she's sick, she'll reassure me that it just means that we have a healthy baby.

Finally, I can take a deep breath again, and do a quick assessment of my body. The conclusion? I'm calm enough that I can snuggle my girl without my racing heart waking her.

Tomorrow, I have to leave Charlie for the first away game of the season. I shiver at the thought of not being by her side. I can't deal with her flying commercial, so I have her booked on a private plane. Her issues during our trip to LA make it easy for me to justify the excess expense. She didn't put up much of a fight when I reminded her of spending the three-and-a-half hour flight sick in a cramped airplane restroom.

Brad is going too. I've shared with him my deepest fears for her safety. He cringed as only Brad can, and reassured me that he'd look after her. They're booked in a suite at the hotel that the team's staying at. Even though Brad is gay, I can't stomach the thought of them sharing a hotel room. However, my issues regarding Brad taking care of her when it's my job have been overridden by my need to know she's safe. What if she needs someone, and I can't get to her? I can't dwell on those thoughts too long because they make me crazy. I've resolved myself to the fact that this is going to be an expensive season.

****

"Yes, I'll take a Whopper with cheese, mayo and ketchup. Extra onions. Extra tomatoes. Hold the lettuce and pickles, please." I add the *please* hoping that she will not floor spice my wife's food.

I haven't even been home yet. Charlie and Brad's private plane landed about two hours ago. The team plane just hit the tarmac, and I raced for Bertha, anticipating Charlie's dietary needs.

The disembodied voice asks, "Would you like fries or a drink with that?"

I chuckle to myself. "Nope. I'll get those at the other fast-food restaurants."

I pull up and hand the lady who looks like she's on my wife's diet, my credit card. She hands me back the card, and the bag of nutrients for my son. I don't really know if I'm having a boy, but the only explanation for Charlie's diet is that we're expecting a three-hundred-and-fifty pound lineman. Secretly, I've been referring to him as Brutus, because really, is there a more perfect name for a gigantic lineman than Brutus? Brutus McKinney. It has a damn fine ring to it.

My next stop is Wendy's. I order Charlie's fries, and wait patiently while the dipshit in the blue Toyota Corolla in front of me digs in his ashtray for spare change.

My phone rings mercifully distracting me from walking up to the car in front of me and handing the asshole a dollar. "McKinney," I respond without checking caller ID.

"Where are you?" the crazed pregnant woman on the other end of the line asks.

"Trying to buy your daily allotment of empty calories and carb-loaded, over-processed, extra-greased shit," I reply, not sounding like the doting husband that I should be.

"Colin, I'm nauseous. I've already thrown up the healthy veggies I had for lunch. Can you hurry?"

I reach up and run my fingers through my hair. *Bald by forty.* "I'm trying to get home, baby." It makes me insane that she's been sick today. I was hoping with the first trimester ending that this shit would be getting better.

"Colin," she whines. "Hurry ... I need my Whopper, fries, milkshake ..." There's a pause, and I can hear the smile in her voice when she says, "... your dick. I've missed you."

We don't get to have our "alone time" we're usually able to find during out-of-town games. Brad is a cock-blocking motherfucker. We'll have a private chat about that later.

In the background, I hear the damn vibrator switch on. "Honey, I'm fucking my BOB because you're taking too long." Then, there's a pregnant pause—pun intended. "Oh God, baby, I'm imaging that your long, thick, hard dick's slamming inside of me." She moans.

My cock presses uncomfortably against the zipper of my jeans, fully aware of what she's saying. I reach down adjusting it. *It's okay, boy. We'll see her shortly.*

Finally, the asshole in front of me finds his fifty-nine cents and goes on with his shit meal. "Charlie, hang in there for me. I'm getting your French fries right now."

I hand the poor pimple-faced kid a ten and snatch my bag of dollar fries before he can hand me the change. I mumble to myself, "Call it a tip."

"What, baby?" She moans into the phone. "Tell me how hard you are for me."

Fuck. I think. *There's a reason that pregnancy is only nine months; because men can't take ten months of this insanity.*

"I'm pulling into McDonalds right now for your shake. Hang on, baby. I'll be home in ten. Then I'll make love to you until you fall asleep in my arms," I try to reason with her.

"But Colin, I need you. I need to fuck you now."

I look down at my poor, confused cock, shaking my head. It had no idea what we were getting ourselves in to when we knocked Charlie up.

"I'm already at the window, handing the nice lady my two dollars. Your milkshake is in my drink holder, freshly frozen, and not melting, just like you like it." I reassure her as I merge into traffic. "Pull that plastic dick out of your sweet pussy. I'll let you ride my hard cock while I feed you your dinner." I roll my eyes at the words that are exiting my mouth. The truth is that I'll do it. I'll set up her smorgasbord of shit on my chest and let her ride my cock while I feed her Wendy's French fries, because I love Caroline Jane Collins-McKinney more than I love my own dignity.

"Oh Colin," she moans. "I'm coming. Oh God, I'm coming. My pussy is gripping the vibrator like it's your cock. I'm pretending it's you, and you feel so fucking good."

I'm half tempted to throw my phone across the car. I just had to listen to my wife masturbate while I'm doing her bidding at fast-food row. Fuck me. This baby can't get here soon enough. I'll trade my sex-obsessed, insatiable, puking wife any day for the rational, self-assured, confident, sassy woman that I married. But, I remind myself over and over, she's growing our child. This is not her. This is her out of whack hormones. I'll have my wife back with the bonus prize of our baby soon.

"Honey, I'm in the driveway. I'm coming to you. I'll be at the kitchen table in three minutes. Let Pancho outside. He can greet me." I try to reason with her.

"Too late," she moans. "I'm going to be sick."

"Fuck my life," I yell as I toss my phone across the car.

****

A few weeks later, it's like a light-switch flipped. She's back to being my sane, rational, Charlie who happens to like at least three to five orgasms a day. She can keep down healthy foods like steamed veggies. I've quit visiting my biggest fans on fast-food row. I tiptoe around the house, afraid to upset the balance, but now I'm getting more comfortable around my new Charlie.

It's a year ago almost to the day that the "break seen around the world" happened. The occasion has been circled on the calendar in my head since the day that it occurred. I know that the media is going to have a field day with questions after the game. So, I've already decided to go to the stadium earlier than usual, in hopes that I can avoid any more press than I'm required to talk to.

Charlie and I are avoiding discussing the anniversary. It's just another game. Another Sunday. My girl in the stands, cheering me on. Just another sixty minutes of football, and hopefully another game in the win column.

I've been awake for at least an hour, watching her sleep. When she snuggles against my chest and whispers in a scratchy voice, "Morning, love" I pull her tightly to me, and sit up enough that I can kiss her shiny, caramel hair. She smells like us, and it's enough that my dick takes notice.

"How did you sleep?" I kiss her full cherry lips and begin to rub my hand over her baby bump. She's had a tough time getting comfortable lately. Her protruding stomach is noticeable in clothes, so she's in maternity jeans that she swears are so comfortable that they may hang around after the baby is born.

"Better." She plants a kiss on my chest that makes me love her that much more. "I finally threw my leg over your thigh, and I was able to get comfy."

"At your service Mrs. McKinney," I say in a goofy accent. Yes. I'm an idiot.

She rolls onto her back. "Let's see if I can wake up our baby this morning." She does this thing where she runs her hands quickly back and forth over her stomach. Sometimes she can get the baby to move. Charlie has been the only one able to feel the action. I desperately want to feel the baby kick.

I can physically look at her and know that she's pregnant. God knows, we've been through the hormonal swings of having a baby, but as the dad, I don't get to do shit. Nothing. Nada. Zip. *Zilch*. I want to feel our son or daughter kick my hand. I want the baby to respond to my voice. Every night I sing to Charlie's stomach, hoping that the little guy is learning who I am.

This baby needs to know that I'm the daddy, and I already love our bean with everything that I've got.

As Charlie moves her hands, I start talking to the bump. "Hey, kid. It's your old man. Today, I've got a big football game. Your mommy's bringing you. I hope you'll cheer me on." Then I pause, and kiss Charlie's belly button. "Tomorrow, we're going to celebrate an early Thanksgiving, because Daddy's playing an away game. You're going to get to enjoy some great food that Mommy and all your crazy aunts and grandmothers are preparing."

Charlie grabs my hand with a squeeze. "Keep talking," she instructs as she places my palm on the right side of her body, about two inches from her center. I hold my breath, waiting, *hoping* to feel the kick.

"Feel that?" she asks with hope dancing in her gorgeous lavender eyes.

I shake my head no, feeling deflated.

"Keep talking," she encourages.

I pick up where I left off. "Then, I'm hoping that I can take Mommy shopping for a new car, because last time I checked, babies can't ride in a two-seater."

Then I feel a slight flutter against my fingers. It's like butterfly wings dancing beneath my fingertips.

"Did you feel that?" she shrieks, with a gigantic smile on her face. "Keep talking."

"Mommy's going to have to get a big, safe car for the two most important people in the world to ride in. What do you think, sweetie? An Audi SUV? A Lexus?" I feel the flutter of movement again.

It's magical. PFM. It's an acronym that the guys use on the team when they pull off a play that is out of the realm of possibility. It's PFM ... Pure Fucking Magic.

I kiss Charlie's full lips, and taste her morning breath. She normally slaps me away until she's brushed her teeth, but she's not pulling that off today. I got to experience PFM. Once I'm done making love to her mouth, I pull back and look into her twinkling eyes.

"Thank you," I can feel the smile on my face stretching from ear to ear, "For sharing this with me. I'll never forget feeling our baby for the first time."

"You have a new job. Every morning, you need to wake our baby up," she says in her know-it-all voice.

"Almost as good of a job as waking up the baby's mother," I say, giving her boob a squeeze.

She laughs and rolls out of bed, heading towards the bathroom. Over her shoulder, she tosses out just before she disappears into the next room, "Don't think for a second that you're getting rid of my car for some slow-moving military-owned tank."

I don't bother to respond. We both know that I'm going to get my way. Plus, I've had the new car, which does look like a tank, on order since the day after she showed me those baby Nike shoes.

I lie back down and stare up at the ceiling. Yup! No matter what the anniversary is, today is going to be a PFM kind of day.

Chapter Four

Charlie

"You look great," Doctor Starr reassures me. "I know that you're experiencing some tightening across your abdomen, but they aren't contractions. They're preparing your body for the birth of your baby. Let me reiterate. You are not in labor. This is perfectly normal for thirty-five weeks into your pregnancy."

I let out a sigh. "Okay. That'll make Colin feel better." I sit up as best as I can, and spread the white sheet over my waist so I can talk to Doctor Starr in a less vulnerable position. I adjust the examining gown, making sure that my ginormous breasts are covered.

Doctor Starr leans against the counter in the examining room and crosses her arms. Her dark hair falls across her shoulders, framing her face in a rather angelic way. "I can't imagine the amount of stress you're under: Colin playing for a trip to the Super Bowl. You're weeks from giving birth, and still working." She unfolds her arms puts her hands in her lab coat pockets. "You're not only growing a human being, but you are trying to be Superwoman. You can't do it all, Caroline. And I've seen Colin at all these appointments with you. Yes. He wants you by his side, but he wants a healthy you and baby more."

I nod my head and tear up. Stupid pregnancy hormones. "I know," I sniff. "I want to be at the game on Sunday. He needs me there as much as I need to be with him."

"Then, go. Go to the NFC Championship game. Come back and see me on Monday. But, no heels. Drink plenty of water, and sleep."

I laugh. "Easier said than done. Sleep is like a mythical creature that lives in the fairy forest and drinks rainbow water."

Doctor Starr kicks up the left side of her lip, and turns her head in confusion.

"Never mind," I respond. I make a note to save that metaphor for Brad. He'll appreciate it.

"On to another subject, how are you doing with your eating disorder?"

Direct much? Why didn't she just ask how many miles I'm running a day? I know that I haven't gained the amount of weight that she would like, but I've been so sick. Even now, if I catch a whiff of Colin's brand of cologne I get nauseous. It's not my eating disorder. It's this pregnancy. "I guess I've finally come to terms that out-of-control is my new normal."

"I want you to consider taking something for postpartum depression after the baby is born. You're a doctor. Do I need to review statistics with you?"

Mentally, I have to catch myself. I'm very well aware of how beneficial antidepressants can be. Doctor Benson has broached the subject at a couple of my appointments. My past issues with control make me more susceptible to PPD. I guess listening to Doctor Benson discuss it with me in the comfort of my home is easier to swallow than hearing the words exit Doctor Starr's mouth in an examining room.

I shake my head. "I promise that I'll discuss it with my therapist, Doctor Benson. Thanks for bringing it to my attention."

I do feel relieved that that's why she asked the question. I can't eat anymore, and I don't need that pressure to shove more food in my mouth, on top of everything else.

She smiles and walks toward the table, offering me her hand. I gladly accept it, and shimmy to a standing position.

"Tell Colin good luck, and go Cowboys," she says, her way of telling me goodbye.

"I sure will." But, I'll leave out the part about postpartum depression. That's the last thing that my husband needs on his plate right now.

Brad's sitting in the waiting room, flipping through a pregnancy-health magazine. Colin has attended every single appointment with me, but he's already left for the NFC Championship game. He was so disappointed that he couldn't make this one.

Brad offered to tag along, so I let him. I can sense Colin's growing uneasiness with the amount of attention and care Brad's been paying to me since I told him that I was pregnant, but there's nothing that I can do about it. Colin pays Brad to be my assistant. He's just doing his job. Right?

I stop in my tracks, taking in the scene. There's a darling couple about my age that are huddled in the corner, looking at something on one of their phones. His arm is lovingly draped around her shoulders, and she is resting her hand on his thigh. There's a very pregnant Indian women draped in her sari. Not even the loose material can hide her very prominent bump. Her husband is playing with their young son at the kid's activity table.

Then, there's my very gay assistant. He has on a pair of Kelly green skinny-jeans with fur-lined leather boots that come up to his calf. He's wearing a white dress-shirt, tucked in with a parrot-colored wool scarf draped perfectly around his neck. His tortoiseshell glasses—for fashion, not vision—rest on his nose. Brad's auburn hair is styled in a perfect, gelled mess. He's letting his auburn facial hair grow to stubble. He says that it makes him look like Robert Pattinson. It so does not, but I can't fault him for trying. I shake my head, and love him even more for embracing exactly who he is. He'll be the perfect Guncle.

He catches me staring, and says, while he checks his watch, "It's about time. I was pretty sure they were keeping you. Then I was going to have to break the bad news to Que Bee. We all know how touchy he gets where you're concerned."

Now everyone in the waiting room is looking at us. *Yes! The best assistant in the world just announced that my husband is a quarterback.* I'm sure that the two dads in the waiting room instantly make the connection.

I roll my eyes and walk to Brad—or, maybe I more waddle, because his head tilts from side to side with my movements. I say, under my breath, "Thanks for letting the cat out of the bag."

"Whatever. You and Colin are on the cover of *Talk Magazine* anyway. They're still speculating on whether or not you're pregnant. Hello … you're either preggers, or swallowed a beach ball." He holds up the magazine, showing me a paparazzi shot of us.

I'm in a light pink button-up maternity blouse and dark jeans. My hair is draped over one shoulder, and my sunglasses are acting as a headband. Colin's in faded, hole-in-the-knee jeans, that I've encouraged him to donate, and an aqua-blue T-shirt that's squeezing his biceps. After seeing this picture, we'll be keeping the jeans. He's leaning up against the brick façade of a health-food store that we frequent. I'm just exiting the shop and walking towards him. The picture was snapped before I entered the weeble-wobble phase of pregnancy. A bag filled with our purchases is in my right hand, and it's slightly hiding the profile of my stomach. My left hand is resting on the top of my swollen abdomen, further obscuring it. But it's the look on Colin's face that makes the picture cover-worthy. He's watching me draw near with a hunger in his eyes that no one can deny. This picture could replace the definition of lust in the urban dictionary.

I'm half tempted to steal the magazine, and frame the picture. It's a candid shot that speaks volumes about Colin's devotion to me, and this child.

The headline reads, "We'll know for sure in a couple of months."

I just shake my head, and walk out of the waiting room while Brad follows, continuing to tell me all the latest gossip about my relationship with my husband.

****

Brad and I had two simple surgeries today after my appointment with Doctor Starr. When we were finished, Carter picked him up from the circle drive out front of the hospital, and the two headed to East Elm to sample the best pumpkin ravioli ever. They invited me to join them, but I decided to head home and spend the evening hanging out with Pancho.

On my way home, I call Rachael. I haven't been able to shake the whole postpartum-depression comment that Doctor Starr made at my earlier appointment. So instead of talking to Janis, who's had four kids and gives sage advice, I call Rachael. Why? Because she makes me laugh. Her ability to marginalize anything is a skill that I wish that I possessed. Really, if someone could bottle it, they'd be billionaires.

"How's my favorite chief of staff to the future President of the United States?" I ask in such a chipper voice that I giggle at myself.

"My feet are on the verge of falling off, because Manolo Blahnik couldn't design a pair of comfortable shoes if his life depended on it. I haven't peed since lunch, and if one more goddamned reporter asks me some asinine question like 'What did the candidate have for breakfast,' they're going to lose talking privileges to me for the next twenty-four hours." She pauses for a second. "You know you're best friends with someone when you can take the phone into the restroom"

A belly laugh comes spilling out of my mouth, and it feels so good. I can imagine my child-sized friend rocking five-inch heels just so she can look at the media somewhere higher than their chests. I'm sure her white-blonde hair is twisted back in a tight knot. She's so polished that somehow Rachael manages to look just as fresh late in the evening as she does when she wakes up in the morning. Sometimes I hate her.

"I don't mind you taking me into the bathroom with you. Go for it," I reassure her.

"How are you feeling? I bet your stomach is absurdly big." Leave it to Rachael to state the obvious.

"I'm good, and yes, I can no longer see my feet." I hear the toilet flush in the background, and the sound of running water. She really did take me to the bathroom with her. "Leaving for the game tomorrow."

"Yeah. About that. Tell Colin good luck from me, and the future President. I, unfortunately, will not be watching it. I'll be attending an all-day campaign event in Florida."

"At least it'll be warm." I try to use her minimizing-everything tactic back on her.

We chat for about ten minutes, which is epically long for us. It's so good to talk about normal things with her. She informs me that she has a new guy in her life. He's actually the Deputy Chief of Staff. Her description: "He's hot, knows how to use his hips and tongue, and doesn't want to marry me. He's perfect."

Rachael asks the most common question these days besides, "How's Colin?" which is, "Any names yet?"

My laugh is over-dramatic, and very fake. I roll my eyes for affect, even though she can't see me. "Not even close. He throws out the worst names for this child. Like he has good taste in every facet of his life, except for baby names. Seriously, if you ever decide to marry, Rach, before you say yes, ask what some of the names are that your future husband likes. I wish I'd known that Colin had such poor taste before I married him."

Rachael laughs. "Remember? No desire to get married, and especially not to have children. I'm looking forward to being an Auntie. I'll swoop in, smother Baby McKinney with love, gifts, and sugar, and retreat back to my quiet townhome."

"Bitch."

"Oh, honey, that's what us aunties do," she says in her best Southern accent.

I reluctantly tell her bye, knowing that I will not see her again until she's meeting her godchild. I miss her so much. She's my anchor when life gets out of control. It makes me sad to hear about the new guy. I guess I still held out hope that Aiden and Rachael would find their way back to each other. I know that Aiden isn't seeing anyone—at least, for more than one night—since they broke up. But Rachael's right, if she and Aiden aren't moving towards the same goal then it's cruel to continue torturing each other.

I pull into the garage, thinking about what I need to pack for tomorrow. My plane leaves at ten in the morning, and I haven't begun to organize my clothes. I'm mentally going through my closet looking for any grey or blue ensembles when I spot it.

Colin's maroon Escalade is gone, and its spot is now occupied with a Mercedes Benz G-class SUV. My first thought is, "It belongs in a jungle, or traversing the Sahara Desert." Then, I notice the six-loop red bow covering the roof that further makes it look like a rectangular box on wheels. The beast is silver, but if it were painted camouflage instead it could be used in a military battle. I can't even imagine what this tank cost. In fact, I don't want to know. *Much more than my Viking stove, and Carrera marble kitchen countertops combined.*

Then, the realization hits me. This is the car he bought for me to drive when the baby arrives. "That bastard," I say out loud as I slam my cute little convertible's door. "He did this on purpose." Colin left for the airport earlier today. He chose to bring this beast home because I'll probably not see him for a couple of days. He's hoping that my pregnant brain will forget our previous talks about buying a baby-friendly car.

We'd discussed purchasing a family-suitable vehicle. I thought we were trading in the Escalade and getting something small that I didn't mind driving, like one of those cute little SUVs. I never agreed to this huge hunk of metal.

I stomp toward the beast of burden, and note that the gigantic red bow on top of it is truly accentuating its box-like structure. I shudder at how horrible this hunk of metal must be for the environment. Then, my eyes are drawn to a yellow sheet of paper taped to the driver's door window.

I stalk over—more like waddle—and rip it off the glass.

"Dear Doctor Collins, I believe that this is the definition of bamboozlement." I pause. I'm so fuming mad that he better be glad he's thirty-thousand feet in the air, and I can't get my hands around his thick neck. "You see, I let you ramble about the small family car that you were WILLING to let me purchase for you. When this has been on order since you showed me the tiny pair of Nikes. Think of this as asking for a postnuptial agreement, but agreeing to drop the fight if I accept Collins as your professional name. I love you, darling, and I love the life growing in your body. This car is so I can sleep at night. Infinity. Colin."

I stand there, staring holes through the sheet of paper. How's it possible to want to smother him with kisses and at the same time long to twist his balls while he writhes in pain?

I reason there's nothing I can do about it right now. Although, there's a brief moment I contemplate going to the nearest car dealership and purchasing the reasonable SUV I agreed to. I quickly dismiss the idea, because I'd be lowering myself to his levels of childishness. When McKinney returns home, and he will have to walk through our doors sooner or later, I'm going to just have to persuade him to return the tank for a practical family car like a *small* SUV.

Crumbling the note into a ball, I toss it toward the recycling bin, noting that at least I'm doing something to save our planet for future generations.

I let Pancho out, and then make my way into our bathroom to change. It takes me just a second to spot the dry-erase marker on my mirror. *Ha! He must be feeling guilty for being an asshole.*

Then, I read what he wrote. "P.S. The Mercedes dealership was given firm instructions that the car cannot be returned, so don't get any ideas."

"Bastard," I mumble under my breath as my lips quirk up into a smile.

"P.P.S. Christen it before the baby arrives. Notice not a question." Then he drew a damn smiley face.

I throw my hands up in the air. I've been beaten at my own game. Except if he thinks that I'm getting rid of my cute little red Mercedes, he's got another thing coming. I've decided to refer to the new tank as the baby's car. Whomever is lucky enough to chauffeur our child can drive it. *Ha!* That should be a good fight when football season is over.

Chapter Five

Colin

Chaos bombards my mind. All I can see is a swirl of whites, greys, and greens. The roar of the crowd is so deafening that I can no longer distinguish a single word; all I can hear is high-pitched yelling. I sink down to the aluminum bench and shut my eyes, dropping my head, fighting desperately to get a hold of myself. There's a camera trained on me right now, capturing every movement that I make. There always is. Even that realization doesn't shake this off. *I just need a fucking minute.*

Someone puts a baseball hat on my head. I don't bother to look up and see who it is. There seems to be a constant sting of slaps on my back and shoulders—I barely feel them. They just magnify the chaotic, out-of-control feelings threatening to overwhelm me. *I don't deserve this. Just getting Charlie back and having her pregnant with our baby was enough. I can't have all of this goodness.* When I do open my eyes, I focus on my right leg. What a fucking crazy fourteen months. I would like to say that I never doubted getting to this moment after the "break seen around the world," but that would be a lie. Oh! I'll probably say exactly that when there's a microphone shoved in my face.

This is so surreal. I've dreamt of this moment since I knew that I was better-than-average at throwing a football. I envisioned this moment a million times in my head. But, never, ever did I have even a fraction of a clue of how amazing it could be. *I just threw the Super Bowl winning touchdown.* Little boys across the country pretend that they're doing just that daily. I actually did it.

"McKinney, come on. They're about to present the trophy. They need you," one of the assistants yells to me. He's the one who I asked to keep my ring for me. If we actually did win the Super Bowl, I didn't want to hold the trophy without wearing my wedding ring.

I pick my head up and nod, stretching my left hand towards him. He unzips the pocket on his athletic pants and fishes out my wedding ring. I slide it on with a pang of sadness that Charlie can't be on the field with me right now.

Standing up, I slip a T-shirt that someone hands me over my sweat-soaked jersey. A camera follows me through the crowd of players, staff, cheerleaders, reporters, fans, maybe—I'm not sure. *Who the fuck are all of these people?* I feel like a fighter being escorted through a rabid crowd to the boxing ring. *Shouldn't "Eye of the Tiger" be playing?*

I make my way up the steps of the platform that's been assembled rather quickly where the commissioner of football is waiting, our team owner, president, GM, Coach, offensive and defensive coordinators, Ty – my best friend on the team, a couple of my receivers, my center, and a couple of the guys on defense.

Apparently, they've been waiting for me to begin the presentation of the trophy. The reporter asks me a question first. "Tell me, Colin, what does this win mean to you?"

I smile at this question. "What a season."

Cheers and screams bombard my ears. This has been as close to a rags-to-riches season as possible. We struggled early on. My leg wasn't one-hundred percent starting the season. I didn't have total confidence in my line to protect me. My receivers didn't have faith that I was going to get them the ball. But every game we got better. Every Sunday, we seemed to gel more as a team. When offense was struggling, defense stepped up. When defense was getting their asses handed to them, offense became resolved to just have to score more points. Perfect season this was not. Hell, we were a wild card team going into the playoffs. No, the season wasn't pretty.

But we found a way to win. The boys standing next to me up here, and the ones whose faces I can see in the crowd played their fucking hearts out. Around week seven it was decided; this is our year, and not finding a way to this spot wasn't an option.

Fortunately, all the following questions go to Coach and the suits. I look around me as they speak, trying to absorb every last detail. The enormity of the moment slams into my chest. Less than fifty times this trophy has been presented. We're bringing it home to Dallas. For the city. For the fans that have stood by me for so many years, and those that haven't. This is for those who've booed when I've jogged onto the field. This moment is for every one of my football coaches growing up who donated their time to us boys. This is for the middle school and high school coaches who believed in me, and spent extra time that they weren't paid for because they saw something special. Fuck. This is for my parents, who've come to my games, worn my jersey, who've believed in me when I didn't have faith in myself. This moment is for Charlie, and our baby, growing in her stomach. Our baby's daddy is a Super Bowl champion. That thought makes the smile already on my face that much larger.

I'm knocked out of my own head when Coach is hitting me on the back and beaming at me like, well, a guy that just won the Super Bowl. "Get your trophy, son, you deserve it."

I look around and see the MVP trophy. What? *They're giving it to me?* I played a great game. My numbers were good, but what about the amazing run that Ty had? He deserves this more than me. I mean, he did, like, gymnastics and shit to get into the end zone.

I take a couple of shuffle-steps back to the microphone, and stand there with a cocky smile on the outside with a world of doubt on the inside. When they hand me the trophy, I hold it up above my head for everyone to see it. Giving it a couple of pumps into the air. The cheers are deafening, *so everyone must agree that I deserve it. Right?*

The reporter starts asking me questions about different plays of the game. I handle those like the professional that I am. Then he blindsides me with, "After last year's season-ending injury, and devastating end to your perfect season, just how much does this mean to you?"

It takes everything that I have to not let my eyes leak on worldwide TV. *What does this mean to me? What does this mean to me? What the fuck kind of question is that?* "It means everything to me. *Everything.* Tonight is what we play our whole careers for. It's why we sweat our asses off in training camp, and spend late nights watching film. It's why we leave our families. It's why we do that one extra rep in the weight room. This is only possible because of the incredible guys that surround me on the field and the support that I have at home." The whole time that I've been standing up here, I've been thumbing my ring. I hope Charlie's watching this, and she sees my gesture of love and appreciation to her.

"So Colin, Chevy is giving you a Corvette. Does that mean that Big Bertha will get garaged?"

I smirk. "I think Bertha is a permanent member of the Cowboys' family." The crowd erupts in more cheers. Bertha is now a legend. The station that carried the Super Bowl hauled her to Miami for promotional appearances. Ford, who Bertha and I endorse, nearly lost their minds at how much free publicity the old girl was bringing them. Charlie just shook her head, but I reminded her that we'd saved enough money from my sponsorship deals for her marble countertops in the kitchen, and the Viking stove.

Finally, after what feels like hours, the ceremony is over. We walk into the locker room, where the celebration is just beginning. There's more interviews, a press conference, coach's team meeting, and champagne is flowing freely. I finally get a shower about three hours later, or maybe four. Hell! It could be next week, for all I know. While the guys are partying it up, I slip out of the locker room to go find my girl.

Turning on my phone is an assault to my senses. I ignore the pings of hundreds of congratulations texts and voicemails.

Me: *Are you at the owners' party?*

I stare at the phone, hoping that she'll respond and not already be asleep. I mean, I wouldn't blame her. She is thirty-seven weeks' pregnant, but I need to see her more than I need to breathe at the moment.

After a few minutes …

Charlie: *Congratulations my love. I'm so proud of you. No. Everyone is back at the hotel, waiting to hear from you.*

Me: *I have to go this party. Do you feel like joining me?*

I feel like the biggest dick-bag for even asking her. She's been having practice contractions. I know she's exhausted. These last weeks have been brutal on us. After winning the NFC title, I don't think that I've actually spent more than a total of five hours with her in two weeks.

Charlie: *I'll meet you there.*

Thank God she said yes. The relief is so strong that I sag against the nearest wall, finally letting my emotions overtake me. *Super Bowl-winning MVP quarterback.*

I climb on the bus with the other guys and head to the club, counting down the minutes until I get to see her, and our baby growing inside of her. The need to touch her soft skin and kiss her lips is overwhelming. I fiddle with my ring, to try to rid myself of my nervous energy. It doesn't help.

I need to physically know that she's okay. My little guy needs to kick my hand. *I've got to stop thinking of the baby as a boy.* Jamie and Brad have been taking care of Charlie, but fuck, I'm glad that this is over. It's my turn. I need a timeout with my wife before I meet this kid.

The club is blasting music so loudly that we can hear it through the bus's windows as we creep closer through the millions of cars crammed on Ocean Drive. We're treated like rock stars as we walk from the bus, down the red carpet, and through the very large gold doors. Ty yells in my ear, "Someday, people will be yelling like this for my mad guitar skills." I smirk at him. My friend, who's a rock star when he's not my running back is really something else. I try to smash down his Cowboy-blue Mohawk, but he swats my hand away.

"Don't touch the do, bro. This took me a good ten minutes with Hard Up Gel."

I just shake my head, and flip him off.

Some of the players are already here. The place is packed. I'd gotten a text from Jamie that my family was in a VIP room on the second floor. I head for the stairs, noting that I look like I should be going more for a run on the treadmill than in one of the most exclusive clubs in Miami.

When I round the corner at the top of the stairs, I see Carter standing next to another shiny gold-painted door. We fist bump a quick congratulations as he opens it for me.

Before I can thank him, my family and friends surround me, yelling their congratulations, and hugging and kissing me like we're at a reunion. My mom nearly climbs me to reach my neck. She's crying, and I smile and hug and kiss her back. My dad gives me a tight hug, and whispers how proud he is of me. Charlie's dad shakes my hand. Carmen kisses my cheek. Charlie's mom wipes tears from her eyes, and pulls me tightly to her. They're all so excited for me, and I love them for it.

But, I want my girl. I can see over the crowd that she's sitting in the corner on a red-velvet bench, with her feet propped up on a metal folding chair. She looks like a dream. Her black V-neck sweater just shows the tops of her more than ample cleavage, and is straining to cover her rounded abdomen. Her caramel-colored hair is loosely braided, and resting on her left breast. *Lucky hair.* She looks serene. Our eyes lock—green to lavender—and her lips turn up into an innocent smile.

Dear God, I need her this moment. She knows what I crave. She's waiting for me to come to her on my terms. She knows that I don't like all the hoopla after games. I just need to be. I watch her right cheek pull up in a slight half-smile as she pats the bench next to her. Her wink is saying, "Come when you're ready. I'll be right here."

I'm ready now. I make a loud announcement, thanking everyone for their love and support. Then I ask all of my guests if they'll wait for us downstairs in the club. I turn, and watch impatiently as they file out of the VIP room, spinning my ring again. Once they're gone, I step outside, and ask Jamie and Carter to make sure that no one enters the room.

As I walk back inside where she's waiting for me, the door slams shut on the rest of the world. I hear silence for the first time in two weeks. The *thump, thump, thump* of the base becomes white noise. No one is yelling my name, or demanding a piece of me. Paparazzi aren't attempting to catch a picture of me doing something embarrassing. No one is asking me if I'm the father of Charlie's baby. Fans aren't demanding autographs or pictures. It's quiet, and peaceful. I'm with my wife, who asks nothing more of me than to support and love her, just as she is.

I walk to the bench slowly drinking in the sight of her. Her eyes travel all over my body, tenderly inspecting me for injuries. She grimaces when she spots the painful bruise near my surgery-incision scar on my right leg. I smile, trying to reassure her that I'm okay.

When I reach her, I lean down and let my lips feel her swollen, soft, cherry colored mouth. She tastes of vanilla sweetness and Charlie. It's so intoxicating that I'm afraid my knees are going to buckle, so I collapse next to her on the bench—the spot that she indicated earlier is mine.

She doesn't say a word. She just lets me use her like she knows that I need at this moment. I explore her mouth gently with my tongue, savoring being this close to her. My mind floods with all that is Charlie: her smell, her taste, and the moan that she makes when I nibble on her bottom lip. The known is so comforting. I cling to it, as the rest of my life is chaos.

Breaking our kiss, I lean down to her swollen stomach, raising her thin sweater and tucking it under her bra. Her abdomen is fuller than when I last saw it. It's beautiful, breathtaking actually. Her body is able to expand itself like this to hold our child.

The skin is smooth, and stretched to the maximum limit across her abdomen. Her belly button is now flat, just slightly protruding, and there's a faint brown line that runs from it to her pubic bone. Sexiest damn thing that I've ever seen.

I plant tiny kisses, starting at the top of the roundness exploring the stretched, taut skin with my lips and tongue. Our baby moves toward me as if he's following my trail of kisses in his warm, safe spot. Then, the baby moves, and pushes with force against my nose. I look up at Charlie who's

INFINITY.

staring at me with soft eyes and a glowing complexion. Love and happiness dance across her beautiful face.

"I think that was the baby's bottom that got you." She smiles. "I've been feeling a lot of arms and legs in my ribs lately. I also know that our little guy's been sitting on my bladder."

I look back at her stomach, watching our baby move just underneath her skin.

"The baby would get particularly excited with lots of movement when you'd score. I'm sure that I'm going to be sore tomorrow from the battering that the bean put me through." She shares this with me as her fingers work through my matted curls.

All I want to do is be alone with her right now, in our bedroom. I want to be inside of her and fall asleep that way. Instead, I'm in a nightclub, after the biggest game of my career, listening to the bass line change.

As if she can read my mind, she says, "Just a couple more days of this, and it can be just the two of us before we welcome our child." It's uncanny how well she knows me.

I need her more than oxygen, food, and water. I need some alone *being* time with just her. I need her naked and pressed up against me. I need to taste her and hold her. God, I just need to sleep next to her again, and wake up with her warm heat cocooning me, her leg thrown over my hip. I need to be the one who cares for her, instead of Brad.

My eyes drift closed as her long fingernails massage my skull. I lay my head on her swollen stomach, inhaling her scent, which is honey and almond-butter from the lotion she rubs on her body, trying to prevent stretch marks.

"How are you feeling?" I ask in a raspy voice.

Her soft chuckle makes her belly dance under me. "Well, strangely enough, half the men here were wearing your cologne. Great for your sponsors, terrible for my nausea. As long as I stayed out of the crowds, I was fine."

Poor Charlie. All of our Christmas shopping this year was done online because she couldn't step foot in a mall. The cologne company has been pimping both the old and new scents because of our winning season—trying to capitalize on my success. It's been great for our bank account/Lake Somerville house fund, but terrible for her body.

"Hopefully, it's almost over, baby. And the contractions?"

"Still practicing." She removes her hand from my hair, and tilts my chin up so I can see her face. In a more stern voice, she chastises, "Quit worrying. I'm fine. The baby is fine. I've taken good care of us while you've been gone."

"I know that you have. I've just missed you so fucking much."

"It was worth it. You're a Super Bowl-winning quarterback and MVP. You know that there's no one who's happier than me. There was no place that I wanted to be more than on the field with you." She pauses as her eyes dance. "I saw you were wearing your ring."

I raise my left hand to her mouth, and she kisses the ring that she had made for me. The gold from her original engagement ring when I used to propose to her every single day. She ultimately asked me to marry her, and now, I see how perfect it really was to have worked out that way. "I wanted you to know that I was thinking about you."

"Always, baby," she confirms as I kiss her very simple infinity wedding band that I had made just for her.

"Go make your appearances. Do what you need to do. I'll be waiting at home for you tomorrow. 'Kay?"

Sitting up, I lean against the back of the bench, allowing my head to bang against the wall behind me. "Fuck, I just want to go home." For a man that just won the Super Bowl and MVP trophies, I sound like a pathetic whiney bitch.

"Go own this time. Honey, you've been working for this day since you were a little boy tossing footballs in the front yard with your dad. Tonight might not ever happen again. We have the rest of our lives to spend holding each other while we fall asleep. Go live it up. Soak in every second, because you've earned it." She says just what I need to hear. Her quiet, even voice knows how to speak to my heart.

I sit up straight and take her lips against mine while I rest my throwing hand lightly across her stomach. Our kiss is gentle, sweet, and filled with love. I want to remember this moment for the rest of my life.

Chapter Six

Charlie

Present day ...

I check my Rolex watch as I walk through the labor-and-delivery double doors heading straight for the nurses' station. Brad's hot on my heels, barking at me to slow down. The irony that I can waddle faster than he can run is not lost on me.

Before I can identify myself, the nurse grabs my chart, flashes me a reassuring smile, and says, "Doctor Collins, we've been expecting you. Please, follow me to your room."

A contraction grips my body and doubles me over. Gripping the wall for support, I attempt to take long breaths through my nose. *You've got this, Caroline.*

The nurse's reassuring smile is gone. "Let me grab you a wheelchair," she says with alarm in her voice.

I shake my head no, and continue to follow behind her. The room she leads me to is large, and some hospital designer has attempted to add homey touches. The walls are painted a light shade of mint green. There's faux-wood paneling behind the hospital bed. The window curtain is open, and the blinds are raised. I have a lovely view of the roof of the next hospital building. I don't care. I want an epidural, and this baby out of me stat, of course, after Colin arrives.

Once she's closed the door behind Brad and me, she introduces herself. "My name is Mary, and Doctor Starr asked me to assist you today with your delivery. Our first order of business is to get you out of those clothes, and into one of our designer hospital gowns," she explains as she hands me a green scrub-colored sheet with arms. "You can change in the bathroom," she says, as she gestures to a door on the other side of the room.

As I'm shutting the door, I hear Mary asking Brad questions about the parade. I'm thankful that Doctor Starr gave Mary the heads up as to who Brad is, and that he's not my husband.

I exit the bathroom a few minutes later with my street clothes in a plastic bag, draped in the ill-fitting sheet with arms. Dropping my belongings in the mauve and faux-wood chair next to the bed, I do my best to scooch to the place that Nurse Mary is indicating that she wants me on the white sheets. I would not refer to myself as very mobile these days.

"I hope you don't mind, but I sent Brad into the hallway. He has your phone. I need to check you," she says preparing me for the inevitable.

I lean back and bend my knees, bracing for any dignity that I have left to pack its bag and run for the border. I throw my head back against the fluffy pillows and look up at the white ceiling tiles, wondering why they don't at least put an interesting sticker up there for anxious almost-mothers to stare at.

After a lot of pokes and prods inside of me, Mary states the obvious. "You are definitely in labor. About four centimeters dilated. You aren't far enough along that you can have an epidural." She removes her gloves tossing them in the large garbage can. Then, crosses her arms over her chest. "Here's my speech on epidurals. They generally slow down labor, but it's your call. You can have one at five centimeters. I'll warn you, it usually takes the anesthesiologist about thirty minutes to arrive, so if you decide that you want one, there will be some lead time."

"Thanks Mary," I say, putting my legs back down. "I'm waiting for my husband to call. I'll keep your warning in mind."

She opens the door, motioning for Brad to come back in. The poor guy looks a little green. He did tell me when I hired him that he didn't do vaginas.

Mary, Brad and I begin chatting about the game, and she asks questions about what it was like to be there, live, watching it, while she wraps a piece of elastic around my gigantic stomach that has a round sensor attached to it.

She sits down on a rolling stool and begins to monitor my contractions and the baby's heart rate. Brad regales her with stories as only Brad can about our time in Miami. It's a nice distraction from my worries and the pain. My husband still has no clue that I'm no longer sitting on the balcony watching the festivities.

As my mind begins to question my decision to not tell Colin I'm in labor, Mary warns me, "You're about to have another contraction."

And boy, do I. Brad grabs my hand, letting me tightly squeeze it, helping me work through it. As I relax, he says, "You're doing fabulous, Caroline. I mean you've got a bowling ball trying to exit your vagina, and look how brave you are."

So they're not the most relaxing words, but for Brad, this is him really trying. Instead of pointing out the crassness of his statement, I mumble a polite, "Thank you. I think."

As my abdomen is relaxing, my phone starts playing "I Just Want to Dance with You." My heart takes flight, battering against my rib cage, and a second later my heart-monitor alarm sounds its warning. I catch Mary shooting Brad a warning look, and he grabs my phone and sprints like he's in the Olympics out of my hospital-room door. *But, I'm supposed to be the one to tell him I'm in labor.*

Mary gives me her stern-nurse glare. I recognize the look. They must teach it in nursing school, because nurses have the look down pat. It's the expression that says, *I've been nice, but you're now on my turf, and playing by my rules.*

"Doctor Collins, Doctor Starr has briefed me on the circumstances surrounding your labor. We aren't worrying about Colin right now. I need you to focus on you and your baby. Brad is going to take care of Colin. When the phone rang, your heart rate went through the roof. If it continues to do that, Doctor Starr will take the baby via C-section, whether or not Colin's present. If you want to do what's best for your family then you've got to focus on your labor. Am I making myself clear?"

I nod my head, knowing that she's right. But, it doesn't make him not hearing the news from me any easier.

She warns that another contraction is coming, and I grip her hand as I labor through it.

Brad knocks, and gets the all clear from Mary before he shuffles in, holding my phone at arm's length from his ear. He doesn't have to say who's on the other end. I can hear his voice across the room, and the phone isn't on speaker.

Brad interrupts the crazed, screaming man and says, "Here she is, Colin," while he hands me my phone like it's toxic. He shakes his head and almost dives for the safety of the sofa in the corner of my room.

I take a deep breath, remembering Mary's lecture, and begin my own. "If you scream at me, I'm hanging up on you. I'm in labor. It hurts like hell. And I will not be yelled at like I'm a child."

I hear him let out a deep breath. In a scratchy, tight voice that makes me worry about his molars, he grinds out, "I'm on my way."

Because I'm a hormonal mess and a little scared, I begin to cry. "I need you, Colin. Tell Jenny to drive fast."

"Why didn't you tell me that it was time?" He sounds so pained, as if I've cut out his heart.

"You needed your moment. It's over. Now, I need you. I'm dilated to four centimeters, and I want to have this baby natural, but I need you here with me. This baby will not be born until you get here. I promise."

Mary interrupts, and says, "You're about to have another contraction."

I hand Mary my phone, and ask her to put it on speaker. Brad rushes to my side, gripping my hand.

"I'm having a contraction. Brad's holding my hand," I yell to Colin, so he knows what's happening. My abdomen is squeezing tighter and tighter.

I'm unable to take a breath, and I clench my hand around Brad's, trying to disperse the pain.

"You can do this, Charlie. You've got this, baby," Colin coaches over the phone. "I know that it hurts, but in a couple of hours we're going to meet our baby, and it'll all be worth it. I'm still in downtown, but I'll be there as soon as I can. I love you, Charlie."

As my stomach relaxes, I lie back against the elevated top half of the bed. Brad starts doing this dramatic shaky thing with his hand as if it's about to fall off. *What a baby!*

"They're getting more intense each time," I inform Mary and Colin, ignoring Brad's dance.

Mary looks at the contraction monitor and agrees with me. "The baby's heart rate is holding strong through the contractions, but let's get Doctor Starr in here and have her do a check up on you."

I nod in agreement as Colin begins rapid-firing questions at Mary. Mary patiently explains to Colin that she must exit the room as I motion for Brad to take the phone.

He picks it up as if it's a snake, and takes Colin off of speaker.

Another contraction hits me before I feel like I've recovered from the previous one. I squint my eyes closed, gripping the sheet as I roll over on my side in the fetal position, gasping for relief.

I know Brad is attempting to calm Colin down, but I can't concentrate on their conversation. Mother Nature is kicking in. The whole world can go jump in a lake. I'm listening to her very stern instructions on what I should be doing.

I find a zone, a happy place, a nirvana, or whatever it is. It's the place that women have been visiting since time began. It's the place that women found before there was such things as epidurals. The surge of hormones makes me tingle and feel as if I've got the best buzz or high in the world.

Each time a contraction grips me I roll into a tight ball, and squeeze the railing of the bed. I use the breathing techniques that they taught us in medical school. I can do this.

I. Can. Do. This.

I'm half aware that Doctor Starr is checking me. I have no idea what she said, and then she smiled and left. That's positive, in my book.

Brad says from some far-off place, sounding like he's in a tunnel, "Colin's in the hospital. He'll be here in just a few seconds, and Jenny's warned me that I need to get lost." He brushes a kiss on my cheek, which I barely feel. "I love you, honey. Be strong."

It registers just barely that Colin just called me. Wasn't he still in downtown? It took us about an hour to get to the hospital. Now, he's at the hospital? Either I've lost time, or Brad and Jenny kept Colin from speaking to me. Don't know. Don't care. Nirvana. Happy place. Mother Nature doing her job. And all that happy shit I read about in my pregnancy books.

When the door opens, I expect to see my psychotic husband, but instead it's Doctor Starr again. *Wasn't she just here?*

She rolls me on my back, and spreads my legs and bends my knees for me. I think that she's explaining what she's about to do, but I'm not listening because all I can hear is the roar of my own blood, and blissing out on whatever fantastic hormones have taken control of my body.

As she's removing her hand from between my legs, the door to the hospital room flies open and my gigantic, crazed husband fills the doorway, looking like an axe murder from some horror flick minus the axe, of course. His hair is a mess of curls from him running his hands through it. His eyes are bugging out of his head, and his mouth is gaping open as if he's about to say something or just finished.

His appearance makes me want to laugh, but not because he looks funny. No, it's more the nervous or inappropriate laugh one has during funerals. I wonder briefly if he's going to yell "Here's Johnny!" I bite the inside of my lip until I taste blood to keep my laughter at bay.

He pauses just long enough to see that I'm okay—there's no baby—and that Doctor Starr is here. He walks to the left-hand side of the bed and stands there, staring down at me as if he doesn't know if he should scream at me or kiss me.

Doctor Starr breaks his glare when she announces, "You're nine centimeters, Caroline. You're progressing. No time for an epidural now. I'm going to get ready. I'll be back in just a few minutes."

Another contraction grips me, and I roll back over on my side and resume the fetal position. Colin's talking to me, but I don't process what he's saying. As the contraction loosens, I finally hear his words. He's repeating, "My brave beautiful girl," over and over again.

I've been silent the whole time through my labor. It's as if I had to be strong for Colin and me. Now that he's here, I can have this baby. Relief washes over me, and I grasp for him as if I'm drowning.

He takes my hand in his, and brings it up to his mouth. He dots the underside of my wrist with kisses, and nips that flood me with serenity. Then, he kisses my wedding ring, and stares deeply into my eyes. "You've got this, Charlie. I'm right here, standing by your side. Let's meet our baby."

"I love you," I whisper as I roll out of the fetal position and onto my hands and knees. I hear the scream registering in my own ears as another contraction constricts my body, and my back bows up like a cat. The gown that I have on is no longer providing modesty, and I feel like it's choking me around my neck, so I grab for it and give it a yank. Finally, I feel like I can take a breath.

Colin carefully removes it from each arm, and then uses it to wipe the sweat off of my face. He holds my hair back away from my clammy cheeks and places his other hand on my back for support.

Another contraction tears through me. When my yells subside, he mops my face again, now using a white towel that materialized from somewhere. At some point, he braids my hair down my back. I know, because I feel the comforting touch of both of his hands on me, and my hair is no longer matted against my sweaty cheeks and forehead.

From somewhere in the recesses of my mind, I hear him bark, "Get her a goddamn epidural, or something for her pain!" He sounds agitated, mixed with terror, but I don't have time to dwell on his emotions as another contraction contorts my body.

Doctor Starr enters my peripheral vision, saying something to Colin. The contractions are on top of each other without giving me a chance to recover. I feel as if my body is going to rip apart. The logical side of my brain has shut off, and the knowledge of the thousands of years of women birthing children ingrained in my DNA takes over.

The most natural and overwhelming feeling baths me again. It's the need to push.

I yell something that's intended to be the word, "Push." But Doctor Starr gets in my face, staring at me with stern eyes, and says, "Wait."

Well, that's like telling a drowning person to give up and start inhaling water. I can't wait. Mother Nature is now running this show, and she's using me as she sees fit.

Awareness that my body is moving grips me. I've gone from all fours to Colin behind me. I'm leaning against his bare chest while he's gripping each one of my thighs in his large muscular hands. He brings my knees up so they're almost to my ears.

I get a moment of clarity, and realize how absurd I must look. I'm naked. My big breasts are pushed up against my stomach, so they're almost to my chin. My unpainted toes are dangling haphazardly, as if my legs belong to a puppet. Doctor Starr is waiting at the end of the bed, which seems to have been partially removed. Mary is next to her to assist. I'm on full display in the most immodest position possible.

I don't give a damn.

A crazy laugh erupts from my chest. I have an out-of-body experience and see the ridiculousness. I'm a Harvard-trained physician. How did I get myself spread-eagled and naked on a table? Oh yeah! Colin Fucking McKinney.

Suddenly Mother Nature grabs my face and says, "Let's get this baby out of you."

They're telling me something about push counts, but I'm not listening. I'm pushing just like Mother Nature is screaming at me to do. I figure she has more experience than anyone in this room. Colin's mouth is pressed against my ear, whispering words of encouragement. "You're doing so well. I love you. So brave. So strong."

I push for God knows how long. My sense of time is completely shot. All I know is that Doctor Starr looks at Colin, and says something. Then Colin whispers to me, "The baby's head is right there, Charlie. Give me three more strong pushes."

Suddenly, I'm so tired that my muscles feel like Jell-O. Three more pushes? Hearing that I have to do this three more times is just too much. My head falls back against Colin's chest, and I feel tears or sweat running down my cheeks. Surely Doctor Starr can do the rest.

When I've all but given up, and don't think that I can push another time, another wave of nature's drugs hit me, and I push with everything that I have.

Colin is in my ear, whispering his words of encouragement. "You've got this … Almost there, Charlie … Two more pushes … One more push, my brave, beautiful girl …"

I can hear the sounds of my grunts filling the room. Then, they're replaced by the most incredible noise that has ever tickled my ears the sound of our baby's wail.

I collapse back on Colin's chest, unable to support my weight any longer. My head flops to the side as Colin kisses my temple over and over again. He releases my legs, and they fall brokenly to the bed.

Doctor Starr places the squirming, pink, bloody angel on my naked chest and says, "Meet your baby girl."

I open my mouth to speak, but all that comes out is, "Girl?"

I run my index finger over her soft skin. She begins to cry again, so I place my hand on her back and snuggle her against my racing heart. She's so tiny. *This was just inside of me.* Once she's pressed against my chest and in between my breasts, she calms down. No more screams, just sweet little content mewing noises.

Colin drops his head to my shoulder looking at our daughter. We're both silent, feeling the love and peace soothe our baby. At some point his tears mix with mine as we stare at our greatest collaboration.

Mary has a twinkle in her eye. "Good job, Mom." It's the first time I've ever been called that. I look up at her and smile.

"I need to take your princess for just a few minutes. We need to give her a bath, weigh her, and some of that other good stuff. You just relax while Doctor Starr takes care of you."

Colin takes this as his cue. He crawls out from behind me, and I flop back against the pillows, missing his warmth and comfort. I wonder briefly if I look as bad as he does. He walks over to the mustard-yellow vinyl couch and sinks into it as much as it will allow. He rests his elbows on his knees, and drops his head in between his legs.

"We have a daughter," I whisper to him.

He doesn't move, or look up to acknowledge me. I watch my tragic hero trying to process the last couple of days.

The room is quiet except for the sounds of our baby whimpering, and Doctor Starr and another nurse talking amongst themselves while they're cleaning the room.

After a measure of time that I can't calculate, Mary hands me a pink blanket with a precious little face peeking out. She has on a pink-and-blue striped hat to keep her head warm. My heart clenches at the sight of her.

"She's probably hungry. Why don't you try placing her mouth near your nipple, and see if she'll nurse?"

Mary helps get her arranged, and since I'm still naked except for a scrub sheet that's been placed over my bottom half, there are no gowns to get in my way. Mary shows me how to hold the baby with one arm, and feed her my breast with the other hand.

When she opens her tiny little mouth and takes my nipple, I ask Colin if he wants to watch. My poor, overwhelmed husband still doesn't answer me.

Mary informs me she's just over six pounds and seventeen inches long. She's tiny, but very healthy. I ask Mary what time she was born at, and am shocked to find out that it's after midnight. She smiles knowingly at me and says, "Caroline you've been in labor at this hospital for more than twelve hours."

I had no idea. I shake my head in confusion. "How long has Colin been here with me?"

She checks her watch. "I'd say for about five hours."

In my mind, everything happened so fast that I would have thought he just made it for the delivery. *Where was he all that time that I was in labor?*

****

After our daughter has taken both breasts, Mary asks, "Caroline, there's a waiting room full of people. What would you like for me to do?" She cuts her eyes toward Colin.

Reading her message loud and clear, I say, "Can you take the baby to the nursery and let them view her through the glass? Tell them that we're doing great, just really tired, and are going to bed. If they want to visit tomorrow, ask them to please text us before coming up here." I make the decision on behalf of Colin. I know that there's no way he can deal with family right now.

Mary smiles at me, and pats my hand as she looks towards Colin sympathetically.

I nod my head, and give her a knowing wink. "I'll take care of it."

Colin hasn't moved from his fixed pose since he assumed it. I don't know what to do with him at this point, so I decide to take advantage of the "complimentary" toiletries that the hospital is probably billing my insurance company hundreds of dollars for.

I gingerly roll to my side and swing my legs off the edge of the bed. I know without trying that my abs are way too sore for me to use them to stand up. I grip the bed for support while I try out my sea legs. I'm a little wobbly, but I can shuffle.

And that's what I do. I shuffle into the bathroom, using the restroom for the first time since the baby stopped sitting on my bladder. It feels glorious. Then I step into the warm shower, and exhale as the hot water washes over me. A shower has never felt this good. My body feels battered and bruised, but strangely enough, I feel like I could conquer the world right now. I just did the impossible. I gave life to a human being. I'd like to see Batman, with all of his gadgets, do that.

I take my time, lathering my hair using my fingernails to work the soap into my scalp, and then rinsing out the soap. The conditioner has a hint of mint, and I work it through my hair using my fingers as a comb. As I wash my body, I note that I can see my feet over my five-month pregnant-sized stomach. Thank goodness Janis had warned me that it takes a while for your abdomen to appear normal again. If not, I probably would have panicked at this point.

Once I'm gloriously clean, I realize with much despair that I don't have anything to put on. I wrap myself in a too-small white threadbare towel, and walk back into the hospital room, feeling much better but terribly sad that I don't have my pretty PJs to comfort me. The thought of putting a hospital gown back on makes me frown.

Then, I spot my hospital overnight bag resting at the foot of the bed. On top is a note from Brad: *Can't have a baby without your hospital bag. XXXOOO, Guncle Brad.* Best. Assistant. Ever.

I unzip my brightly-colored floral-print tote and spot the PJs that I purchased a couple of weeks ago. I carry them, along with other necessities, back into the bathroom to dress. Once the door is closed, I drop my towel and slide on a pair of my favorite pregnancy panties, and slip the light pink, silk pants on my legs, and button the top across my straining breast. I make quick work of throwing my wet hair in a clip that I found in my travel bag and slip back in the hospital bed, pulling the sheets over me.

Colin still hasn't moved, or spoken, or hell, at this point, he may not have breathed. I've left him alone, to just *be*, long enough. This baby doesn't have a name. She doesn't even have a place to sleep. We were going to take care of all of that this week. I get it. A lot has happened in the last seventy-two hours. Now, it's time for him to be my partner, and this baby's daddy.

"Colin," I coax. "Come crawl in bed and snuggle with me before they bring Elizabeth back for another feeding."

He picks his head up and looks at me with haunting, empty, eyes. "Charlie," he warns. "I don't have it in me yet to discuss names."

I smile sweetly. "All the more reason that I should go ahead and fill out the birth certificate." I've chosen Elizabeth because it's Liza's full name, and she helped me remove my wet clothes. Plus, it's a really great name.

He stands and walks toward the bed, doing his best impression of a little old man. His shoulders are slumped, and his head is hung. I use my hands and arms to move my sore body all the way to the edge, making enough room for him to lie on his side.

He's still shirtless, and I notice that there are traces of dark brown blood on his blue jeans. I'm not sure whose blood it is, and I don't dare ask. Colin is not mentally ready to acknowledge the blood yet. That I do know.

He lies down on his side on top of the sheets, and he gingerly rolls me so that my back is to his front. He drapes his left arm over my body, resting his massive hand on my deflating abdomen.

I know that I'm going to have to be the one that does the talking. He's still not ready to verbalize what he just witnessed. "So, you got a daddy's girl, huh?"

His light chuckle presses his chest tighter against my back. "After the amount of Whoppers, fries, and shakes that you ate, I was expecting a twelve-pound offensive lineman."

"Disappointed?" I ask keeping my voice neutral, but hoping that he's not.

"Are you kidding me? Daughters love their daddies forever. No. I deserve her after the horrible thoughts I've had about your father, and the way that I treated my ex-wife. God's laughing," he whispers with a hint of sourness in his voice.

I hate that he mentioned his ex-wife. It's not that I'm jealous or bitter that he was married before. Colin feels a tremendous amount of guilt when it comes to her. I've agreed with him that some of it is merited, but he's got to let it go. The birth of our daughter should mark the time when he forgives himself for hurting her.

Just as I'm about to tell him all this, he continues, "She's going to be dating some douchebag like Aiden or me, and he's going to make her cry, and I'm going to behave just like Jack Collins, except I'll probably kill the fucker."

We lie there in complete silence, and it's the most peace that I've felt since Colin and the boys started their playoff run. The lights are off in the hospital room except for a nightlight that's casting odd shadows on the ceiling from some of the medical equipment left in the room. The blinds are closed and curtains drawn, so we don't even have moonlight.

As my eyes drift closed, in a choked voice Colin says, "That's the most intense thing that I've ever experienced." He pauses and swallows deeply, and keeps going. "All the blood ... and your yelling ... and I couldn't make it better for you ... I couldn't help you."

He pulls me tighter against him. He whispers so quietly that I'm not certain that I'm actually hearing him. "I asked God that if I could only have one of you, that you'd be okay."

He buries his face in my wet hair that's slipped out of the clip holding it at bay. "I can't watch that again, Caroline. You can't put yourself in a situation that made me witness my greatest fear."

He swallows deeply again, and then chokes out, "I thought you were going to die."

"Honey," I try to reassure him. "You just witnessed childbirth without drugs. Doctor Starr would never have let anything happen to me or the baby."

"Don't. Fucking. Care," he spits out.

When I open my mouth to say something else on the subject, he cuts me off. "Stop," he yells making me jump. "I can't discuss it anymore. It's over," he says in a normal talking tone. "You're fine. You're here with me. But, so help me God, Caroline, you need to give me some time to cope with the birth of our daughter. If that makes me a little more neurotic with you then get the fuck over it."

Well, I guess I just got put in my place. I lie there silently, feeling his heartbeat race against my back. My mind is turning over ways that I can help him, to reassure him that I'm okay, but I keep coming up blank. I pray that just me lying next to him is enough.

"Yesterday was the worst day of my life." He drops a statement like that and doesn't follow it up with an explanation, but the tightness of his body betrays how truly upset he is. I can almost feel him vibrating with tension.

I wait a couple of beats and then ask, "Do you want to tell me why?"

The room is silent for what feels like an eternity. "You made a choice for me, and by making that choice, Caroline, you made my recurring nightmare come true. I had to stand there and face the blackness that enters into my dreams while I was surrounded by a million-plus people watching me." He says the last part so quietly that I can barely hear him.

Then, I realize what I've thought was his need to "be" is actually Colin extremely upset. Panic grips my heart, and I try to roll over to look in his eyes. His eyes are where I can read Colin's truths. As if he knows what I'm doing, he prevents me from turning over, gripping me tighter while holding me in my same position. "I … I'm …sorry …" I stammer.

"I couldn't get to you." His hot breath all but burns my scalp. "There were fans pulling at me, and reporters yelling for a statement. I was surrounded by people blocking me from getting to you." His hand on my stomach grips the material of my pajama top. "Why didn't you tell me? Let me make the choice. Let me be a partner in this." His angst-ridden voice is slicing me open and gutting my insides.

"I thought …" I start, but have to swallow the lump in my throat. "I thought I was making the best choice for us. I knew that I had some time before the baby arrived. I wanted you to have your victory moment. To enjoy the success that you've worked so hard for," I plead with him to understand where I was coming from when I made the decision.

"Goddammit, Caroline!" he bellows making me cringe. "Do you think that moment will ever be happy for me? Do you think that I will ever look back on the victory parade and my address to the fans as positive? I couldn't get to you." He takes a deep breath, and then continues. "I finally yelled, 'My wife is having our baby. Move the fuck out of my way.' Do you think that that's how I wanted to tell the world our joyous news?"

Oh, God! I feel so awful. I can picture in my mind my big, strong, tough husband losing his cool in front of the cameras, and I begin to cry. In my mind it was so perfect. I was letting Colin have it all.

"Then, they wouldn't let me talk to you until I cooled down … There were so many people keeping me from you. I rode here in a fucking police car," he finishes speaking and crawls out from behind me, leaving my back frigidly cold. "A fucking police car."

I roll backwards, pulling the covers up around my chin, watching him pace back and forth in front of my hospital bed and run his hands through his hair.

He's shirtless and his jeans slip to his hips, revealing the top of his perfect V. His boots *clomp, clomp, clomp,* as he paces. And in this state, I can't appreciate the beauty of his body. He obviously has more to say. I'm just not sure that I want to hear what it is.

He opens his mouth and closes it again. Just when I'm to the point that I want to beg him to forgive me and reassure him that I'll make this better, he stops pacing, and places both of his arms on the bottom of my hospital bed, bracing the upper part of his body. He looks menacing. This is the "I'm furious" football expression.

"You know what's the worst? The absolute fucking worst part."

I hang on every word, waiting to find out what could possibly be the worst thing I've done in this whole mess because for the life of me, I can't figure out what it is.

"Brad is who was with you when you went into labor. Brad is who brought you to the hospital. Brad is who got you settled in, and helped you through your first hours of contractions. Brad is who held your hand. Brad. Did he wipe the sweat from your brow, Caroline?" He pauses and stands to his full height staring down at me as I lie in bed feeling minuscule and obsolete. I'm inwardly beating myself up for my choice.

"Last time that I checked, Brad is not our baby's father. Brad didn't pick you up crap food every night. Brad didn't massage your swollen feet, or help you shave your legs. Brad certainly wasn't there when we created our daughter. So fuck Brad. I earned the right to be a part of the day that my daughter entered this world. I earned every blessed second of it, but it was taken away from me."

He turns away from me, and walks toward the bathroom. Before he enters, his shoulders tense as he says without turning around, "And I'll never have the time back."

He slams the door behind him.

Sobs consume my body. This is not what I thought the birth of our baby would be like. I thought it would be a fantastic day, filled with love and joy, and family and hope. I thought Colin and I would hold our child and marvel at whose eyes she has, and does she have a half-smile like her daddy's? It never occurred to me that the birth of our baby would bring sorrow and angst to our family.

When he exits the bathroom, his hands are no longer balled into fists, and his posture is a bit more relaxed. "I had no idea, baby," I plead sitting up as best as I can. "I promise. I just thought I was doing what was best for you. You can't be this upset with me." I pause and swallow my sob. "I'm scared to death, Colin. Our baby is coming back in this room any moment, and we have to figure out how to take care of her. I need you right now. Please be on my side. Please help me." The sob escapes my lips as I beg again, "I need you."

He doesn't respond, and walks back over to the couch, sitting down with a thud. He drops his head back against the top of the cushion and shuts his eyes. I lower the back of the bed into a flat position and lie there, staring through the ceiling.

The air is thick with tension, hurt, and unspoken anger. I decide that the best thing that I can do is just give him time.

After a few minutes, there's a soft knock on the door, and a young nurse rolls in a plastic bassinet filled with a squirming little blanket. I sit up and fix the back of the bed in an upright position, and adjust my pillows behind me. Then, I flip a spotlight on so I can see my baby girl.

The nurse reaches into the bassinet and cradles my baby against her as she walks her to me. "She's hungry, and ready for her mama." She smiles so sweetly that I latch on to her positive energy and try to absorb it.

"I'm not sure what to do," I state apprehension cutting my voice.

She places her in my arms, and I cradle her tiny body to me. I unbutton the top two buttons on my pajama top, and she helps me position my breast near the baby's mouth and shows me how I have to entice her to take my nipple.

When she seems to be drifting off to sleep instead of eating, the nurse unwraps her, which angers my little squirming person. As she opens her mouth to let out a big yell, the nurse puts my nipple in my baby's mouth. Apparently, she got her father's appetite, because she knows exactly what to do.

The nurse, who I've come to find out is named Becca, sits with me while I nurse her. She gives me a tour of the drawers in the bassinet, showing me how to use a blue sucker thing and take care of our baby's belly button. Becca gives great tips on how to change diapers, and prepares me for what will be happening until I'm released.

I latch on to Becca as if she's a life preserver. Before she leaves, she writes her name and phone extension on a dry-erase board in my room, and says that I can call her anytime. I no longer feel so alone.

When my sweet baby has taken both breasts, and I've burped her like Becca taught me, I place her against my heart, and loosely drape the swaddling blanket over her back.

"Colin, why don't you come join us in bed and see your daughter? You haven't held her yet." He picks his head up, and opens his eyes, giving both of us a haunted stare. He shuffles each foot forward as if they're made of lead and slides in bed.

I scoot over, making sure that he has enough room. "Would you like to hold her?"

"No. She's looks comfortable right where she is." He laughs, but when I look at his face, his smile doesn't meet his eyes. "Apparently, she likes your boobs as much as I do." It might not be a sincere laugh, but it's music to my ears.

She makes these soft little mewing noises that remind me of Pancho when he's having a good dream. I wonder if our baby is dreaming right now.

"Her hair is so dark," Colin comments with a touch of awe in his voice. "I just thought that with our coloring, she'd be a blonde."

I reach up and pull her little cap off so I can get a better look at her hair. It is very dark. "Who knows? I've read that babies lose the hair that they're born with. It could grow back in blonde."

The longer we sit next to each other, the more okay he seems to become. I leave her cap off and stroke her hair, hoping to reassure her that she's got a mom and a dad who love her to pieces.

Colin shifts behind me and uses his left hand, his throwing hand, to touch her for the first time. His long pointer finger moves back and forth over her tiny arm in a stroking motion. He brushes it against her pink cheek. When he moves his finger over her hand, she opens her tiny little fingers and grasps it, holding onto to it for dear life.

That's when my hulking quarterback breaks. He shifts behind me and wraps one arm around my shoulders in a fierce embrace while his other hand is grasped just as firmly by his daughter. My husband drops his head against my hair, and wracking sobs over take him.

We haven't slept for more than twenty-four hours, after not sleeping much the forty-eight before that. My husband has experienced the highest high and confronted his worst nightmares in that time period. He's gotten the titles that he's wanted most bestowed on him—Super Bowl and MVP-winning quarterback and Daddy—it's too much.

As his breathing returns to normal, we scoot further into the bed, getting comfortable. That's when we eventually fall asleep. Colin leaned against the back of the bed, me lying against his chest in between his long legs. His arm is wrapped protectively around me, and resting on my stomach. Our baby is pressed against my heart, in between my ample cleavage, clutching her daddy's finger.

Chapter Seven

Colin

"Colin, I need to speak to you," Jamie says when I answer my phone. After a brief pause, he adds, "Alone."

Charlie's on her morning run, or should I say, walk. I thought her boobs were huge when she was pregnant. Then her milk came in, and they doubled in size. They dwarf the baby's head. Charlie says that they're too heavy right now for her to jog, so she's just been walking around our secured, gated neighborhood, while I have alone time with my angel and spoil her the fuck rotten.

"Sure," I reply, instantly filled with dread. Anytime Jamie wants to talk to me alone, something bad has happened. "Charlie's out for a walk. I'll come to the pool house."

I place Charlotte in her baby carrier and buckle her in, just in case. I know that we're only walking about forty yards, but I take no chances with her.

Charlotte is not her actual name. It's just what I refer to her as. Charlie and I have the distinction of being the only patients of Doctor Starr's that have left the hospital without giving their child a name. We've been home for two weeks today, and we're no closer. There hasn't been any screaming and yelling over baby names. No. This is more passive-aggressive guerrilla warfare.

I shake my head at the sight of us. "Alone" these days is defined at Charlotte in my arms and Pancho on my left side.

When I enter the pool house Jamie has a grim look on his face, and two men in dark suits are standing beside him. Instantly, my stomach fills with dread. *Is this about the sip-and-see?* Today, we have a meet-the-baby party, or some shit like that. All I know is that Jamie has been less than thrilled with the idea of fifty of our closest friends converging on our home.

We haven't allowed any visitors, much to the chagrin of the new grandmothers. Yes. It means that no one but the two of us have held our baby. It's been too much. We've taken these two weeks since Charlotte was born to just be. I needed this time to come to terms with being a Super Bowl MVP and Daddy. I also needed to forgive Charlie for not telling me she was in labor, and my jealousy over another man being the one to take care of her. The what-if scenarios that have run through my mind are enough to add to the nightmares that I now have every night, but I'm finally coming to terms with the past. Staying mad at Charlie and jealous of Brad gets me nowhere except in a shitty mood, and I don't want my daughter to feel anything but love from me. All is forgiven, but definitely not forgotten.

I place Charlotte, in her carrier on the couch in the pool house, and Pancho jumps up to lie next to her. *That's my boy. Always watching out for his baby sister.*

"I'm assuming the guys in suits aren't here to discuss the menu for the party today?"

Jamie ignores my comment and nods to one of the suits. "Mr. McKinney, I'm Agent Dunham with the FBI. Unfortunately, this is not a social call to congratulate you on your Super Bowl win and new baby."

I figured as much, but my heart rate still elevates as I ponder his intentions.

"What we believe to be a credible threat made against you and your family has landed on my desk." I drop to the couch next to Charlotte and cradle the carrier to my side.

"A man stated that he was going to kidnap your newborn and wife, and hold them for ransom." His tone is even with a hint of apology thrown in for good measure.

I almost roll my eyes as my heart beats its way to normal at this guy's big revelation. Kidnapping threats made against me, my wife, and now my daughter are a weekly occurrence. Usually, it's some hard-up drug addict who needs a few bucks for his next high. They make the statement being a verbose asshole, and someone reports them. Then I spend a couple of thousands of dollars proving that the guy is indeed full of shit. Legitimate threats have been made in the past, and those are the ones that cause my nightmares, but they are few and far between.

Agent Dunham continues, "Jamie has made us aware that since you announced that you're married and having a baby that the threats have more than doubled. The reason that we're taking this particular one seriously is because a man fitting the description of the person who bragged about kidnapping your wife and child attempted to enter your gated neighborhood yesterday."

My palms become sweaty, and I rub my fingertips over Charlotte's soft hair, reassuring myself that she's okay. Any momentary calm I just experienced is completely gone. I swallow the extra spit in my mouth and ask the next logical question. "Was he arrested?"

Jamie, glances at Agent Dunham and the other suit, and then speaks looking, very guilty. "You see, Mr. McKinney, we didn't know about this possible threat, so we turned the guy away, assuming he was paparazzi. However, my guy has given the FBI a description, and we recorded the van's license plate which, of course, has been turned over."

Van? Some sick fuck had a van to kidnap my family.

"Mr. McKinney, we're taking this attempt very seriously. With your private security team's great work, we should have the guy in custody soon." Agent Dunham reassures me.

Standing up, I begin to pace. This is more than I can take. Charlie needs to get home, now. I grab my daughter's carrier and whistle for Pancho. "Sounds like you guys are on it. Thank you." Then to Jamie, I turn and say, "Keep me posted."

I can't escape the pool house quickly enough. I almost sprint Charlotte into the master bedroom, sinking down into the plush cushion of the red college chair. *This is our safe place.*

Immediately, I unstrap my baby girl and lift her to my chest, cradling her sleeping body against me. I'm half surprised my racing heart doesn't wake her. I feel sick to my stomach. *A kidnapper almost gained access to my family.*

The only thing that keeps me from seriously losing my shit is the less than ten-pound angel in my arms. She needs a daddy who's strong, and fights for her. That means that when Charlie returns from her walk, she's not going to know any of this is going on. It means my daughter will never live in fear, imprisoned because of my career.

I give myself a mental pep talk about being a man, and the head of this family. A man protects his wife and child. I'll tell Charlie once the bastard has been arrested, and not before. I'm not ready for the bullshit that surrounds us to intrude in our bubble we've been living in since Charlotte came home from the hospital.

As the minutes tick by, I actually start believing what I'm selling myself. Denial is a beautiful thing. Today, is the day my daughter will be introduced to all the people who deeply love her. It will not be clouded with my real world problems.

I have to trust Jamie to do the job that I handsomely pay him to perform.

I glance around our bedroom, noting that it appears that a baby-store bomb went off in here. The sitting area has been turned into a temporary nursery. I had Jenny move all the furniture except for the red college chair into storage. Brad and Charlie's sisters took my credit card and went on a baby shopping-spree. I swear our baby has more crap than me and Charlie combined.

When Charlie returns home, we have important things to do today, like naming our kid, and not worrying about all the sick fucks in the world.

Let Jamie and the FBI do what they do best—catch the bad guys.

We plan to announce her name at the party. But first, we've got to decide on said name. Today, is the deadline that we set for ourselves. I have a feeling that this battle might be one of our ugliest.

Charlie made the first shot across the bow by dressing her in Dallas Cowboy footed-pajamas. I'm not the sharpest tool in the shed, but I recognize this for what it is. Charlie's manipulative attempt to get her way. She thinks that I'll be distracted by our daughter's cuteness, in my team colors so I won't notice when she writes down the name of her choice. I've been bamboozled before by the likes of Doctor Collins (should be McKinney). I retaliated a bit with the baby's car, but in my defense, that car was bought with my family's safety in mind. I will not be manipulated when it comes to naming our daughter.

Who knew naming a kid could be this difficult? Or maybe we're the two most stubborn people in the world? Charlie may be, but I'm not.

Charlotte and I two-step into the living room as I sing her an old George Strait song. I don't know any lullabies, so I assume that old country is just as good as anything. Charlie bought me this harness-like thing to put Charlotte in so I can carry her and still use both hands, but it sucks. My baby knows who her daddy is, and she likes to snuggle into my chest hair, not against some padded material.

Dear God, I'm grateful we live inside the gated neighborhood, and my security team is so good.

"We're in here," I yell when I hear the backdoor slam. "And I think Charlotte is ready to eat." She makes the cutest little sucking face when she's hungry.

"Tell Elizabeth that I'll be right there," Charlie says. I hear the refrigerator door close. Hopefully, she's eating something. I've been watching her like a hawk to make sure that she has a balanced diet. Doctor Starr put Charlie on an antidepressant as a precautionary measure against postpartum depression before we left the hospital. She talked to both of us about how pregnancy is a huge trigger for Charlie's disease. I encouraged Charlie to take it. We agreed on a six-week timeframe, and then she can reevaluate with Doctors Benson and Starr.

I watch her walk into the living room, looking like a porn star. Her tits are huge, and further accentuated by the tight maternity sports bra that she's wearing. I don't know if my cock can take four more weeks of this dick tease until we can resume showing how much we love each other. Charlie and I need the physical connection to know that we're okay.

Her stomach is already flat again—she doesn't agree—and she's lost her pregnancy weight, thanks to her aversion to my cologne while she was pregnant. She argues that the scale is wrong, because she still feels fat.

Discreetly, I adjust my semi-hard cock, and ponder if I might have to "make a call" while she's feeding the baby. This six-weeks-without-making-love-to-my-wife thing sucks.

Charlie flops down in one of the oversized chairs in the living room and unzips the front of her sports bra, freeing the beauties. I involuntarily lick my lips, which causes her to shoot me a disgusted look. "They're for Elizabeth."

I shrug. I'm a guy with a hot wife that now has tits crafted by the gods—so sue me. That's my only excuse. I stand up and carefully bring Charlotte to her, feeling a sense of loss as I place her in Charlie's outstretched arms. And because I wouldn't be me if I didn't, I reach down and cop a feel, giving her my panty-dropping half-smile. She rolls her eyes as she adjusts Charlotte on her breast. Two can play her little game of manipulation—*Dallas Cowboys PJs indeed.*

"Today's the day," she says. "Let's make this official. Elizabeth Colin McKinney. Great name. We can call her Liz, Lizzy, Beth, Eliza, Liza, Libby, Betty—she'll have tons of nicknames."

She's chosen Elizabeth because she feels like she owes it to Liza. My kid's name is too important to choose it because it settles some arbitrary debt.

I flop back down on the couch across from her and lean back, getting extra comfortable, preparing for the epic battle of wills. "While those are all great points, Doctor Collins, Charlotte Jane McKinney is a beautiful name. Named after her mother's nickname, blessed with the middle name of my gorgeous wife. Perfection!"

I watch her try to open the lid of her water bottle with one hand. I rise to my feet to help her when she raises her eyebrows and drops her chin. "Sit back down. You're going back to work soon. I've got to figure out how to do stuff one-handed." Then, she smirks, and adds, "You've spoiled me."

She places the water bottle between her knees and uses her left hand to twist off the cap. She holds her water up, imitating my now famous pose when I won the MVP trophy. I can't help but laugh at her flattery attempts.

"Okay, so we are at a complete impasse. My mom and dad named us after president's kids. We could take that route," she suggests.

I mentally go through their names in my head; Chelsea Clinton, Caroline Kennedy, Julie Nixon, Amy Carter. Then, before I can stop myself, I flash her my shit-eating grin. It's the full smile that makes my eyes crinkle. "What about Jenna, then?"

If looks could kill, Charlie would have just crucified me on the couch. She picks up one of the throw pillows from her chair and hurls it at me left-handed. I must say, she's got quite an arm on her. "Speaking of Jenna, would you like to write the thank-you note for the congratulations flowers, or shall I do it?" She bats her long eyelashes as a sugar-coated grin spreads across her gorgeous face.

"I'll have Jenny send her a form thank-you note." I make a dismissive gesture, making sure she knows that this subject is closed.

The flowers Jenna sent were obnoxious, over the top, and stunk. The card read, "All my love to the new little family, Aunt Jenna." I intercepted them before they were delivered to Charlie's room, and had them disposed of.

Jenna's still trying to get back in my good graces after the stunt she pulled last year. Inviting my wife and paparazzi to our meeting at the hotel pretty much moved Jenna to my "I don't give a fuck" list. Although, Aiden did convince me not to take her house and car away from her. His reasoning was sound. Everything she owns, I've purchased for her. If I had taken it away, I had nothing to hold over her head to keep her quiet. We moved all the monetary assets that I'd given her into a trust. She plays nicely for the next five years, she gets it all, plus a hundred-thousand dollar bonus. Hopefully, it's incentive enough.

Without missing a beat, I get us back on the important subject at hand: naming our daughter. "Should we go through the baby-naming book for the billionth time?"

"No." She shakes her head. "I never want to see that dog-eared thing again." Then she pauses. Her lavender eyes grow wide, and a twinkle appears. "If I can't have Elizabeth Colin, what do you think about naming her after Aiden?"

I feel like Pancho, trying to interrupt what these stupid humans are saying. My head cocks to the side, and I raise my lip and eyebrows. She's got to be crazy if she thinks I'm naming my baby girl Aiden.

She continues. "Ainsley is the female name for Aiden. He's been such a good friend to both of us, and I rather like the name. Ainsley McKinney has a nice ring to it. It's different, but not different like no one's heard it before. It's cute for a little girl as well as an adult professional. It doesn't rhythm with anything, so that limits what she can be called on the playground."

That's been one of my huge issues with choosing a name. I'm already saddling the poor kid with a famous dad and paparazzi-favorite parents who've had every conceivable lie printed about them. Hell, Charlie and I had to sneak our baby out of the hospital using a delivery entrance in the middle of the night, for God's sake. I don't want to add a poor name choice on top of her inherent-by-birth baggage.

I say the name out loud, "Ainsley." It's pretty. It has a nice ring to it. Of course, Aiden will get a kick out of us naming our baby girl after him. I think that I love it. "Ainsley," I repeat out loud. "Ainsley."

I jump off the couch and into the air, yelling, "Sold!"

It startles Ainsley, and she yelps. Charlie shoots me a dirty look as she soothes our baby.

I sit back down, and say, "Ainsley Jane McKinney … perfection."

Charlie corrects me, and says, "Ainsley Elizabeth McKinney."

While Charlie finishes feeding Ainsley, I slip out the backdoor and confer with Jamie on what plans he's put in place to keep my family safe.

Jamie is sitting at his desk, reviewing video footage from the guard shack. "Anything new?" I ask as I take a seat across from him.

He looks apologetic and shakes his head. "Sorry, Mr. McKinney. We're working our tails off."

I nod. I know he is. Jamie takes his job very seriously. "What's the plan for the party today?"

He diverts his gaze from the screen and leans forward on the desk, looking me in the eye. "Your guests will pass through two security checkpoints. The caterer is leaving the food at the guard stand. There's not enough time to complete background checks on all of the caterer's employees. Everyone that enters your home will have either passed a previous screening like Alice and Chef, or be on your invitation list."

"Sounds like you've got it under control," I reply. As I stand up, I reach out and shake Jamie's hand. "I appreciate what a great job you did training the gate guards. Make sure they get a bonus on their next paycheck from Doctor Collins and myself."

A smile breaks out across his face, and he says, "Thank you Mr. McKinney. They were just doing their job, but I know they'll appreciate it."

As I turn to leave, Jamie yells, "One more thing."

I stop, and spin around. Poor guy looks like he's scared to say whatever it is. "You're going to have to inform Doctor Collins that she can't jog around the gated neighborhood anymore without taking one of the security guys. Also, I'm assigning two of my men to her and Ainsley at all times when they leave the house."

No wonder the guy looked petrified. Charlie will not be pleased, but she's just going to have to suck it up. After the asshole has been arrested, I'll tell her what a close call we had.

I sigh as I walk back to my home. This is my life … all because I can throw a football.

Our family and friends don't mind passing through the added security measures when they arrive for the party. Everyone is too excited about meeting Ainsley Elizabeth Jane McKinney. We reasoned if the future king of England can have multiple names, so can Miss Ainsley.

****

My first full day away from Charlie and Ainsley is much harder than I'd thought that it would be. I text her fifty times at least. Finally, her sister Amy texts me back, and says I have to stop because everyone is trying to nap.

Amy has been a gift from God. She's an elementary education teacher who worked at a pre-school. After nine straight nights of not sleeping more than a couple of hours, Charlie called her and begged her to help. Amy quit her job, and moved in upstairs.

She's great. She keeps to herself and doesn't need for us to entertain her. She's working on her masters, so she's busy with her online courses, but can pause her work if we need her.

We discussed having my mom or Charlie's mom come spend some time with us, but we both decided that it wasn't a good idea. Susan and Charlie are not on the best of terms because my mom can be a clueless ditz. I love Charlie's mom, but my mom would get her feelings hurt if we didn't include her.

By hiring Amy, we soothed our mothers, are actually sleeping, and have given Amy an opportunity to focus on school. Win/win situation for all parties involved.

Today, is Charlie's first day off of the antidepressants. She seems to be doing okay. I've watched her like crazy to make sure that she didn't slip into old habits. She's been eating, and kept her exercise to reasonable levels. I've been so proud of my girl. The only bad habit she's picked back up is her coffee. Frankly, I'm surprised that she made it through her pregnancy without having a cup.

I toss my phone on Coach's desk, making it clear to everyone in the room that I plan on answering it if it rings. The team president, GM, Aiden, and Mark are already there. We're just waiting for Coach to finish up a phone call.

I have a feeling I know why they called this meeting. This is the last season that I'm under contract. They're going to offer a contract extension because they don't want my status with the team to be a distraction next season. And it shouldn't be. Super Bowl, MVP-winning quarterbacks should be taken care of.

This is a damn good position to be in. The last time I had to worry about my contract, we'd had another almost, this-close season. My divorce had been recently finalized. I'd been on a path of destruction, doing whatever and whomever I pleased. What a difference the years make.

Coach comes walking into his office with his jaw set in a tight grimace, and running a fist over his heart. The team president asks before the rest of us can, "Are you okay?"

He laughs, and flops back in his quilted leather executive chair. "I'm too fucking old to eat chicken wings anymore."

Everyone nods their heads in agreement. Coach starts talking, "So Colin, we obviously want you to be our franchise quarterback for as long as you can play. Let's cut to the chase. We want to offer you a contract guaranteeing that you'll retire from football in a Cowboy's jersey."

Aiden and Mark let out an audible sigh behind me. This is obviously the best-case scenario.

I smile, and reach across the desk and shake Coach's hand. "That's what I've always wanted. Cowboy for life."

The conversation then moves into contract specifics, and things that I let Mark and Aiden handle. I grab my phone and check for any messages. Like the dream that she is, Charlie texted me a picture of Ainsley, Pancho, and Amy lying together on the couch. *Life is good.*

****

Another drab, generic hotel room with popcorn ceiling. This isn't the first time I've had to leave my girls overnight, but I've limited my trips to as few as possible. The fucking nights are the worst. During the day, I'm too busy to remember that Charlie and Ainsley are at home and not with me. I'd gotten so used to Charlie traveling to all my games that it never occurred to me that once the baby arrived, her days of traveling would be over.

Kissing my girls goodbye and climbing into my truck was one of the hardest things that I've had to do to date. It's the first away-game of the season, and this hotel room couldn't feel lonelier if it tried. I hate that I will not get to read to Ainsley, give her a bath, or tuck her in.

Is Ainsley sleeping right now? Was she good for Charlie in the bathtub? What did she think of the new baby food that Charlie was going to try introducing? Is Charlie asleep? Can she sleep without me next to her? Is she missing me?

I look at the clock. The red numbers scream at me, "Go to sleep, fucker, you've got to play football tomorrow." But I can't. I've lost the ability to sleep when she's not next to me.

I grab my iPad, and decide to distract myself with some world news. Unfortunately, I scroll to the entertainment section, and see a news story about Charlie and me. I click on it out of morbid curiosity, and read the headline. "Is Charlie Already Stepping Out on Colin?" It's a picture of Charlie with Brad. He's pushing Ainsley in her stroller, but thankfully, Charlie has a light blanket thrown over the compartment so you can't see my baby's face. Her arm is looped through Brad's arm at the elbow. She's dressed in exercise clothes and he has on pair of jeans, navy T-shirt, and sunglasses. I'll give the photographer credit. It does look like her and Brad are lovers. If I didn't know for a fact that he was one-hundred percent devoted to Carter and has only platonic love for my wife, I might just kill the fucker right now. But that twinge of anger, maybe jealousy, which still gnaws at me about Brad being the one to take my wife to the hospital to have our daughter is still there. It was Brad who'd held her hand, and helped her through her early contractions. The thought of Brad being with my wife while she was in labor with our daughter makes me crazy.

Because I'm a sadist, I scan the story further, adding a match to my combustible feelings. It mentions Charlie and Brad shopping for antiques while "taking Colin's baby for a stroll." They dined outdoors and sipped champagne - although in the picture it's just Brad with a glass in hand. Then it notes that Charlie breastfed our baby at the table while Brad seemed to not care. I roll my eyes. I'm sure parent groups are going to be up in arms that my wife dared to sip champagne while breastfeeding even though there's no evidence that she actually did.

I decide to forward the link to the article to Brad and Charlie with a note. "Ah ... young love."

I leave it at that. They can interpret my message any way they choose.

No more news for me. I open my word-find game app and lose myself for more than an hour, searching for words that I don't know the meanings of.

****

God, finally the first away game of the season is over, and it was brutal. The lonely hotel room and missing my family was the cherry on top of a shit game. We lost. I sucked. I couldn't seem to scramble away from the defenders and find a receiver, even if the other team had removed two players from the field. The plane ride home was so fucking quiet it was scary. No one sat near me. I think my team might be scared of me.

All I want is for my wife to be naked in the hot tub, waiting for me. It's the thought that kept me from losing my fucking mind after the game. I've come to just expect that when I pull into the driveway after a game, my girl will have the hot tub turned on, a champagne bucket of iced-water bottles, old country music playing over the outdoor speakers, and she'll be in some sort of string bikini contraption that's for my viewing pleasure only.

As I turn into our neighborhood, my dick gets hard in anticipation of seeing her. I can almost feel her surgeon's hands working the knots out of my sore muscles. Staring down at my over eager cock, I chuckle. Who says that the sex goes downhill after kids? Geez, we took six weeks off for her to heal and then picked up right where we left off. That's because we were made for each other.

Bertha gives me a moment of protest and then decides to behave herself. I finger my wedding ring in anticipation of seeing Charlie in just a few seconds. I'm giddy, a little boy on Christmas morning who's hoping against hope for a new bicycle.

But, as I walk through the backyard gate, I don't hear Merle Haggard or Willie Nelson. The water isn't bubbling in the hot tub, and it's empty. Like there's water in it, but no hot blonde in a bikini. Then, I panic. What if something's wrong? With her? The baby?

I unlock the backdoor like a lunatic and it flies open, hitting the stopper and catching me on my shoulder. The pain barely registers. I jog through the house as much as my sore ankle will let me, and throw open the bedroom door, hearing my pulse pounding in my ears. Trying to calm my racing heart, I grip the door handle, and have to catch my breath.

She's in bed sound asleep. The lights are completely off. The curtains are pulled so the only light in the room is from the bedside clock, and the baby monitor power light, indicating that it's on.

Once I've recovered from my initial panic and confirmed that both my girls are okay, the disappointment sets in. Hell! Pancho didn't even get up to greet me. So much for him being man's best friend. *We lost. I played for shit. And no naked girl in the hot tub.* Fuck my life.

I walk back to the kitchen and grab a couple of bottles of water out of the refrigerator, and take a seat at the kitchen table.

What did I do after football games before Charlie? It's been so long that I hardly remember what life was like before she stepped on the elevator in Los Angeles. I think that I might have soaked in my bathtub, filled with Epsom Salt. Did it work to keep me from getting sore? Shit. I really don't remember. I quickly down the first bottle, and toss it toward the garbage can with my right hand, but I miss. I'm a lefty through and through. I take the lid off the second one, and drink it more slowly. My house is so quiet. Was it this quiet before Charlie? Once again, I don't remember.

What about when I was married to my first wife? What did we do after games? I keep drawing a blank. *What did we do?* Then it hits me. We fucked like bunnies in heat. *God, how could I have forgotten that?* Oh, yeah. The girl asleep in the other room has hijacked any part of my life that she wasn't in, and filled the gaps with everything that makes her the one for me. I guess my time without her was so meaningless that my brain cells don't care to store the knowledge.

Maybe the reason that I always had so many people at my house was because I didn't like this level of quiet. It's a halfway decent theory. What did Charlie call my house when she first moved in? A country club? A home for wayward boys?

That makes me smile as I slump back in the kitchen chair. My ribs hurt like a motherfucker. Taking a breath is becoming difficult. I know that if I don't do something, I'm going to be worthless at practice tomorrow. I decide to soak in the Jacuzzi bathtub for old time's sake.

When I stand, and take the first step on my right leg, pain shoots up to my hip. It's been almost two years, and it still aches every damn day. The doctors, including Doctor Collins, say that this is about as good as it's going to get unless I want to quit playing football. Not an option. All my Super Bowl win did was give me a taste for more gold rings.

Grabbing two more water bottles, I limp towards our room.

Charlie doesn't stir as I drag my pathetic self through the bedroom and into the bathroom, shutting the doors behind me. Hobbling to the bathtub, I turn on the water as hot as I can stand it and add the lavender-scented salts. Next, I line up my water bottles on the edge of the tub and pull another one out of the mini refrigerator that we keep in the bathroom. My water bottles have been shoved to the side, and replaced with bags of breast milk and a half-drunk baby bottle. I smirk and shut the door.

Just as I'm sinking into the tub of water that's so hot that I can feel my skin pinking, Charlie opens the master bathroom doors and shuffles in, immediately shielding her eyes from the bathroom light. She's obviously been in a deep sleep. Her hair's a rat's nest, and her face is pillow creased. But she's still the most beautiful girl in the world.

"You can turn the light off, babe."

She mumbles a thanks and hits the light switch, but not before I get a good look at her. She's got on one of my white T-shirts that barely covers her bare behind. I briefly wonder what happened to her panties, but frankly, I don't care enough to ask. They just get in the way.

The street lamp outside filters in through the glass bricks over the bathtub, casting just enough light so I can watch her shuffle towards me, taking a seat on the ledge. She leans back against the shower stall and pulls her knees up to her chest.

Now, it's very evident that she has no underwear on, and my dick stands up to get a better look.

Speaking first, I say, "Sorry, if I woke you. I tried to be quiet."

She folds her arms over her knees, and rests her head on her elbow, looking sideways at me. I can tell that she's exhausted. "I was trying to stay up until you got home, but I couldn't keep my eyes open. Sorry about the loss."

I'm not in the mood to discuss football, so I ignore her condolences. I move my hands in the water, feeling the waves of heat tumble over me. "I missed you in the hot tub."

"Yeah, about that," she sighs, "Ainsley spit up all over me after dinner, and I had to bathe both of us. I just didn't feel like getting wet again. I'm sorry. I'll be waiting for you after the next game."

"No need to apologize, beautiful girl." I lean forward, and run my wet hand over her shin. "You've spoiled me."

Her mouth turns up in a beautiful pleased smile that meets her eyes. "I'm glad that you think I spoil you. I know having a baby has changed so much of our lives. Our focus. But, I don't want to lose our time for just the two of us." She picks her head up, and says in a quiet voice, "I missed you."

I lie back in the hot water, noting that it's already less painful for me to take a breath. Hot water, or Charlie's presence? I'm not entirely sure. "I missed you too. Shit, I didn't sleep last night. For some reason, even though we never shared a room when you came to road games, just knowing that you were in the hotel, and I could get to you, if I needed, made me able to sleep. Last night I was fucking miserable."

She giggles her precious Charlie laugh and says, "It's because we had to sneak around to be together. Kind of like we were horny teenagers still living with Mom and Dad. I liked all of our hotel sex."

I smile at the memory of some of our stolen away-game moments. It never occurred to me that they would be coming to an end once we became parents. "Do you think that you'll be able to come to any away games this season?" I almost hate to ask the question because I dread the answer.

She lets out a sigh, and her lavender eyes look up at the ceiling before she speaks. "I don't know. As long as I'm breastfeeding, I don't see how I can come without bringing Ainsley. Then, do I really want to haul our baby on a commercial flight, bring all of her gear? And who watches her during a game? I'm not leaving her with just anyone. So we'd have to bring Amy with us, and Amy really likes having her weekends off ..."

I throw my hand up, stopping her. "I get it. Doesn't seem possible this year." I contort my long limbs in the bathtub so I'm able to slip under the water. My blood is boiling. She told me no, that she's not coming to my away games. I know it isn't rational. I know her reasoning is perfectly logical and makes sense, but damn, it doesn't make it any less easy to hear. She's my breath, my soul. I need her with me.

When my head pops out of the water, she's gone. I look around the bathroom and don't see her anywhere. "Charlie," I call.

No answer. I assume that she went to check on Ainsley. I look down at my dick, and we're on the same page. She might anger us, but it's been two days since we had any attention. I bet that I can talk her into some we've-been-apart lovin'. Maybe? God, I hope so.

I lean forward and start draining the water when she comes into the bathroom holding Ainsley, who's covered in baby vomit. "Oh no. Is she sick?" I ask, like an idiot. It's obvious that she is.

"I think that it's just teething, but her bed is a mess." My dick deflates at her words. It's time to be a dad.

I climb out of the tub, and grab my seven-month-old squirming angel that is the perfect mix of her mother and me. I refill the bathtub with much cooler water, and remove Ainsley's messy pink footed pajamas and her diaper, tossing the latter in the special garbage can.

"Thanks," Charlie calls over her shoulder as she walks out of the bathroom. "I'm going to strip her bed."

I press Ainsley to my chest with my left hand, and slide us both into the warm water. She coos and grabs a fistful of my chest hair, giving it a tug. It makes me wince, so I gently open her little plump fingers and extract my hair. She smiles at me as if she wants me to see her swollen gums. I kiss her white-blonde hair that replaced her dark hair which fell out when she was a couple of months old. She's so gorgeous. She's got her mother's lavender eyes, and my olive complexion. I hope that she'll have Charlie's long legs and perfect ass. At the moment, she's a chunky little thing. Fat rolls on top of fat rolls. I love every cell of her body, but damn, I wish she'd quit raining on my alone-time with her mother.

I slide us a little deeper into the water and reposition her on my chest so she's facing away from me. She slaps the water, giggling each time water droplets sprinkle her face. Using my right hand to cup water, I pour it over her head, careful to avoid her eyes. She slaps the water double time, letting me know that she likes it.

Grabbing the baby soap and pink and white polka-dotted washcloth, I begin to bathe her. Once I have her backside, I lay her back against my chest so I can wash her tummy, arms, hands, and legs. I assume that her feet are still clean from her earlier bath.

"I missed you, baby girl," I coo to her. She looks up at me with Charlie's eyes, and pats my face with her chunky hand. I capture it with my lips, and pretend to eat her fingers. She loves this game, and squeals with such delight I want to do it again and again.

Charlie walks into the bathroom looking haggard. Dark circles surround her bloodshot eyes. Her shoulders are slumped. "Go to bed. I'll take care of Ainsley," I encourage her.

She walks over and plants a kiss on both of our foreheads. "Thanks. I appreciate the help. By the way, I hope you know that the article you sent me was nothing."

The picture of Brad and Charlie walking so close is not defined as *nothing* by me, but now is not the time to discuss their relationship. I just smile and lean forward for a goodnight kiss, which she brushes across my lips.

Ainsley and I watch her change her T-shirt, still neglecting underwear. Damn her. I'm going to be tempted to wake her up once Little Miss is back in bed.

We play in the bathtub for about ten more minutes before I get us both out, drying her using a pink hooded-towel that makes her look like a kitty-cat. I show her the reflection in the mirror, and she claps with delight.

Gently, I place her on the floor of my closet while I quickly towel-dry, and throw on some boxer briefs. Then I scoop her up in her kitty towel, and head upstairs to put her back to bed—hopefully for the night.

Pancho, who's shown no interest in this tonight, follows us upstairs as if to make sure that the little person gets back in bed.

I put a fresh diaper on her, and pick out my favorite pair of footed jammies. Clay gave them to us. They're pink and read, "Better looking than Daddy."

Because I've missed out on two nights of bedtime stories and snuggles, I rock her in her pink-and-green striped chair and read her *Goodnight Moon*. Before the end of the story, she's fast asleep in my arms.

I hold her for longer than I should. If Charlie were here, she'd admonish me that I'm spoiling her, and she shouldn't be rocked to sleep. But, I'm her dad, right? Isn't that what dads of baby girls are supposed to do—spoil them rotten?

My ribs scream in protest as I place her carefully in the crib, so as not to disturb my sleeping angel. Ignoring them, I lean over the bed railing to give her one more kiss.

By the time I hobble to the bottom of the stairs, I'm not sure that I can walk anymore. My leg is so swollen around the ankle that I can't flex or point my foot. Instead of going to bed and snuggling with my wife, I make my way to the freezer and grab a package of frozen peas.

I limp back into our bedroom, and flop down on the sitting room couch that's just recently been returned from storage. Propping my leg up on the armrest, I place the peas over the most tender part. I have to stifle a moan. The cold feels so good against the burning heat of my injury it borders on sexual. I grab the throw blanket from the arm of the couch, and cover myself with it as much as I can. Pancho makes himself comfortable on the ground next to me and begins to snore. *It must be nice to feel that content.*

As I drift off to sleep, I turn over in my head just how much more pain I can tolerate. I refuse to take the painkillers that they've prescribed to me for obvious reasons, but Aleve isn't cutting it anymore. Blessedly, the ice dulls the pain enough that I can sleep, or maybe I'm just so worn out that I fall into a coma.

Chapter Eight

Charlie

"Put the baby down and let's go," I order Brad.

He's holding Ainsley above his head and wiggling her back and forth.

"Guncle Brad loves you to pieces. Yes. He does. Yes he does." Then he says it again. And again. And again.

I swear to God, if this baby's first word is anywhere close to Guncle or Brad, I'll smother him in his sleep, or Colin just might beat me to it.

He reluctantly hands Amy his goddaughter, and kisses her five more times on the head before he'll even acknowledge my presence. He puts his hand on his hip, finally turning to me. "Come on, Doctor Buzz Kill. Let's go fix bones."

"If you can't learn to leave in a timely manner, I'm going to stop letting you come over when we have to be somewhere." I shrug my shoulders as I walk into the utility room to grab my purse.

"The patient's unconscious. Don't be such a Scrooge. It's not my fault my goddaughter is ridiculously precious," he hollers behind me.

I walk back through the living room and give Ainsley one more goodbye kiss. Amy works with her to wave "bye-bye" to us. It's so cute because she opens and closes her hand in front of her face as if she's waving to herself. My heart floods with love, and a strong desire not to leave her. I went back to work two months after she was born, but I'm still not used to telling her goodbye.

"Call me if you need me, Amy," I instruct.

She kisses Ainsley's cheek. "We'll be just fine."

Miguel and Jamie are waiting for us outside. The number of threats that Colin and I receive has gone up drastically since Dallas fell below a .500 record. Jamie started traveling with me exclusively at Colin's request after we had the near kidnapping attempt. I shudder at the memory. I can't believe how close some crazy got to our home. Our daughter. I was glad Colin waited until the guy had been arrested before he told me.

But, now that Colin has angry fans, Miguel has joined my security detail. When I demanded to see the specific threats, Colin's face grew pale, and assured me that I did not need to. For once, I didn't argue, and took his angst at face value. They're bad, and probably directed toward Ainsley and me.

Brad and I slide into the back of the black Range Rover with limousine-tint on the back windows. Miguel drives, and Jamie takes the passenger seat. This has become such a part of my life that I no longer blink at being chauffeured, followed around my job, and not let out of the large mens' sight.

Brad starts gushing about a new restaurant that he and Carter tried last night. Apparently, it's the new place to go and be seen, so Colin and I will not touch it with a ten-foot pole.

"How's Que Bee?" Brad asks as he turns towards me, adjusting his seat belt.

"Do you want to hear 'fine,' or do you want the real answer?" I ask, avoiding his gaze by looking out the window.

"Let's go with the real answer for five hundred, Alex," he quips, chuckling at his joke.

I look at him and decide to unload my worries on the best assistant in the world. "Physically, his ankle still swells after every game and most practices. He doesn't complain, but I know that he's hurting. He walks with a limp most nights."

"You're a doctor. What do you think?" Brad asks, genuinely interested in my opinion. He leans forward as if to hear me better.

I sigh. "It's not going to get any better. He had a compound fracture, and has a steel rod supporting the bone. If he were my patient, I'd tell him to play football as long as he can live with the pain, and when he can't take it any longer, then it's time to quit."

"And as his wife?" Brad asks, raising his eyebrow.

"I tell him that I love him. What else can I do?" I shrug. "Mentally, he seems spread so thin. He's trying to be at home as much as he can. The team is demanding more and more out of him, trying to get this season back on track. His sponsors are asking for him to step up his public appearances because of his successful last season."

I stop and swallow hard to keep my tears at bay. Brad reaches out and grabs my hand, giving it a squeeze. "Whatever new security threat that is keeping him up at night is bad. He doesn't know it, but I've woken up to him racing upstairs to check on Ainsley just to come back and fall on the sitting room sofa, taking deep breaths and sweating profusely, as if he's having a stress attack. All winning the Super Bowl and having a baby did was make us bigger targets for the press and the crazies."

Taking a deep breath, I let it out slowly. "I think that the hardest thing to watch, though, is that he's lost the gleam in his eye. His playfulness is gone. He walks around like a man who has the weight of the world resting on his shoulders. Although, he's still so sweet with Ainsley."

As the car exits the freeway for the hospital, Brad asks, "How did he take you missing his home game today?"

I think that's the crux of the problem. When I apologized to Colin and told him that I had to go into the hospital because my specialty was needed for this particular patient, he just shrugged his shoulders, and kissed my forehead. Colin of last season would have thrown a fit, and at least asked if there were another surgeon that could fill in for me. Then he would have pouted, and tried using some sort of sexual diversionary tactic to try and persuade me.

"He said that he understood."

Brad's mouth drops into a frown. "That sounds nothing like him."

"I know." I nod my head in agreement. "I'm hoping that taking Ainsley trick-or-treating tomorrow will cheer him up."

Brad and I found her a precious butterfly costume. She loves wearing it, and laughs like crazy when I show her how cute she is in the mirror. We discuss how darling she's going to look until we arrive in the hospital parking lot.

Brad adjusts his clothing once we get out of the car. The man is trying to make green scrubs look good. There's no point. I flash him my *you've got to be kidding* look. His auburn hair is in a perfectly gelled mess. "Just in case your media fans are waiting for us. I like to look good when I'm accused of stealing you away from Que Bee."

I roll my eyes, not caring in the slightest what I look like. I gave up that fight long ago.

Jamie is on guard, and looking around us. He flanks me on my right side while Miguel takes the left. I'm ushered quickly through the parking lot, with Brad following behind me. No media today. I quip to Brad, "Looks like you got pretty for nothing."

He just laughs.

I'm looking forward to this surgery. The patient was injured in a motorcycle accident. It's going to be a challenge to put him back together, but I feel pumped to try.

My phone rings in my purse right before we walk through the sliding glass doors. It's Amy's ringtone. I quickly grab it to see what the emergency is, hoping that Ainsley is okay. I really don't want to hand this case off to another doctor.

"What's up Amy?" I ask.

She's crying, and my heart falls to my stomach. "Oh God. What's wrong with my baby?" I scream into the phone. The four of us stop walking. Brad, Miguel, and Jamie surround me, staring, with concern deeply etched in their faces.

Breath doesn't leave my body while I wait for her reply.

"Ainsley's okay," she sobs. My next fear is Colin, so the split second of relief that I just felt is replaced by gut-wrenching terror.

"Colin," I sob, and Brad takes the phone away from me.

"Amy, it's Brad. What's going on? You're scaring Caroline to death," he says with a protective edge that I'm not used to hearing present in his voice.

There's a long pause. Brad is making calming hand gestures, as if Amy can see him. I stand there with my nails digging into my palms, teetering on the edge of a precipice. *What's making my sister so upset?*

"Okay, sweetie. Okay. We're coming home. Get Ainsley packed. We'll be there in twenty." He instructs her.

I stand there on the razor edge of fear, staring at Brad. He pulls me into his arms, and begins rubbing my back. "Your dad has suffered a massive heart attack. They don't know if he's going to make it."

****

I've made the drive from Dallas to Houston hundreds of times. It's a long stretch of flat highway that passes through a few towns. There's nothing particularly interesting to look at. Traffic flows well. Everyone goes about seventy miles per hour so I can set the cruise control and just drive. And think.

Today, however, we're in Ainsley's tank. I'm driving like a crazy person with my hazard-lights flashing. Brad is in the passenger seat on the phone with Methodist Hospital where they took my dad trying to get an update. Amy is in the backseat, giving Ainsley a pacifier, attempting to soothe her until we arrive in Houston, and I can feed her. None of us thought to grab the extra bags of breast milk or snacks before we raced out of the house.

I left security in Dallas because we all couldn't fit in this car. Colin will be livid, but he's just going to have to get over it.

Brad says into the phone. "Okay. Thanks for the update. I appreciate it, Leslie. Make sure you tell your brother hello for me."

When he hangs up, he says, "Doctor Collins is still in surgery. That's all that I've got. Sorry ladies."

I let out a sigh, and grip the steering wheel, willing the eighteen-wheeler in front of me to move to the right lane so I can pass him. Finally, I get sick of waiting, and pull an action-movie worthy maneuver to scoot past.

The jerk of the car makes Ainsley cry … of course.

"Look, he's in surgery. Let's stop at the next exit so you can feed her. There's nothing you can do at this point." Brad tries reasoning with me.

As Ainsley's screams pick up, I know that he's right. We take the exit for Buffalo, Texas, and pull into an Exxon station. Amy volunteers to go inside and buy us drinks while I feed little Miss Angry Pants. I no longer cover myself in front of Brad. He knows to look away until Ainsley is settled.

"Have you told Colin yet?" Brad asks once I have Ainsley situated.

"No. I want to wait until after half-time. I'm afraid that if he finds out before he'll leave, or not be focused on the game. He has so much pressure on him right now. As you said, there's nothing any of us can do," I reply as I reposition Ainsley. She's getting too big for me to keep nursing her. She's going to be tall, like her daddy.

Brad scrolls around on his phone, and says, "Looks like half-time is almost over. Want me to call Jenny, and ask her to get in touch with the team?"

Nodding my head, it does cross my mind that I didn't even ask Brad what the score is.

****

You wouldn't think that the Houston Medical Center would be crowded on a Sunday, but we sit in traffic for ten minutes just trying to turn into the hospital's parking garage. As I impatiently tap my finger on the gear shift, my phone rings. Amy and I both take a huge gulp of air and wait while Brad speaks to whomever is on the other end.

"Thanks for telling me," Brad says. "Yes, I'll let them know."

Brad hangs up as I'm taking the parking garage ticket from the machine. "That was my friend, Leslie." He pauses, and swallows the lump in his throat.

I know instantly that my dad didn't make it. A giant hand reaches into my chest and grips my heart, squeezing it so tightly I'm not sure it can pump blood any longer.

I gasp as Brad confirms my fear. "I'm sorry, but there was nothing they could do."

Amy drops her head into her hands and sobs. It's a gut-wrenching wail that further breaks my heart. *My poor baby sister.*

I stare ahead, focused on doing one thing at a time. Right now, I need a place to park this tank. Yes. That's my focus. I'll think about my father passing away in a moment.

By some miracle, I spot an open place on the second floor. Once we're parked, Brad rushes to comfort me, but I wave him off and point at Amy. My next focus is to take care of my daughter. I walk to Ainsley's car seat and carefully unlatch her, and cradle her against my chest. Her warm little body snuggles against me, calming me instantly. She's got a large happy grin on her beautiful face, and reaches out to pull a piece of my hair that has escaped from my ponytail. *How sad, baby girl, you'll never get to know your grandfather. He didn't even live long enough for you to say his name.*

Grabbing a blanket out of her diaper bag, I throw it over her. It isn't particularly cold outside, but I know from lots of experience that hospitals are always chilly. I don't want my baby unhappy. My focus is to make sure that Ainsley is comfortable.

I've dealt with death before. My chosen profession exposes me to it more than, let's say, Colin's profession exposes him. I always wondered how I'd handle it when I lost one of my parents. Would I fall to the ground and cry uncontrollably like I've seen others do? Would I politely thank the doctor delivering the devastating news as if they baked me a fresh batch of chocolate-chip cookies? I do none of these things.

What I do instead is go into doctor mode. Let's fix this. Let's deal with the crisis. I decide to make a list of what has to be done.

Console my sisters.

Console my step-mom, Carmen.

Check on Mom. How's she going to feel about her ex-husband passing away?

Make funeral arrangements.

Write his obituary.

Get him buried.

Deal with the medical practice.

As we enter the hospital, Colin's number flashes on my phone screen. He's not going to be pleased when he realizes that I sent him to voicemail. I'm not ready to be consoled yet. I don't have to listen to his message to know that he's jumping in the car and will be here as soon as possible. He loves me. He loves Ainsley. That's great and all, however right now, I'm trying to find out when the hospital will release my father's body to the funeral home so we can start making arrangements.

Doctor mode.

The best assistant in the world gets Ainsley and I situated in the waiting room and takes the key that I was smart enough to grab from the junk drawer in the laundry room, the one to my old townhouse, to make sure it's stocked with everything Ainsley and I'll need to call it home for a while. They say that money can't buy happiness, but it can purchase the baby gear that I'll need for Ainsley, clothes for both her and I, toiletries, and food for all of us. Right now, I wouldn't call those things happiness, but they sure do bring some stability to this unbelievable rabbit hole I feel like I've fallen through. *My father is dead. I'll never see him again.*

Everyone has gone back to Carmen's home. Is it strange that I'm already not thinking of it as Dad's house? Brad is accepting furniture deliveries at my townhome. Ainsley is asleep in my arms as I wait patiently for the funeral home to claim my dad's body.

The nurse asked me a few times if I wanted to see him. All my sisters went in and said their goodbyes. I didn't. The last time that I saw my dad, he'd come up for one of Colin's home games. He sat with me in our box. We talked football and medicine. He held Ainsley and gave her "Poppy" kisses. He'd hoped that she would agree that Poppy was a good name for him. I smile, thinking about his next comment. "If she's anything like you six girls, she'll come up with the name that sounds the least like Poppy." He actually even went into the locker room to congratulate Colin on a good game before he left to return to Houston.

I have no reason to see my father's lifeless body. I've accepted that he's gone. I know that he loved me. He knew how happy my life is with Colin. He met his first grandchild. He died on the golf course, playing an exceptional game of golf according to the scorecard that I found in his bag of personal belongings. No. Jack Collins and I were and are in a good place. No regrets.

I'm mentally and physically worn out. Just as I put my head back against the wallpapered wall and shut my eyes, Colin's presence wraps me in warmth. The hair on the back of my neck stands up, and his smell rolls over me, making me feel peaceful inside.

"Hi," I greet him without opening my eyes.

He kisses Ainsley on the head, and then I feel his warm, soft lips on my cheek. "I'm so sorry, baby. I tried calling you a couple of times, but you sent me to voicemail."

There's a hint of hurt in his voice, but I ignore it. I can't deal with Colin's bruised feelings at the moment. "It's been crazy."

"What can I do?"

I open my eyes for the first time to look at him. He's in his after-game gear. His hair is a mess. Leaning into his shoulder, I inhale. "Did you not shower?"

His face is etched with concern. He rubs my leg and says, "I just had to get to you."

For some reason, those words break down whatever "doctor mode" wall that I've built, and I begin to sob. Colin takes a sleeping Ainsley from me, and places her on a loveseat right by us, covering her with the baby blanket I brought in. He pulls me into his lap and holds me while I finally let out the sorrow that I'm feeling for losing my dad. He rocks me like he rocks Ainsley, and there's something about that motion that brings me the comfort that I'm desperately craving.

My emotional breakdown is interrupted by the very kind social worker, letting me know that the funeral home just left.

Sitting up, I scoot off of his giant lap. There are strategically placed tissue boxes all over the waiting room so I grab a couple of handfuls and begin to try to clean myself up a bit. Thankfully, we're alone in this room, because I don't think that I could deal with Colin's biggest fans at the moment.

Once I've given up on making myself presentable, Colin picks up our sleeping princess and says, "Let's go home, baby."

I watch with a heavy heart as he walks in front of me, favoring his very swollen right ankle, carrying our beautiful daughter snuggled into his chest, while Miguel follows us to my car.

****

Brad should work for Disney, because the man makes magic happen. As I steer the tank into my old driveway, I note that he's turned on lamps so I don't have to pull up to a dark, empty house. It's such a small gesture, but it reaffirms how much Brad means to me. He's thoughtful enough to take the time to do the little things he knows mean so much. I make a mental note to take him out for a very nice dinner when we're back in Dallas.

Colin hobbles toward the backseat of the tank as if he's going to get a still sleeping Ainsley from her car seat. "Colin, go upstairs and ice your leg. I'll get her," I tell him as I gently block his path.

He shoots me a very ugly glare, but has the good sense to not argue with his very tired, tear-stained, mentally worn-out wife.

I do my best to not rattle Ainsley as I take her baby carrier out of its base. "This, baby girl, is where your mommy proposed to your daddy. This is where we became a family," I tell her sleeping form as I enter through my old front door.

Brad, my fairy godfather, waved his magic wand, and turned my old home into a beautiful place again. My former couches that are now in the pool house in Dallas have been replaced with a similar-looking sofa and loveseat from the local retailer who promises same day delivery and no backorder slips. Brad bought a couple of issues of current sports magazines that now are displayed in a fan-like pattern on my new round coffee table.

There's a red crockpot on the counter that is slow cooking something that smells delicious. The scent reminds me that I haven't eaten since the poached egg that I had for breakfast. *God, I don't even know what time it is.* I place Ainsley, still in her carrier, on the floor next to the couch where Colin is already flopped with a bag of frozen corn on his mid-calf.

I toss my purse on the island—about the spot where Colin introduced me to the pleasures of oral sex again—and open my refrigerator. Just as I suspected. Brad has it stocked with all the foods that Colin and I keep at home. When I move to the pantry, an entire shelf is filled with Ainsley's vacuum-sealed packages of organic baby food in all the flavors that she likes. The comfort that I feel knowing that my family has the basics is overwhelming. *One less thing to worry about.*

When I turn to look at my dining room table that still shows the scars from Colin's attempt at a romantic dinner—the knife marks from where he tried to get the candle wax off the wood—I see the same highchair that we have at home.

My eyes fill with tears. This is no longer where I live, but Brad did everything that he could to make it a home away from home. God bless him.

My nostalgic revelry is broken by the sounds of my phone ringing. I grab it out of my purse, and check caller ID. I don't recognize the number and toss it to Colin. "I'm going to get us settled. Would you play secretary, and watch the baby?"

He flashes me his half-smile. "Is she going to do a trick?"

"Yeah," I reply as a small smile touches my lips. "Hopefully, stay asleep."

I hear enough of the conversation to know that word of Doctor Jack Collins passing away is spreading. Colin does a great job of thanking whoever it is, and reassuring them we'll let them know the funeral plans.

I spend a long time upstairs just sitting on my old bed that Colin says is too small, and staring at the wall in front of me. Colin and I only lived in this house for one week, but we made a lifetime of memories here—good and bad. I still remember how nervous I was the night before I saw him again after Los Angeles. There was beautiful lovemaking that happened in this room. There was also loneliness, and doubts about us and our future. This is where difficult conversations and demands for more information were made. There were surprises, like when he turned my bedroom into a rose garden. But there was also the awful fight with my father downstairs.

In this house is where my now husband and my deceased father came to blows over me. God, now that I'm a mother I can see my dad's point of view so much better. Even though I wish he would have let Colin visit me when I was hospitalized for my eating disorder, I can now fully appreciate why he didn't.

I think about Ainsley downstairs. The idea that some jock with a cocky attitude will one day be chasing after my daughter makes me shiver. Dear Lord, I hope that he doesn't make her cry. Her daddy might do worse than Jack.

Right after Ainsley was born, Colin said that she was Jack's best revenge. Colin will one day know what it's like for his daughter to date someone who he doesn't believe is good enough for her. And let's face facts ... nobody is good enough for Ainsley McKinney. No one.

The sound of my husband's breathtaking voice singing to his angel tickles my ears, shaking me from my thoughts. A part of my heart is shattered by the loss of my dad, but I will always be thankful that he was able to attend my medical school graduation, walk me down the makeshift sort-of aisle when I married Colin, and meet his beautiful granddaughter. All three milestones my five sisters will not get to share with him.

I very quietly whisper, "I love you, Daddy. Faults and all."

****

"Colin, you've got to go back to Dallas," I plead with him the next day while he's changing Ainsley's diaper, and I'm applying my moisturizer.

"Coach approved a leave of absence. We're fine. Calm down," he says as he bends down and blows raspberries on her tummy, making her shriek with happiness.

"All I'm doing today is making the funeral arrangements. Brad's going to help me make phone calls. Amy said that she can watch Ainsley." I wipe my hands on one of my old white hand towels, and turn to Colin. "Trust me. Everyone is so grateful that I'm taking over this job. They'll bend over backwards to help me. I want you here for the funeral. I don't need you today."

"Is Mommy the most stubborn woman we know?" he says in his high-pitched *Daddy is being a patronizing ass* voice as he continues to tickle Ainsley's tummy. "Yes, she is. Yes, she is."

This takes my frustration level, on a day that's already one of the hardest of my life, to atomic levels. All sass and spunk have left my body, and I begin to cry. I stand in the middle of my bathroom, with just a towel wrapped around me and sob pathetically, not knowing what else to do.

"Please go," I plead. "Save days away from the team for when I really need you. Please," I beg. "Today's not one of those days."

He places Ainsley on her tummy on the carpeted floor, and sets a red lion in front of her just out of her reach. "Let's do some tummy time, sweet girl. Try to get the lion," he says while giving it a shake.

Then he walks to me, and pulls me against his chest. My cheek lies against the thumping of his heart, and the sound is like a drug for my soul. It's my lullaby, calming my frayed emotions. He strokes my hair. "You sure you don't need me to stay, beautiful girl?" He pulls away from me and tilts my head up so he can see my eyes. "You could've fooled me."

He's right. If he were an engineer, or had any other normal job, I'd have him take a week off of work and help me though this, but he doesn't have a normal job. He's the Super Bowl-winning MVP quarterback for a team that is fighting for every win this season. He can't just take a week of paid vacation during the season. The only acceptable reason to miss a game is injury, and we certainly don't need any more of those.

"I need you every damn day, Colin, but so does the team. Hop a plane to Dallas. Go to practice. I'll text you as soon as I have the funeral details worked out. There's nothing that is missing-practice worthy today. I promise."

He pulls me to him again and strokes my hair. "I'm a phone call away. I'll give one of the assistants my phone. Call me."

I nod, feeling relief in my heart that he's leaving.

"Do you want me to ask Jenny to come down?"

I think about it for a moment. "Yeah. Why don't you have her come for the funeral? She can watch Ainsley."

The rest of the day is a whirlwind. Fortunately, Dad and Carmen had already purchased their burial plots—how morbid, but helpful to us children. The funeral service will be held in a Methodist Church; it's near their home, and they're members of it but never attended. Brad rented out my dad's favorite restaurant for the after-funeral luncheon. I can't bring myself to call it a reception.

I went to my old medical practice and personally told the staff of my dad's passing. Most of them had already heard. Apparently, my father's death made the Sunday evening news here in Houston. I had them reschedule appointments, and make all the necessary phone calls to close the practice until next Monday. Brad personally called all of the high-profile athletes Dad worked with, and invited them to the funeral on Wednesday.

I called Clay and Janis. I think, for one of the first times since I met Clay South, he didn't have a crass comment. They assured me that they'd be at the funeral.

The next time I check my watch, it's after eight o'clock at night. Amy has already fed, bathed, and put Ainsley to bed. My breasts ache from not feeding her enough today. I plop down on my new couch, put my feet up on the coffee table, and grab my glass of red wine. *I can't wait for Wednesday to be over.*

It's not until I hear, "I Just Want to Dance With You" that I remember that I haven't talked or texted with Colin at all today. I'm sure he's unhappy with me.

"Hey, baby." I sound as exhausted as I feel.

Colin and I spend the next thirty minutes on the phone getting caught up on each other's days. He was only an hour late to practice—thank you, Southwest Airlines. He'll be back late tomorrow night for the funeral on Wednesday. Aiden's coming, which makes me smile. He's a calming presence in our life. Also, Rachael will be in town. I'm still holding out hope that they'll reconcile.

I reluctantly tell Colin goodbye when Brad saunters into the living room, and joins me on the couch with a flop.

The two of us polish off a bottle of wine, and we watch old reruns of *Sex and the City*, complaining about how terribly they've been edited for basic cable. Brad and I've watched them enough that we fill in the missing words, or quote the deleted scenes.

Apparently, my breastfeeding days are over. No pump, half a bottle of wine, yup … Breastfeeding is over. I made it almost nine months. I'd self-congratulate more if my heart weren't so heavy.

Brad is staying in the guest room, or Colin's former office/back to guest room. I hug him goodnight, and thank him for all of his help today. Literally, I couldn't have survived without him. He's amazing.

I walk upstairs to my daughter's crib in the corner of my old bedroom where the red college chair used to reside. She's sleeping so peacefully, on her back, head tilted to the side. Ainsley McKinney is a gorgeous child. I'm not just saying that because I'm her mother. She got the best of her daddy and me. I kiss two of my fingers, and touch them to her forehead. "Sleep tight, precious one."

****

"Hello everyone." I clear my throat and adjust the height of the microphone so I don't have to stand on my tiptoes. "For those who don't know me, I'm Doctor Caroline Collins-McKinney. I'm the second-oldest daughter, if you're keeping score on the cards provided." I attempt to make a joke. Fortunately, everyone is kind enough to at least chuckle.

Carmen asked me to speak at my father's funeral. She wanted his eulogy to be meaningful, and reflect who he was. I reluctantly agreed. Wiping my sweaty palms on the black dress that Brad bought for me, I note how loose it's fitting. I've got to start eating again, and scale back my runs before Colin notices. *Push that thought aside and focus on your notecards.*

Clearing my throat, I continue. "Looking out at your faces in this packed church just confirms what a full life my father led. Some of you he knew through his practice, and can thank him for his healing touch. Others met Jack through us six girls. I see our tennis coach that taught all of us how to swing a racket. Then there's the golfing gang that he played with a couple of times a week." The guys that he was playing with when he collapsed are sitting together, and wearing their golfing attire. Their eyes are bloodshot, and their faces are grey. I can't imagine how hard this must be on them. "Hello to my father's business associates and neighbors.

"My point is that Doctor Jack Collins was everywhere. He was passionate about medicine and sports. He loved his community, and was involved wherever he thought he could make a difference. But, above all else, Jack cherished his wife, Carmen, and his girls."

It was really hard for me to write that part last night. Finally, Colin looked at me and said, "Jack loved you the best way he knew how." After reflecting on Colin's words, I know that he was right. Was it shitty for him to leave his wife and four little girls for his pregnant nurse? Yes. Did he love Carmen the rest of his life, and my two half-sisters? Absolutely. I let the anger go, and feel ten pounds lighter.

"I was fortunate enough to work with my father at his medical practice. In fact, I recognize a lot of you here today. It would mean so much to Jack that his former patients attended his memorial service. Thank you, on behalf of our family." I scan the audience and see Clay wiping a tear from his eye. My heart swells for the gentle giant, whose retirement from football brought me back into the arms of my husband. My eyes lock with Rachael, who's sitting next to my mom, and Chelsea, blending in with my family as if her last name were also Collins. Next to Chelsea is Amy, and Aiden has his arm draped around her shoulder, comforting her. *Interesting.* Last, but not least, my eyes lock with my husband. He looks so dignified in his Armani charcoal-grey suit. The green tie that he's wearing making his eyes sparkle. Right now, the love and devotion for me written on his face almost brings me to my knees.

I have to pause for a moment and collect myself. *I will not cry. I will not cry.* It's my mantra for today. "When I was five, I proudly told my dad that I wanted to be a doctor, to follow in his footsteps. In typical Jack fashion, he asked me what it meant to be a doctor. I told him that I wanted to be just like him, and make people feel better. My dad decided that if I wanted to go into medicine, he'd do everything in his power to help me, but I got no pass for being the daughter of a doctor. Dad made sure he loved us enough every day so us girls would have successes and failures. He never propped us up using his money or influence. Instead, he gave us opportunities to help ourselves.

"Yes, he gave me a job in his practice. However, it was made clear to everyone who worked for him that just because I shared his last name didn't mean that I should be granted any special privileges. It was through my first job in his practice that I met my husband. So, even when I was a bratty teenager, annoyed at the crummy car he gave me, and the minimum-wage job I had to drive two unpaid-hours to work at each way, I can say that I learned work ethic from him. I learned medicine. I found my husband, and I hope to take the life lessons he tried to instill in us girls, and pass them on to my daughter."

Yes. I think that's about as politically correct as I can say it. I take a deep breath and deliver my finishing remarks. "My trim, fit, healthy father was taken from us too soon. He was always too busy to get the heart scan that Carmen bugged him about. He felt that because he was a doctor, he was immune to such things as heart attacks. If I could turn back time, we'd all badger him until he had the quick procedure done. Who knows? We might have avoided this gathering today. Unfortunately, I can't, so as a doctor, I tell you all to get your heart checked yearly." I add a bit of humor by shaking my finger at the crowd.

"In conclusion, I'm going to share with you what I've written to my daughter about how I want her to remember her grandfather." I pull out the sheet of notebook paper that I scratched some words to Ainsley on. Memories will fade, so I wanted to do this while they were still fresh. I plan to put the letter in an envelope, and place it in her baby book. One day, she'll ask me about her grandfather, and I'll share the words that I've written with her.

Unfolding the paper, I don't dare look at the crowd. I know that I'll not make it through this if I see my sisters crying.

"Dear Ainsley." I pause, swallowing my tears one more time. "Today, your grandfather and my dad, Doctor Jack Collins, passed away. He died doing what he loved—playing golf. He wanted you to call him Poppy, which is about the craziest name that I could imagine for him. He wasn't a Poppy. Maybe Doc would have suited him? Grandfather? But not Poppy. I'm sure that you would have chosen the perfect name to call him.

"He loved you so much, baby girl. The first time he held you, he got tears in his eyes. I asked him if he was disappointed that he didn't get a grandson. You know what he said? Absolutely not. With a twinkle in his eye, he said, 'I was made to be the dad and poppy of little girls.'

"You'll miss out on visiting him at his doctor's office. When I was little, he kept jellybeans in his desk. For you, it probably would have been unicorns and rainbows. You'll miss out on him teaching you to play golf. Your grandfather was an excellent golfer, but an even better teacher.

"Most of all, you'll miss out on his wise advice. He always knew what to say, even if it was hard, and it would make you cry. Your poppy, or whatever you would have named him, loved you. He was silly and fun when he visited you. He smothered you in kisses, and told you how much he loved every little hair on your precious head. He carried pictures of you in his wallet. I know he showed them to any poor soul who dared to ask about his first granddaughter.

"Never doubt that Doctor Jack Collins loved you like he loved nobody else. I'm sorry that you will not remember him, but don't you worry. Your crazy aunts will make sure that you hear all the great stories."

I fold up the letter, and whisper through my choked-up voice. "I love you, Daddy."

I all but run back to my husband and his open arms. As soon as I'm seated, Colin pulls me to him, kissing my hair. "You're my MVP, Doctor Collins. Well done." I collapse into his side, feeling the air being sucked from my lungs. My shoulders fold into my chest. It's over. Finally, I can grieve for my father.

Chapter Nine

Colin

It's been five days since I kissed my daughter goodnight and made love to my wife. I had originally planned to leave Wednesday night after the funeral, but dammit if I could bring myself to call a town car to take me to the airport. One more night with Charlie. One more morning to give my sweet baby girl some tummy kisses.

Brad had fed Ainsley breakfast while I made love to my wife. In the shower ... in the closet ... on her too small bed ... If it's possible to store up sex like camels do water, then that's what we were doing. Telling her goodbye when I saw the black town car arrive out front gutted me, because I didn't know when I'd see her or Ainsley again. I still don't.

Charlie is staying in Houston and working at her dad's office until they can either hire more doctors, or they sell the practice. Apparently, Jack had not been as great with his money as Carmen had thought. He'd just taken out a second mortgage on the monstrosity house to fund the new rehabilitation equipment. That's the equivalent to a financial ouch.

Miguel stayed in Houston to watch over my girls. There's no room in her townhome, so I got him a hotel room near her place. He reports to me every day how they're doing, and briefs me on any threats. The level of comfort this brings me is minimal, but it's better than nothing. And the facts are clear, I'm far from over the almost kidnapping attempt when Ainsley was two-weeks-old.

Today was Charlie's first day in the office. I sent her a dozen red roses with a note that says, *Keep your chin up, Infinity. Colin.* She knows that she's lost the professional athlete patients. Her goal is to keep the active patients, and the practice going. I'm hoping that she finds another doctor soon, because this coming-home-to-an-empty-house is bullshit.

I roam through this place like the damn ghost of Christmases past. I feel like I've got a chain wrapped around me, making it hard to breathe. I'd thought coming home to a sleeping Charlie was miserable after my games, but coming home to an empty house is a million times worse. It's just Pancho and me. He at least keeps me company by lying next to the bathtub while I soak. I flipped on the TV in the bathroom, and lay there watching *Sports Center*. I'd much rather be staring at my hot wife.

Jenny's tried to cheer me up in her Jenny-like ways. She offered to take me to dinner. Who wants to eat? She rented a movie that we watched in the movie room. I couldn't tell you what it was about. I felt like throwing a temper tantrum. "I. WANT. MY. WIFE. AND. KID. BACK!"

I check the clock on the oven in the kitchen. It's almost seven o'clock. I have a computer date with my girls. It's pathetic how excited this makes me. I let Pancho out fifteen minutes ago so he could do his business, ensuring that nothing interrupts my time with my loves.

This is the plan that Charlie came up with last night on the phone so I'm not so miserable. I'll get to visit with Ainsley while Charlie gives her a bath, and gets her ready for bed. Then I'll read her a bedtime story, before Charlie tucks her in. At least my daughter will be able to see me, and I'll get to feel like I'm with my family. Or so Charlie says. Nothing replaces actually holding, touching, and kissing my girls.

At 6:59, Pancho and I are in the kitchen at the counter with my iPad, waiting to get the Facetime request. At thirty seconds to go, I grab a bottled-water out of the refrigerator. At 7:00 on the nose, I'm sliding on to the bar stool, drumming my fingers against the counter, waiting for the request ding. Inpatient? Yes. FIVE DAYS WITHOUT MY GIRLS!

At 7:10, I can't wait any longer. I call Charlie. Brad answers, sounding slightly annoyed. "Hey, Brad. I'd like to talk to my ladies this evening." *See, I'm being polite.*

"Sorry about that. Ainsley made such a mess at dinnertime out of herself and Caroline that she just decided that the two of them would take a bath together. I'd bring her the phone, but well … you know."

"Yeah … Yeah … I know. Please don't bring her the phone," I say, with a little too much angst in my voice. "Just tell her that I called."

"Will do," he says before the phone goes dead.

I drop my phone on the counter and rest my forehead against the granite, banging it a few times for good measure. This sucks. I'm not an asshole. I know that Charlie needs to be in Houston with her family. They all need her right now. Ainsley needs to be with her mom, but at this moment I don't care about any of that. I didn't get married and have a child to not be a part of their lives.

The silence of our home is deafening. There should be laughter, and baby giggles. Toys should be squeaked and rattled. Hell, at this point, I'm even willing to hear *Twinkle, Twinkle Little Star* on repeat. I miss the day-to-day routine that we'd fallen into. I'd even take tears as opposed to this silence.

Standing up, I turn around in a circle, looking at how pristinely clean everything is. There aren't any baby bottles in the sink. No toys on the floor for me to trip over. Charlie's medical journals aren't littering the kitchen table. Our home feels like a show house, one of those places that my real estate agent took me to view already-built homes. I half-expect to see images of some random family in the picture frames that are lining the bookcase in the kitchen.

Picking up my water bottle, I throw it against the cabinet, feeling a little better as I watch the water race down the slick wood surface. *Model homes don't have water-stained cabinets.*

I grab Pancho's leash, slip on my running shoes, and take us for a light jog around the neighborhood. Purposely, I leave my phone at home, hoping that Charlie will call—a bunch of times—and I will not answer. She needs to feel some of the misery, loneliness, and angst that I'm feeling right now.

Petty.

Yes.

Bratty.

Yes.

Don't care.

Pancho and I complete about three miles. I know that he's missing his morning runs with Charlie, and he makes me stop two houses from ours and remove his leash so he can run to the house, just as she's taught him. He waits by the back gate for me to let him in. I get a twinge in my heart when he checks the cars in the garage, and runs in the house. "There's no one for you to find, boy. It's just us," I say to him.

The first thing I do when I walk into the kitchen is check my phone. There are no missed calls, but I did get a text from Charlie.

Charlie: *It's been a hell of a day. Thanks for the flowers. I'll call you in the morning.*

Fuck my life.

Chapter Ten

Charlie

Wake up.

Quick run with Miguel trailing me.

Brad feeds Ainsley, while I take a shower.

Get Ainsley clean from breakfast.

Get Ainsley dressed.

Get me dressed while I have my first cup of coffee.

Drop Ainsley off at my mom's house for Amy to watch her.

Try to keep my father's failing medical practice in the black.

Deal with patients who are upset that my father is dead. *Not my fault!*

Fight insurance companies.

Calm a panicking Carmen that she's not going to lose her home.

Pick up Ainsley from my mom's house.

Feed Ainsley, Brad, and myself.

Bathe Ainsley.

Put Ainsley to bed.

Collapse on the couch with Brad, and drink wine until my heart rate returns to normal.

Give Colin thirty minutes of my night, even if sometimes I find it difficult to speak because I'm so mentally drained.

INFINITY.

Crawl into bed.
Repeat again tomorrow.
And the next day.
And the day after that.

Chapter Eleven

Colin

Charlie and Ainsley have been back to Dallas once since her father passed away, and that was for only two nights. I'm counting down the days until Thanksgiving. She's closing the office for the week. I get my girls for eight days. Of course, I have two football games in those eight days, but I'll get to fall asleep and wake up with the two most important ladies in my life—thrilled is an understatement. The word ecstatic comes to mind.

Pancho and I've been spinning like the Tasmanian Devil through the house, trying to spruce it up. Alice is right alongside me, shooing me out of the way, but I can't stop. It's nervous energy.

I keep reminding Pancho that today's the day Charlie and Ainsley are coming home. By the time that practice is over, they should be here. Chef is preparing one of our favorite meals. Alice has brought a few of Ainsley's most treasured toys downstairs so we can all hang out in the family room after supper. Jenny offered to keep Ainsley for us so Charlie could come to my game tomorrow. I'm hoping that we can decorate the house for Christmas while she's here. This will be Ainsley's first Christmas, and I want it to be perfect. Only Charlie can put those special Griswold touches to our house that makes it feel like home around the holidays.

I make our bed, and tighten the sheets. Charlie likes the sheets tight. Pancho and I've been living a bit like bachelors, so I check under the bed to make sure that there aren't any socks or dirty underwear that have accidentally wandered there instead of the dirty-clothes hamper. I discover one of Pancho's rawhides. Charlie makes Pancho enjoy those delights only in the laundry room or outside. I pull it out, showing him the evidence of our bachelor ways. "Dude, these have to stay in the laundry room, or your mom is going to kill us."

Pancho hangs his brown-and-black spotted head as if he understands every word that I'm saying. He knows that he's being chastised. He could be in Mensa for dogs.

I go back under the bed skirt, looking for incriminating evidence, and find two random socks, and a pair of skin-colored G-string lace panties. They make a huge shit-eating grin spread across my face as my dick reminds me how they got there. Just as I'm bringing out the proof of my last tryst with my wife, Jenny clears her throat.

I belly crawl out from under the bed before I sit up on my knees to see what she wants. Her hair is a very normal shade of platinum blonde today. I have to say, I miss the colors when she decides to go conservative.

"You're going to be late for practice," she scolds. Her arms are crossed, and she's leaning against the wall with a smirk on her face as she plays some stupid game on her phone.

"Yes, Mommy dearest," I reply as I hurl one of my dirty socks at her. I'm in such a good mood today that nobody can piss on my party.

She lets out a surprisingly girly squeal, and ducks before my sock can contaminate her. "Colin, that's disgusting, and you're an asshole. Seriously. Are you sixteen? And now you made me lose my game," she says in a huff as she turns to walk away, shaking her head. Then, she pauses. "Oh. By the way, Aiden called, and asked who's coming to Thanksgiving," she states without an ounce of concern in her voice. Before I can reply, she continues, "I told him that if he meant was Rachael going to be here, then the answer is yes. Not sure if he's still coming. You might want to call him"

I sit back on my heels and sigh. "Thanks for letting me know."

149

It's been a year and half since Rachael told Aiden that she wasn't going to marry him. They've seen each other twice. Once, when Ainsley was born at our two-week Meet Our Kid party, and at Charlie's dad's funeral. Both times Rachael was fine, but Aiden looked like he had a bad hangover. I don't know what else to say. I've spelled it out for him: the girl you love doesn't love you back. Move on.

Even I know that's much easier said than done. Exhibit A: My first marriage. Exhibit B: My overdose. Exhibit C: Sleeping with random women and Jenna.

Just the thought makes me shudder.

Jenny checks her watch, and from the safety of our living room says, "Seriously Colin. Get your ass in gear. You're bordering on tardy, and I'd hate to see you have to stay late today of all days."

She's right. I'll just have to trust Alice to debachelor my pad.

****

The definition of insanity is doing the same thing over and over again, expecting different results. That's what I feel like I'm doing at practice.

"Quit checking your watch, asshole. I'm going to think that you have a hot date," the quarterback coach teases me as he hands me another ball to throw.

I drop back and toss it as far as I can, hitting the upright. That was a long fucking throw. I even surprised myself. "I do. I've got not one, but two beautiful blondes waiting to welcome me home."

He laughs, and lobs me another ball. "Twenty bucks says that you can't hit the upright twice."

Is he kidding me? I smirk, drop back, and throw the football. I watch it rotate through the air and hit in the exact same spot the last ball did. I'm on fire today.

I lean toward him, making the money sign in his face while I do a bragging victory dance. "Pay up, motherfucker," I taunt him.

He laughs. "How about if I keep my twenty, and you can cut outta here a little early?"

He doesn't have to offer me that deal twice. I don't even bother showering, just grab my stuff out of my locker, slip my wedding ring on, and head for Bertha. I say to myself, "Watch out ladies. Daddy's on his way home."

It's a gorgeous November day in Dallas. The sun is shining. I have my windows rolled down, enjoying the breeze blowing through my truck. Old Pat Green is singing his heart out through the truck's speakers. Life is good.

I let my mind wander. Maybe I should get a convertible for days like this. I donated the Corvette that I won for being named Super Bowl MVP to my charity. They raffled it off, and someone bought it for almost three-hundred thousand dollars. Shocked the hell out of me. The winning bidder asked if I'd sign the leather seats. Umm ... sure. *You just paid three times what the car is worth. I think that I could be bothered with my signature.*

When I drive through the open gates of our neighborhood, my left leg begins to bounce up and down with nervous energy. I find myself trying to see around trees, and through shrubbery. I want a glimpse of what Charlie calls The Tank. Then I know my girls are home.

The closer I get to my house, the tighter the knot becomes in my stomach. Unfortunately, what my brain realized was obvious before my heart is that my girls aren't here yet. I check my watch, knowing they should've arrived two hours ago.

I grab my phone, and hit Charlie's number.

"Hello?" she sounds harassed. I flood with relief. At least they're okay.

"Hey, baby, it's me," I say, sounding like an idiot. Of course it's me. Who else has my George Strait ringtone?

"Look, Colin, the doctor will be in any second. I'll call you when we're done here," she says, clearly annoyed with me. I'm not sure what I've done, but it's something that's pissed her off. Then the meaning of the words that she's said register in my head. Doctor? In any second? That means she's not on the road.

"Wh ... What?"

"The voicemail that I left you." She pauses for a heartbeat. "You haven't been home yet, have you?"

"No. I'm just pulling into the driveway. What's going on?" I ask as my heart starts racing. I park Bertha in the driveway. Fuck the neighbors if my truck doesn't fit in with their pristine community.

"I think Ainsley has an ear infection. Brad and I were in the process of loading the tank when she just started crying, and wouldn't quit. I called her doctor, and she said to bring her in. Brad and I are in an exam room now."

"Poor baby. How is she?" I'm flooded with worry. My baby hasn't had more than an upset tummy. I can't imagine her crying, and Charlie not being able to console her. Just the thought makes my stomach clench.

"Brad's bouncing her while they look at animal artwork that lines the halls. She's at least calm now."

Then it dawns on me. How can Ainsley be at a doctor's office in Houston? Her pediatrician is here, in Dallas. Charlie and I interviewed numerous doctors before we chose Doctor Kaufman. Charlie clearly said that she called Ainsley's doctor. "Who's seeing Ainsley in Houston?"

"You mean what doctor?" She keeps talking before I can confirm that yes, I mean what doctor are you taking my daughter to that I don't know. "She came well recommended by one of the nurses at the office. I haven't met her yet. Oh, Colin, she's coming in. I have to go."

The phone disconnects before I can even tell her goodbye. I sit in my truck, and stare out the window at my empty fucking house for longer than I care to note.

Helpless. That's a good word to describe how I'm feeling. Motherfucking helpless. My baby girl is in pain, and I'm not there to kiss the ache away. *It's my fucking job.* My wife's assistant is holding my daughter and bringing her comfort, and I'm paying him for that privilege. My wife is frazzled, and I'm not there to hold her hand, and stroke her hair, telling her that everything is going to be okay even if I don't know that it will be. The two most important people in my world are four hours away from me, being comforted by Brad. Fuck my life.

I let Pancho out with zero enthusiasm, and sink into the living room couch while I grip my phone. She's got exactly thirty minutes to call me back before I do something really stupid like drive to Houston when I have to be at the stadium at seven-thirty tomorrow morning.

I sit there in my quiet, still house, smelling the wonderful dinner that Chef prepared for us. Too bad it'll go to waste. In the corner are some of Ainsley's favorite toys. It's even more depressing, seeing them piled up neatly instead of strewn all over the living room rug. I check the time. Charlie has ten more minutes.

Should I do a NASA countdown clock? I remember watching the space shuttle launch when I was in school. They had this huge digital clock that would tick down the seconds until launch. A space shuttle launch and football game are both very similar in a lot of ways. Most importantly, ten minutes on the countdown clock, and ten minutes left in a football game both don't really mean ten minutes. There are a lot of time-outs and clock stops. What I mumble to no one in particular is, "Ten minutes now really means ten fucking minutes."

Five minutes …

Four minutes …

Three minutes …

"How is she?" I ask when I answer before the phone has a chance to complete a ring.

Charlie lets out a sigh. "Double ear infection. We have numbing drops, and an antibiotic, because she also has a stuffed-up head." Before I can say anything, she continues. "Colin, she's fine. She has a cold. She's not the first kid to have an ear infection, and she will not be the last." Charlie's using her "I'm the doctor, and everything is fine" voice.

I growl. It's probably not the correct response, but I can't help it. "I don't care. She's my daughter, and this is her first time sick. I. Want. My. Baby." I open and close my fist, knowing that this is so much more than not being with my sick child. This is the frustrating month of not seeing my family but once since the funeral. This is the disappointment of not having them waiting for me when I arrived home from practice. This is every time that I talk to Charlie, hearing what Brad's doing with MY daughter. This is my loneliness and frustration that I can't get in the car and drive to them because I have to toss a ball in twelve hours.

Charlie begins to cry, which makes me feel like a dick, on top of my frustration and disappoint. "Look, I'm going to put Ainsley to bed. We'll get up early tomorrow, and drive straight to Dallas. I think that I can still make it to your game."

I stand up and walk around the living room, running my hand through my hair. In a much more resigned voice, I sigh. "If you can make it, then that's great. If you can't, or if you have to drive fast, don't worry about it. There will be other games."

She sniffs. "I miss you."

I reply very quietly, "I miss you too. Kiss A for me."

"I will."

We both linger, not wanting to say goodbye. It makes me feel marginally better that she's missing me also. Finally, I tell her, "Put Ainsley to bed and call me back. I just want to talk to you before I go to sleep."

"Okay," she whispers.

Then, I hear Brad in the background mumbling something. "What did Brad say?"

"He's telling me that he has her bathed and in PJs. She's ready for her night story and Mommy time."

The words "Mommy time" open the gaping wound back up in my chest. I want to scream, "What about Daddy time?" Little girls need their daddies just as much as they need their mommies. It should be me that bathed her, and put her in her jammies.

I found a new book at the bookstore to share with Ainsley. It has a dog in it that looks like Pancho. There's this battle raging in my head between being grateful that Charlie has Brad to help her out, and being insanely pissed that some other man is doing my job. I tell her bye before I say something that I'm going to seriously regret.

The images of Charlie, Brad, and my daughter, shopping and having lunch, pop to the forefront of my brain. The tabloid speculation is like a brush fire burning out of control that our marriage is over because Charlie is living with Brad in Houston. The pictures of Brad pushing Ainsley in her stroller through a park near Carmen's home. Charlie and Brad having sushi together at a restaurant in Houston. Brad pushing Ainsley in a toddler swing in Charlie's mom's front yard.

I laugh ruefully at myself. I'm fucking jealous of Charlie's gay assistant. He may not be fucking my wife, but he's stepped in and taken up my jobs in every place but the bedroom. That's bullshit. Ainsley has one father. Charlie has one husband. Brad needs to step back, and figure out his place.

My heart is attempting to beat its way out of my chest. Sweat starts pouring off of my forehead. It's difficult for me to breathe. My dream, the one where Charlie tells me that I'm not good enough for her and Ainsley, floods my mind in crystal clarity.

"It's coming true," I say out loud. "My dream is coming true. The vines are carrying her away from me. Charlie is leaving me for Brad."

I flop back against the couch, and stare at the ceiling. When that does nothing to calm me, I lean forward, putting my head in my hands, trying to take a breath. "Why does she even need me? She has her toys. Brad doesn't have a mistress job. Brad is there to take care of every one of her needs. Brad is her protector. Brad is her partner. I'm just the motherfucker who brings home the paychecks."

Here's the best part. I've paid the asshole to take over my role. I handed him my daughter and my wife on a fucking silver platter.

I grip the arms of the sofa, willing my lungs to expand. The tightness is about to overtake me. *Fuck Colin. Calm down.*

I try to push the pain out of my heart and think good thoughts …

The day that Charlie and I got married.

The night she told me that we were pregnant.

Hell, seeing her on that elevator for the first time in eight years.

Our kiss in Clay's brag room.

Dancing with her at the George Strait concert.

She loves you. She wants and misses you.

Slowly, slowly, I begin to take in air, and my heartbeat returns to a non-sprinting rhythm.

I fall back against the couch, and turn my head to stare at the first family picture that we took right after Ainsley was born. Charlie is dressed in a white blouse, and black pants. I'm wearing a vibrant blue shirt, and nice jeans. My gold Super Bowl ring gleams in the light.

We're sitting on the fireplace hearth. She's holding Ainsley, who is dressed in a long ivory gown, in her arms, and I have Pancho on my lap. Just a hint of his Dallas Cowboy's dog collar is visible. We look so happy. Charlie has a contented smile, and her eyes are bright lavender. She's wearing her infinity necklace, diamond earrings, wedding band, and past, present, future ring that I had given her about a year prior. Ainsley's eyes are closed, and she looks to be dreaming of angels. Even Pancho appears to have a smile on his face. Our house was so calm and peaceful that day. Charlie is looking at the camera, but my eyes are cut to the side; I'm staring at my girls.

When the photographer showed us the proofs, Charlie immediately grabbed this picture and said, "That's the one."

I'd raised my eyebrow, questioning her choice. "I'm not looking at the camera."

She'd leaned over, and kissed me on the cheek. "Yes, but the devoted look on your face says everything that I choose to remember about the birth of our daughter."

It struck me for the first time that maybe Charlie had to forgive me as much as I had to forgive her.

She has to end this living apart bullshit. It's been almost a month since her dad passed away. It's time. Hire a new doctor, sell the practice, do something, but I've been a supportive husband for long enough. I've offered to give her money, if that's what Carmen needs. The world is hers if she'd just move back home. It's time to reclaim my family.

Chapter Twelve

Charlie

The Tank is loaded down. My well-drugged baby is secured in the backseat. Brad is DJing from the passenger seat, and I've got the cruise-control set. Barring any issues, I should be able to make it to the second half of Colin's game.

Jenny is waiting for me at our home. Miguel is going to drive me to the stadium so I don't have to worry about parking. Carter is anxiously waiting for Brad, and a little reunion time.

The sun is shining, and it's another gorgeous late fall day in Texas. In two short hours, I should see my husband in his very sexy football pants and tight jersey. Yum! Five or six hours after that, I might get to actually kiss him, and say hello properly.

Colin must have been a miserable SOB lately because Jenny offered to stay at our house tonight and take care of Ainsley for us. When we announced that we were expecting, we were informed that Jenny's job description did not include nanny responsibilities. I can only think that Colin's been such a bear that she feels like she's taking one for the team by giving us some time away from parenting.

Brad checks the clock, and finds the game on the local radio station. We hit the outskirts of Dallas right when I was expecting. I do a mental fist bump with myself. The Cowboys are about to kick off.

Everything goes as planned. Brad stays to get Jenny and Ainsley settled while Miguel and I race to the stadium. I flip down the mirror and check my appearance, just in case the paparazzi are waiting for their high-dollar picture of me arriving at the game.

Then, I send Colin a text.

Me: *The eagle has landed. Pulling into the stadium lot now. Love you to infinity.*

As I flash my ticket and have my bag checked, the butterflies in my stomach begin beating their wings in time to the fan noise. It's been fourteen days since I've seen him. I want my husband. *Desperately.*

I enter our suite to the shrieks of Liza and a couple of the other players' wives that I've become friends with. This feels so normal. I did this every home game for two years. Normal is such a foreign feeling that I'm not sure what to do with it.

Then it hits me. Nothing since my dad passing away has felt right. Gosh, I could even go all the way back to becoming a mom, or finding out I was pregnant. My life has changed so much in a year and a half. Right now, in this second, I feel like the old Caroline. The one who attended every one of her husband's games. The girl who lived and breathed Colin Fucking McKinney.

I'm the girl who's practicing the kind of medicine that I love again. The one who walks through the practice doors every morning, and feels alive. I'm no longer just biding my time, keeping my medical license active. I'm developing relationships with patients—watching them heal because of my care.

The feeling of normalcy is so foreign to me that it almost barrels me over. I grab the granite countertop in the suite to steady myself. Since I dropped Ainsley off, I haven't thought about her once. I've only been focused on getting to my husband. I let out a sigh, realizing that this is what the old Caroline felt like, and the best way to describe this sensation is *right*.

"You okay?" Liza asks. Her face is tight with concern.

I smile, and it's not forced. "Yes. I think that I am."

"Read your card. Our curiosity has almost gotten the best of us." She motions to a vase filled with mixed colored roses that I honestly hadn't even noticed.

I grab the envelope that reads *Charlie* in Colin's script.

Carefully, I remove the card, and read his awful left-handed penmanship. "My heart only beats for you." Then he drew the sideways number eight, and signed it CFM.

I'm smiling like an idiot as I bring the card to my chest, pressing it against my heart. Dear God, my whole body tingles with love for that man.

I pour myself a glass of wine, and say hello to Colin's parents before I settle into the open seat next to Liza to watch my man play football.

****

"Hey handsome, care to join me in the hot tub?" I ask my gorgeous husband, who's already ripping off his clothes as if they're on fire. I'm wearing nothing but a smile. I'd advised Jenny earlier that she should probably not look in the backyard tonight. I couldn't promise that Colin and I wouldn't be making a porno. I also told the two security guys in the pool house to turn off the backyard cameras.

This is our first time seeing each other in a couple of weeks, and I want and need my husband. I'm craving his touch on my skin, his warm breath on my neck. I want all of him. I want to bask in his attention.

I've got an old country Pandora station playing on the outdoor speakers. The hot tub is bubbling at a fantastic ninety-nine degrees. Our Waterford crystal champagne bucket is filled with bottles of water for Colin. I've an open bottle of Malbec wine sitting next to the champagne bucket, and a halfway empty glass in my hand. It's just like old times, except we're parents now, and my dad is dead.

Colin leaves his clothes on a sun-lounger so I get to watch him walk towards me in all his naked glory. My nipples tighten into sharp points, and it's not from the chilly night air. His body is perfectly sculpted as if he's been carved from a block of solid marble. His abs ripple as he moves closer. Involuntarily, I lick my lips, wanting a taste of his full lips, pec muscles, and the very hard cock that's standing at attention. *That's my husband, and he wants me just as much as I want him.* I'm so aroused I'm even able to ignore his limp.

"See something you like?" he asks as he flashes me my half-smile. Those green eyes of his twinkle in the moonlight. Dallas won. He played an inspired game. Ainsley and I are home. Colin's happy.

He climbs into the hot tub, sinking into the bubbling water, and lets out a very contented sigh. His long, muscular arms rest outside of the hot tub on the brick surround. I scoot next to him, snuggling up to his side, noting that we fit together perfectly after all this time. Two halves making one whole.

His pec muscles beg me for attention, so I bring my tongue and lips to his nipples and begin to suck and nip the one closest to me while I pinch the one furthest away. Colin's groans of appreciation bathe my insides with hot liquid lava. I long to feel his pulse against my lips so I kiss my way up his toned chest to his heart. His rhythm tells me that he's as turned on as I am.

We need to reestablish this connection. I don't want to talk about football, or Ainsley. I can't give him his being time. Not now. I need to feel him against me—every muscular inch.

"You haven't even said hello to me yet, wife of mine." There's humor and love in his words.

I ignore him and climb on top, placing my knees on either side of his thighs. He grabs my waist and pulls me to him, using his tongue to slowly make love to my mouth. Our kiss takes on a comforting yet desperate edge that speaks volumes about what we're feeling. It's *I missed you more than I can articulate,* and *I love you more than myself.*

His erection is pinned between us. Even through the numbing effects of the water, his hardness throbs against my stomach in anticipation. My hands go from lovingly massaging Colin's scalp and running my fingers through his dark-blonde waves to gripping his back muscles as I rub my hips against him, craving the friction of his erection against my clit. His soft moans of pleasure make me ache to have him. God, I've missed this. *Colin.* It's one simple five-letter name, but the man behind it is anything but simple. He's intense and moody, he's passionate and loving, he's private and public; the five-letter name that defines my husband is my drug of choice.

I still haven't spoken a word to him. I prefer to let my body do all the talking for me. I begin to rotate my hips, using my core to massage his penis. Colin uses the weightlessness of the water to move my slickness up and down his length. I throw my head back, breaking our kiss in ecstasy as his erection puts just enough pressure against my bare, exposed clit.

We're home. This feels like what home is supposed to be like. I grab his face in my hands and lean in, giving him a soul-searing kiss. I don't want to tell him how much I need him. I want him to feel my desire, my love, my want, my *need* for this. What we have between us in this moment is not defined by time or space. It's love and lust, tied up in a gorgeous box labeled passion.

He kisses me back, matching my intensity perfectly. I feel him guide my hips up a little higher and then bring me down, encasing his erection inside of my heat and wetness. I moan into his mouth as he brings me down further and further until I'm sitting on his thighs, filling me with himself, his hardness.

I let him move my hips up and down and rotate me on his erection. I've given my whole self over to him for him to use as he wishes. And for my own needs. I don't want to be in control of this. I'm in charge of so many things in my life right now, I just want to turn my pleasure over to Colin and let him bring the love and release that I crave.

Our movements, or should I say my movements, become more frenzied. Water sloshes around us, stirring up the hot tub enough that we're splashing over the edges. It's perfect. Wordlessly, I let go of my body and give into the orgasm that is building deep inside me. I don't tell Colin that I'm close, but he must sense it, because he begins to drive harder inside of me while he maneuvers my hips. When I know that I'm seconds away from coming, I lean forward and take his swollen lips, mimicking our movements with my mouth. We're frenzied without making a sound or breaking our connection. I silently orgasm as he thrusts inside me one last time, flooding my insides with himself.

Our kissing becomes gentler, sweeter, calmer, but no less loving or affectionate. I don't want this to end. I'm not ready to discuss our real life outside of this hot tub. I don't want to read "the end" on our fairytale.

He's the first one to pull away. When he does, he takes my chin so he can look into my eyes. It's a half moon out, so we have a soft spotlight overhead. There's no doubt that his eyes are soft, dewy, with love for me. "Welcome home, Mrs. McKinney."

Chapter Thirteen

Colin

As holidays go, Thanksgiving is one of my favorites. There's no gift-giving pressures. There's not much decorating. Plus, everyone comes to our house to celebrate with us if I'm playing at home. If it's an away game, then we pick a night earlier in the week and celebrate it then.

It just so happens that this year, it's a home game, so everyone, except for Amy went to my game on Thanksgiving Day. She decided to be the awesome aunt that she is and keep Ainsley company.

Fortunately, everyone is sleeping at a nearby hotel but Amy and Aiden. Amy is back to playing nanny—which is a gift—and Aiden and I have some business that we need to take care of, so it made more sense for him to stay with us.

This is the third time that Rachael and Aiden have been around each other since his marriage proposal took a gigantic shit. This is also the first holiday that they've spent with us since that momentous day. I had to have the bro talk with Aiden. The one that starts off with "I've got a nine-month-old kid. You can't get so shit-faced that you pass out on the stairs again." And ends with "She's moved on. It's been a year and half. You should too." So far, they've been awkwardly polite to each other and have avoided being in the same room. Success in my book.

Charlie and the gang are in the kitchen, putting the final touches on our Thanksgiving feast, and I'm trying to work out the soreness in my ribs from today's game. I'm feeling pretty damn lonely in the hot tub without my best girl in her string bikini, but then again, I'm sure our family doesn't want to watch us have monkey sex while they eat their turkey. No, even I can admit that it's best that Charlie stays out of the hot tub when our family is awake. But I will say that I've got some new spank-bank material from our last hot tub experience for when she leaves me again on Sunday.

"Hey, dick cheese! How'd you get out of making cream sauce for the broccoli?" Aiden asks as he pulls a chair over to the edge of the hot tub.

Ewww. *Not a great comment, Aiden.*

"I got punched in the ribs for sixty minutes by some asshole lineman that kept blowing snot on me anytime he got close." Aiden's eyes grow wide with horror, and apparently he decides to change the subject before I further explain the other grossness that happens during a game.

"It's now perfectly clear why you keep playing football," he quips as he forces a smile. There's obviously something that he wants to discuss. He's been acting odd – even for Aiden. I've watched him open his mouth as if to speak, just to shut it again. It's been on the tip of his tongue since he arrived, but whatever it is, it's obviously something that he doesn't want to bring up.

Well, that doesn't sound positive. "What the fuck have you done?" I ask preparing myself for another, "Aiden, you're such a smart guy. How do you get yourself in these fucked up situations?" speeches.

"IsleptwithAmyafterthefuneral," he rushes out, looking like he has a bad case of food poisoning.

"What? Is that English?" I take a swig from my water bottle and finish it off with a gulp before tossing it into the garbage pile I've started near the bushes by our bedroom.

He takes a deep breath and lets it out. "I slept with Amy after the funeral." His head drops like Pancho's when he knows he's supposed to stay off the couch, but he just can't help himself.

My jaw clinches, and I feel like pummeling my best friend. "You did what?" I grind out.

Aiden puts his hands up defensively. "Look, I really like her. It's not like I just fucked her because she's hot."

I've come to think of Charlie's sisters as my own. Amy in particular, because she's lived with us for a while. I'm an only child. I can't even pretend to know what it feels like to have siblings, but I do know that I will kill any motherfucker that makes the Collins' girls cry.

My molars crunch together. "I'm going to give you thirty seconds to explain why I shouldn't beat the shit out of you."

Aiden knows that I'm dead serious and starts spilling his guts. "You're the one who keeps telling me to move on from Rachael, and I've been trying. I've gone on some dates with girls in LA, but they all seem to have an angle. 'Oh! You're McKinney's agent? Does he need a model for his next line?' You know, that kind of shit."

He leans forward and begins to fidget with an imaginary thread from his pants. "Every girl that I've met seems so fake. I've gotten to know Amy over the years, and have always really liked her. She's got such a sweet, gentle way. She's kind and beautiful. She laughs at my jokes and calms me when I'm upset. Frankly, she's the polar opposite of Rachael."

I will definitely agree with him there.

He pauses for a second, clearly getting into uncomfortable territory again. "I saw her so sad at her dad's funeral, and I got this overwhelming feeling of just wanting to hold her and kiss her tears away. It's like I didn't even notice that Rachael was a couple of people from me."

My surprise at his statement must show on my face, because he says, "I know. Can you believe it? Seeing Rachael didn't even make me want to discover the bottom of a whiskey bottle. Anyway, after the lunch thing was over, I asked Amy if she'd like to go for a walk. And she said yes. We walked around some park for a long time and just talked to each other. Then, I asked if she wanted to come back to my hotel and watch a funny movie."

Aiden's eyes grow wide clearly about to defend himself. "I had no intention of sleeping with her when I invited her. I really just wanted to make her feel better."

I've known Aiden for most of my life. I can tell how sincere he is. Now, that I'm really looking at him, he does have that dopey, I'm-in-love look about him.

"We ordered room service and bought a comedy on pay-per-view. It was just so natural. I snuggled her to my side, and one thing led to another."

I throw my hand up, stopping him. "No more. I get it. Could you stop fishing in ponds so close to my wife? Find a beautiful blonde that isn't Charlie's best friend or sister?" Seriously, this is ridiculous. He lives in LA. There has to be a blonde there who won't want him for just his ties to the entertainment industry.

"I know how this looks, but it's really not like that. We've talked every night on the phone. When it's time to say goodbye, I don't want to hang up. I find something beautiful, and I want to buy it for her, or take a picture because I know that it'll make her smile. I can't believe that I've fallen for a girl that is the polar opposite of Rachael, but I think that it's a good thing."

I almost feel sorry for the guy. Almost. He fucks Amy over, and there's going to be huge tension in our house. However, Aiden is a great dude. I know he wants to be married and have a family. Amy is a dream of a girl. I can see the two of them getting along well. "Don't dick her over, okay? The surest way to get uninvited from family holidays is to piss off Charlie. She'll have your nuts made into a keychain for The Tank if you fuck over Amy. That's her little sister." I lecture him, doing my best dad impression. Then it hits me. What would Jack think of my best friend dating his daughter? I laugh, knowing he'd be livid.

Aiden shakes his head and his face begins to relax as it occurs to him that I'm not going to beat his ass. "I know. And I have no intention of doing that. But, here's the thing: Amy is afraid that you and Caroline are going to fire her if you find out."

"Fire her? For what? Picking the wrong guy?" I couldn't help but get my jab in. "She can't help it that you drugged her drink."

"It wasn't like that, Colin, I swear. She ..." Aiden starts pleading his case, again looking as innocent as can be.

I cut him off. "I know. I was kidding. As long as Amy is putting Ainsley's needs first, I'm not upset that she's seeing you." I pause a heartbeat, and add, "But let me be clear, Aiden, you're treading in dangerous water. I'm not kidding. You fuck her over and we will choose her over you. I don't give a fuck that Ainsley is named after you or that you're her godfather. Hell hath no fury like a pissed off Caroline Jane McKinney."

Aiden nods and offers me his hand. I shake and give it one final, hard squeeze. "Let me be the one to break the news to Charlie."

He looks very relieved.

****

Sunday, feels like a goddamn morgue in our house. All the family is gone but Aiden and Amy. I haven't shared the news about their relationship with Charlie yet. Selfishly, I didn't want to give us anything that might cause a fissure to form in our perfect week together.

When Ainsley began to babble in her bed this morning, I turned off the baby monitor and raced to my angel. She's sitting up banging a soft toy that must have gotten left in her crib. Her gorgeous chubby cheeks light up when she sees me, and she reaches her arms out for me to pick her up.

Charlie keeps lecturing me. "Colin, she's never going to learn to crawl if you carry her everywhere." My reply, "Haven't seen a kindergartener yet who couldn't walk in to school on the first day."

Ainsley babbles to me, and I swear that there might be a "da da" in the mix, but I refuse to count it until she looks at me and just says, "Da Da." Then, my heart will overflow with joy.

"How's Daddy's baby princess this morning?" I ask her as I kiss both of her rosy cheeks. I carefully place her on the changing table and remove her night diaper. Then, I blow thousands of raspberries on her round tummy.

She kicks and wiggles with excitement, and it just eggs me on. I savor each Ainsley giggle, knowing that I won't have them for another two weeks or even longer, and sadness grips my chest.

I remove her from her lavender PJs and replace them with an outfit that either Amy or Charlie left out for her to wear today. Her and I sit down in the middle of her room on the pink flower rug and choose toys that we want to play with. I find a set of stacking cups and show her how you can place them on top of one another, building a tower where I'm going to lock her up to keep nasty boys away. Once again, the thought of Aiden and me as teenagers flashes through my head and I shudder.

As if the kid understands me, she gives me a half smile and then uses her fat little hand to knock the tower down. The clanking sound must wake Pancho, because he quickly joins us for playtime.

I observe how gently she pets him. It's really more like a very soft pat, but Pancho freaking eats it up. He begins to smother her face with licks, and she laughs harder, letting him bathe her with his tongue.

Noting the time, I know that these precious moments with my baby are coming to an end, so I pick her up and cradle her against me. "Daddy loves you with all of his heart, pumpkin. And you and I are going to be together every day very soon. I'm going to read you books every night, and sing you songs every morning. And I'm even thinking about teaching you how to two-step, but you've got to learn to walk first."

She reaches up and grabs a bit of my hair that's fallen on my forehead and gives it a tug. She laughs at how the curl springs back up. I hold her tightly to me, trying to memorize every inch of her. When I see her again, she'll have grown. She'll have learned a new skill and changed in appearance. I want to remember everything about how she feels in this second. I memorize her weight in my arms, and I inhale her fresh baby scent.

I begin to sing "Love Without End, Amen" by George Strait to my baby girl. It's been our song since she came home from the hospital. I figured she should love George just as much as her mother and I do.

"I hate to break up the party, but we've got to hit the road," Charlie says from behind me, sounding as sad as I feel.

Battery acid floods my stomach, and this all-consuming feeling of loneliness drowns me. I think about throwing something crazy out there, like, "Don't leave. Let's take Ainsley and disappear to another country." Or, "Fuck football, I'll go to Houston with you."

I don't do either. I get my breathing under control before Charlie notices. It's not like she needs to add another stressor to her life. She's already working herself to the point that I'm concerned about her. She's so damn thin, and there are dark circles under her eyes. I'll be glad when her dad's practice is back on solid ground for more than just the obvious selfish reasons.

Charlie has mentioned more than once the obligation that she feels to her family and her dad's memory to ensure that the practice he built is strong and in good hands before she turns it over. It's admirable, really.

I begrudgingly pick up my daughter's suitcase and carry it down the stairs while I balance Ainsley in my other arm, not wanting to let her go. *My daughter has a fucking suitcase to come to our house.* The irony is not lost on me.

Once we reach the foyer, I drop the pink-and-white polka dotted bag by the stairs and grab Charlie's arm, spinning her around and pushing her up against the front door. "Look, if this is about money, just tell me how much. I'll pay off the loan on the rehab equipment. Tell me what I have to do to keep you and Ainsley here with me." It's a plea, and I hope she hears the desperation in my voice.

She tries to take Ainsley from me, but I don't let her. She's not going to use the baby as a shield. Her eyes cut to the ground as if our foyer marble is the most interesting thing on the planet. "You know that this isn't completely about the money. I want to leave the practice as strong as it was when my dad died. No one can do this but me. Plus, Colin, I'm enjoying this challenge. I like seeing my patients' progress, and knowing that it's because of me."

Charlie just confirmed what I've been suspecting. This whole getting her father's practice in order is about Charlie wanting to do right by her father, but it's also practicing the kind of medicine that inspires her again. My gut acknowledges what my mind isn't ready to admit yet. *This isn't going to end. She's going to slowly move my daughter to Houston, four hours away from me, for her career. I did move her away from her dream for my job.*

Charlie continues to drill holes in the floor with her eyes, and it's killing me. I adjust Ainsley on my hip and use my free hand to raise her chin. Her eyes are glassy with unshed tears, and I fucking hate it. "Hey, don't cry. I'm just tired of telling you goodbye." Then, I give her my half-smile and chuckle. "Thought I'd make one last-ditch attempt to keep you here."

I kiss her lips, not wanting to let her go. I don't want us to end this magical week together angry at one another. If she is wanting to stay in Houston permanently, ten minutes before she leaves me again is not the time to fight about it—even I'm smart enough to realize that.

She's the one who pulls away first. "You know we got distracted and never discussed the Lake Somerville property site plans."

She's at least thinking about our future if she's talking about the vacation home.

"Damn distractions." I smirk, staring directly at her tits.

"Maybe we can get to it next time we're home." *Please let it be for good next time. Prove me wrong, Charlie. Come on, baby, show me that you aren't karma's best revenge.*

She turns, brushing against my crotch as she wiggles away from me. "One more bathroom break. Can you put Ainsley in the car?" Neither one of us moves for a couple of heartbeats as I absorb her smell, and feel the lingering remnants of her touch on my cock.

She breaks the spell and heads toward our bedroom. I pick up Ainsley's suitcase. "Come on, baby girl. Time to tell you goodbye."

My heart is heavy as I carry my daughter to The Tank. I can do this for a finite period of time, but this can't be my life. I can't keep giving Ainsley goodbye kisses. I'm not willing to give up my relationship with my daughter or wife for Charlie's career.

Brad and Carter are having a heated goodbye make-out session in my driveway, and only stop when I begin to load the back with my wife and daughter's things.

Amy and Aiden join us on the driveway. Amy is flushed and her lips are swollen. They must have said their goodbyes in the privacy of one of their rooms.

I strap Ainsley into the car seat, checking the restraints to make sure they're secure across her chest. Next, I lean over, giving her a kiss on tip of her nose. She giggles and bats at a toy that Charlie has suspended from the roof of the car. I can't stand it, so I lean in for two more kisses and a nose rub. "Bye, Daddy's angel. I'll see you soon."

Brad takes the passenger seat, and Amy slides in the back next to the car seat.

Now, I must tell my beautiful girl goodbye. I pull her to me and hold her tightly while I kiss her lips. I silently pray into her hair that I'm wrong, and that she's going to come back to me.

Her arms, wrapped tightly around my chest, give me the reassurance that this is as hard on her as it is on me. *My feelings must be wrong.*

She pulls away first. "I love you."

I smile, not wanting to make it any harder on either of us. "Infinity."

"Infinity," she repeats as her fingers brush over her necklace.

Then, Carter, Aiden, and I stand like the pathetic fucks we are watching The Tank, filled with our loved ones, drive through the security gates while Miguel follows them. *Another man who is taking care of my family.*

Chapter Fourteen

Charlie

Wake up.

Quick run, while Miguel and I ponder the meaning of life.

Brad feeds Ainsley while I take a shower.

Get Ainsley clean from breakfast

Get Ainsley dressed.

Get me dressed.

Drop Ainsley off at my mom's house for Amy to watch her.

Have the most fun that I've had practicing medicine.

Brainstorm ideas with Brad on how we can bring in new patients to the practice.

Talk shop with the physical therapists about our patients. See their progress.

Fight insurance companies.

Put out mini-fires in the office amongst the staff.

Pick up Ainsley from my mom's house.

Feed Ainsley, Brad, and myself.

Bathe Ainsley.

Put Ainsley to bed.

Collapse on the couch with Brad, and drink wine until my heart rate returns to normal.

Give Colin thirty minutes of my night.

Crawl into bed.

Repeat again tomorrow.

And the next day.

And the day after that.

But much more enthused about practicing medicine.

Chapter Fifteen

Colin

Since Thanksgiving, Charlie and I have Skyped or Facetimed every night without fail. It's my favorite time of the day, and I plan around it like the pathetic fuck that I am. I've rearranged film-watching with my coaches, I've canceled dinner meetings, I've blown off sponsors' events, and I've ignored Jenny's repeated requests to try and entertain me.

Hearing the trill of the Skype request has turned my dick into Pavlov's dog. It instantly gets hard knowing that we're going to see Charlie. So far, we haven't had sex over Skype. She's suggested it more than once, but I'm not sure I can handle watching her come on a dick that isn't mine when I can't touch her.

I get it. She's explained it to me. She'll be pretending that it's me, but I know that it's not, obviously, and as of right now I just don't think that I can handle it.

Charlie and Ainsley haven't been home since Thanksgiving, a month ago, and it's killing me. It's no one's fault. My football schedule has taken me away from Dallas every weekend. It sucks. I haven't gotten used to my empty, quiet, lonely house. Thank God for Pancho. I can't imagine what a miserable bastard I'd be if I didn't at least have him.

Every time I talk to Charlie, I see the gleam in her eye she gets when she's talking about the practice. I know in my heart that it's what she wants to do. I'm just at a loss with what my next move is. Am I a complete dick and demand that she moves home? I don't want her unhappy. Then there's the nagging voice in the back of my head that reminds me that she chose medicine over me once before. My ex-wife politely reminded me of that fact when I told her I wanted a divorce.

She put her career first and dumped me like yesterday's news. If I push her, will she choose being a doctor again over me? Can I survive her leaving me twice in one lifetime? Fuck. I don't think so. But can I survive not having my daughter with me, not watching her grow up? Absolutely fucking not.

I can't dwell on these thoughts too much. If I do, I'll lose my shit, which won't do anyone any good. *One day at time … One day at a time …*

And now, it's slap-a-fake-smile-on-my-face show-time …

"Hello lovely ladies," I greet my precious baby, who's in red-and-white striped Christmas jammies, and her gorgeous mother, who has on a baggy sweatshirt and yoga pants. She's still so hot that my dick twitches.

We talk about the normal stuff. How our days were. Anything interesting that might have happened. We ignore the media reports that I've contacted a divorce attorney, and Charlie is pregnant with Brad's baby. You know, the normal things that every couple deals with.

Then, I ask the absolute wrong question. "What fun did Miss Ainsley have today?" Simple, obvious, easy question, right? Wrong!

Charlie's cheeks begin to glow, and she's almost bouncing she's so excited. She turns to Ainsley and says, "Want to tell Daddy who you met today?"

Ainsley smiles and reaches for the computer screen. I reach back, longing to feel her chubby fingers around mine instead of the flat, cold, monitor glass. I can tell that they're in Charlie's kitchen, and I spot Brad in the background, doing something on the stove.

"Ainsley met Santa today." Charlie oozes Christmas joy that I'm not feeling. "Didn't you, baby girl? Didn't you, baby girl?" she coos to Ainsley.

My stomach instantly knots. "I thought we were taking her to see Santa when you come home for Christmas?" I'm rather proud of myself. My voice is steady, and doesn't betray how upset I am.

"Well, honey," she's instantly defensive, "Santa was coming to my office building, and Amy brought Ainsley up to see him. I couldn't very well tell her to shield Ainsley's eyes from the fat man in the red suit."

Her tone really pisses me off. It's condescending, like I'm an idiot for wanting to take my daughter to meet Santa Claus for the first time. "I don't know. I just thought that it was going to be something special that the three of us did together." I don't add *because you've taken my child away from me for the last two months to accommodate your family, your father's memory, and your career instead of your husband, and your assistant is playing the part of Ainsley's father.*

Brad moves from the stove and off-screen, probably heading to the refrigerator that's nearby. Then I watch my daughter lift her eyes above the computer screen and point at Brad. She says the words that I've longed to hear. Ainsley says, "Da Da," but she says it to Charlie's best assistant in the world instead of her father.

"I have to go," I spit as I disconnect from Skype, angrily mashing the button.

I'm in shock. I sit at my breakfast bar staring at the screen. My daughter just referred to Brad as her father. I become so queasy that for a moment, I think that I might puke. My daughter just called Brad Da Da. *My. Daughter. Called. Brad. Da Da.*

My phone rings and I send Charlie to voicemail. I don't care to hear her pathetic excuses. I know exactly what I just witnessed. Ainsley wasn't looking at me. She wasn't babbling. She clearly lifted her lavender eyes over the laptop and looked at Brad, calling him her father.

Next, the house phone rings, which I refuse to answer. Charlie begins pleading on the answering machine for me to pick up. It's really a bad move on her part. Right now, I'm so upset that phrases like "You have twenty-four hours to bring me my child" are running through my head. There's even an "I'll fight you for full custody" that enters in my thoughts.

I grip the edge of the granite, attempting to anchor myself. My heart is thundering in my ears. There's no calming myself down at this point. I'm too angry, and hurt, and enraged. I ignore the texts messages that are flooding my phone. This is the straw that broke the camel's back. I've been the supportive husband through this. I've played nicely. I've let my wife and daughter leave me under the guise of saving the medical practice, and immortalizing Jack Collins. Game's over. My daughter thinks Brad is her father. Game motherfucking over.

The walls of the McMansion are moving in around me—crushing me. I know that if I don't get out of this house and away from my technology that I'm going to do something that I'm going to regret tomorrow, like calling Charlie and making threats that, as of right now, I have every intention of following through with.

If she thinks for one fucking second that I'm going to let her ride off into the sunset with our daughter, she's got another thing coming. I worship the ground that Charlie walks on, but Ainsley is my blood.

I slip on a pair of trainers and leash Pancho. My run begins around the gated neighborhood. It does nothing to calm me down, so I put Pancho in the backyard. Just as I head through the security gates, Jamie reaches me, dressed for a run.

"Not tonight. I'm going by myself." I don't look at him, or acknowledge his presence.

"But sir, we discussed the reasons to accompany you at night ..."

"I said, 'not tonight.' Leave me the fuck alone," I growl.

I see Jamie nod out of my peripheral vision, and turn around to jog back to the pool house.

Just to torment myself, I run past the home that I bought for Brad. Carter's living in it while Brad's sharing living quarters with my wife. *And playing Daddy to my daughter.*

What an idiot I've been. I handed him my family—hook, line, and sinker. The tabloid stories swirl through my head. I've never doubted for one minute that Charlie was loyal to me. Never. On this run, though, I begin putting pieces together. Pieces that my rational mind would discard.

Has Brad been turning my wife and daughter against me? Is he taking what's mine?

I think back to the conversation that Charlie and I had when Ainsley had her first ear infection. Charlie called the pediatrician "Ainsley's doctor." Did she know then, that she was taking my daughter away from me? Had she already interviewed doctors in Houston? Is that why she called her Ainsley's doctor?

My worst nightmares, the ones that cause panic attacks, are coming true.

Is this what my ex-wife felt like when I told her I wanted a divorce? Was she this hurt and devastated? Maybe this is my karma. If so, I've paid the ultimate price. My daughter's first word was to call another man "Da Da." I scream out loud, and hit my chest while I'm running, "Fuck you, karma."

I pound the streets of my subdivision, thinking things that I shouldn't until I spot a restaurant and bar. I haven't drank since I found out that I have Celiac Disease, and before that I hadn't had more than a glass of wine since the night of the Clay South retirement dinner, when I poisoned myself to keep what's-her-name from trying to fuck me. Turns out she didn't care that I was sick and still made a play, setting in motion the events that led to the world knowing about my relationship with Charlie.

I pat my pockets, and find that I don't have a credit card on me, but I'm Colin Fucking McKinney, the Brad Pitt of football. I brought this town a Super Bowl; surely the bartender will let me have a tab.

I walk in, huffing, trying to catch my breath as I grab a seat at the bar. The place is some chain brew-house. The name escapes me. I've never been in here before, but I've driven by it millions of times when I was a slave to fast-food row while Charlie was pregnant.

Immediately, the very pretty blonde bartender with giant fake boobs smiles and slides a glass of water in front of me. "What'll it be?" She's got enough makeup on that I'm sure it leaves smears on the sheets.

"Jack on ice, but hey, I don't have my card on me. Can you start a tab, and I'll settle it tomorrow?"

She winks a heavily-mascaraed eye. "It's on the house, Colin."

The first taste swishes around my mouth and burns like red-hot candy. I feel it sliding down my throat and into my stomach. The burn mixes with the battery acid, and begins to neutralize it.

The second sip lingers just inside my mouth for a moment. Then I swallow it, and feel the battery acid retreat a little more.

There's a second of clarity when I question what the hell I'm doing here. I look around the restaurant and note that it's painted a red color that matches my anger. There are a few other people sitting at the bar with me. One's an older guy. He looks like he'd really like to talk to me so I ignore him, refusing to make eye contact. The pretty redhead, at the end of the bar, appears to be waiting for someone. She's nervously tapping her foot and checking her watch. Then there's the couple in love, practically dry-humping as they share a bar stool. It's as if they've been sent by God to mock me.

I take another sip and don't bother savoring it. I have no car, and it's only about a three-mile walk/run/stagger/crawl back to my house. I've survived being hung over at practice many times before. It's either I get shit-faced here, or I drive to Houston and take my daughter away from her mother, which will only end badly for all of us.

Slamming the glass down, I ask the *Playboy*-looking bartender for another. Here's the pathetic thing: I have no alcohol tolerance. I'm feeling it, and I've only had one drink. Aiden would call me a pussy, and rag me like crazy if he were here. But if he were here, he wouldn't let me do this, so I'm glad he's in Los Angeles.

The older guy who's been itching to get my attention finally grows a sac. "I really enjoy watching you play."

I hold my glass up to him and say a polite "thanks," hoping that he'll now leave me the fuck alone.

"That play you made in the Super Bowl was unbelievable." So much for him keeping his mouth shut.

"Yeah. I was just as stunned as everyone else." I'm trying to sound humble here, and that this guy's got to catch the clue and leave me alone.

"What'd you do to piss off Charlie?" He's got a snide look on his old, wrinkled, smug face.

Just hearing her name come out of a stranger's mouth makes me insane all over again. "Don't say her name," I growl as I grip the edge of the highly-polished wooden bar until my knuckles show white.

The old man holds his hands up as if he's surrendering. "Sorry, I meant no harm. She's hot. If she were mine, I'd make sure that I stayed on her good side."

Before I know it, I've got the geezer pressed up against the bar, twisting his white, stained T-shirt tightly in my fist. He reeks of booze and fear. His watery eyes are bulging out of his head, and his mouth is hanging open like I'm choking him. "Don't ever talk about my wife again," I say through gritted teeth.

Two burly men are approaching my right side. I'm coherent enough to know that I don't want any trouble, so I release the asshole, throwing my hands up. "Sorry, just a misunderstanding."

The restaurant has gone silent, except for the diners holding up their phones and snapping away. *Great. I'm going to be breaking news again on the morning talk shows.*

I can tell the large men really don't want to be the bouncers that throw the city's Super Bowl-winning MVP quarterback out of their bar. Instead of messing with me, they whisper something to the old guy, and he follows them out.

The pretty bartender hands me a fresh drink as I sit back down on the bar stool. "I get off in thirty minutes if you need a ride home," she says with a sexy little wink.

Do I need a ride home? Yes, because I have no money, ID, or phone. I can't call anyone to pick me up. Do I need a RIDE home? No, as pissed as I am at my wife, I don't want to fuck some random chick.

I down my third drink and can no longer feel my toes. "I could use a lift, but I'm not going to fuck you," is what I'm sure that I said. What came out sounded like, "I cud us a fit, but I emmm not gonnnna fuck ya."

She hands me one more and a glass of water. "Let me tell my boss where I'm going."

She flounces back with one of the big guys who helps me to the bartender's car. Just my luck: it's a VW Beetle. The big guy puts me in the front seat where my knees meet my chin, and climbs in the back. God only knows how he fit. The bartender starts the car, and pulls into traffic.

Next thing I know, Big Guy is hitting me on my arm, and asking me to talk to the security guard. Something incoherent spills out of my mouth, but it's good enough to gain us entrance to my neighborhood. It does occur to my alcohol-infused brain I never told the bartender my address.

I point to my house as I feel my eyes growing heavy again with sleep. Big Guy helps me stumble to the back gate, while Bartender opens it and my unlocked backdoor. Big Guy puts me on the couch with a thud. "You okay, man?" His voice is gruff.

I must give a satisfactory enough answer, because they leave me there. Pancho jumps on the couch, licking my face, but I swat him away. Standing up, I play pinball between the walls and furniture as I make my way into the bedroom. The last thing that I remember is shutting the door on Pancho.

****

I know that I'm sick, and I know why. I crawl back into bed and pass out.

****

My next coherent thought is "Why is Jenny standing over me?" Then I remember my daughter calling Brad *Daddy*. My run comes back to me. The bar. The altercation. My stomach turns as I'm reminded of the Jack Daniels.

When I open my eyes, Jenny says, "Caroline called. She's beside her self." Jenny's hair is still a normal shade of charcoal black. *What an appropriate color.* My head throbs too badly to ponder if she dyed it in my honor.

Fuck Charlie. Let her be worried. How'd she feel if Ainsley called Jenny *Momma*? I roll over, trying to get away from the wicked witch of the west with her Goth-black hair.

"Shall I tell her that you reek of booze and vomit?" She's using her "catch more flies with honey" voice.

I pull the covers over my head, and beg the jackhammer between my ears to shut itself off.

"Can I confirm for her that the news stories are true; that you got into a bar fight and were taken home by a blonde waitress?" Jenny says, pulling the covers off of me, tapping her foot with her hands planted on her hips.

I reach down and am relieved to discover that I still have my running shorts on. The thought of Jenny seeing me naked makes me shiver.

"Answer me, Colin. You have to be at practice in an hour. I suggest you do something with yourself, because you look and smell like a New Orleans Bourbon Street homeless person."

I mumble, "Go the fuck away," as I pull a pillow over my head, trying to find the jackhammer's off button.

She shuts the bedroom door behind her. I gingerly roll to my back so as to not upset my stomach, but I know that before I go to practice, it's going to have to be agitated. Fuck. All boozing it up did was add a sick stomach and pounding head to my shattered heart.

I yell to Jenny that I'm getting up so she won't come back in here. My voice sounds like I've eaten glass. I test out my sea legs. Fortunately, I don't think that I'm still drunk. I start my shower water, and then make my way to the toilet. Fuck, I'm regretting my decision to get wasted.

It doesn't take much for me to get sick. When I'm sure that I'm done, I open a bottle of water and drink it, waiting patiently for it to come back up. I'm not disappointed.

When I'm finally finished, I drag myself into the shower and let the water spill over me until it runs cold.

Next, I brush my teeth, and then take inventory of myself. Physically, I'm much better. Stomach is settled. Headache is now a dull throb. Mentally, I'm a dark nightmare that resembles a Tim Burton film.

I walk into the living room, dressed for practice. Jenny's sitting at my kitchen table, talking to whom I can only presume is Charlie, because Jenny says quietly, "He's here. I'll call you back."

"*E tu Brute*?"

"Fuck you," Jenny replies. "She's worried about you."

"She's worried enough that she put my daughter in the car and drove to Dallas to check on me? No. No, she's not that worried. She's worried only enough to call my assistant. I see." I know that I'm being a gigantic asshole, but I don't care. I'm pissed and hurt. Fuck her. "God forbid that she should leave her dad's practice for a day to check on her husband." The word "husband" comes out of my mouth sounding like poison. I pull the egg whites out of the refrigerator and begin making an omelet.

"She told me what happened." Jenny pauses as if she's waiting for me to respond. "Babies babble. I'm sure what you heard was Ainsley just babbling."

I expected more from Jenny.

I clench my hands into fists, and lean forward onto the balls of my feet, slamming my whisk against the edge of the bowl. Jenny's face morphs into a questioning look. She's never seen me really pissed off. "Jenny," I squeeze out through clenched teeth. "If you wish to keep your job then stay. The. Fuck. Out. Of. It."

For the first time in our working relationship, Jenny doesn't have a snarky retort.

****

I'm a lunatic at practice. I know that I'm trying to escape the pain. Maybe if I do ten extra pushups, I will not feel it anymore. If I can just run a little faster, I'll leave the pain in my chest behind me.

It's no use. The ache never dulls, and I only get madder.

When I'm home, I finally check my phone. My voicemail is full. I erase every message without listening to them, and ignore all the texts from Charlie. I only reply to Aiden and my parents, letting them know that I'm alive.

I'm not fine. In fact, *fine* jumped on the last train headed west. I'm a goddamn heap of mess. I don't bother eating dinner, because my appetite is also on the proverbial train. I take a shower while I plot out my next move.

The water beating against my back adds a level of clarity that I desperately need. It's obvious that something has to give. My schedule isn't flexible. I don't have the ability to hang out in Houston while Charlie fixes her dad's shit, or decides to permanently remain there playing head doctor. Charlie's life is flexible. I decide to give her a deadline. Thirty days. That seems more than fair. Then it will have almost been three months since her father passed away. She needs to figure out if she wants to run the medical practice and give me custody of Ainsley, or bring herself and my baby back to Dallas. Charlie's choice. But in thirty days my daughter will be living with me again.

I call her instead of Skype for our seven o'clock appointment. This is in no way, shape, or form a date.

She answers as if she's been sitting by the phone. Her melodic voice fills the line, and what's left of my shattered heart clenches. My system floods with need and hurt and want. It's a confusing mess that ultimately washes out in sadness.

I cut off her pathetic explanation ramblings. I don't care. No excuses. There's nothing short of "I'm moving back in with you" that will soothe me at this point. "Listen, Caroline." I rarely use her given name so when I do, she knows that I'm serious. "I have nothing to say to you, other than I expect you and MY daughter," I emphasize the hell out of the word my, "to be here in two days for Christmas. But, your clock starts now. You've got thirty days to clean up the shit storm that Jack's death dropped in your life, or I keep our daughter with me."

"Is that a threat, Colin?" she asks, in a voice so cold that it could freeze ice.

"Not a threat, darlin'. It's a motherfucking fact. Remember my 'I don't give a fuck' list you like to tease me about? Well, my daughter isn't on it, and you sadly miscalculated if you thought she was." I'm sitting in my home office, staring out the window at the oak trees I had planted. They're too immature to give me the feeling of stability that Doctor Benson's old oak did. Then it hits me. What a fucking perfect metaphor for my relationship with Charlie. Even though I've known her since she was nineteen, we've only been back together for less than three years. I don't fully trust that she's not going to break my heart again. Would I be okay with her taking Ainsley if we'd been together ten years? Probably not, but at least maybe I'd feel like I knew the motivations of the person on the other end of the line.

She begins to cry and plead with me, but it does nothing to soften my heart. It can't. It's too broken. In the middle of some sort of begging, I interrupt with, "Goodbye Caroline. I'll see my daughter in two days."

Clicking end on the phone call is brutal. I love that woman. She's been my one true love since I was a kid in college. She's been my obsession—my fucking *oxygen*, since I took my first breath and discovered what love felt like. All I've wanted since I was twenty-one was to be married to Charlie Collins. Hell, I asked her every single day to be my wife. I've dreamt of being a father to our baby. But, and I plan on making this crystal clear, Ainsley is my blood. She's my daughter. She's half of me. I will not lose any more time with her. I will not be relegated to a paycheck-earner role in her life. I am her daddy. When she cries, I comfort her. When she's sad, I cheer her up. When she's sick, I mop her forehead. She's just as much mine as she is Charlie's—that I have no doubt about.

Chapter Sixteen

Charlie

Colin and I are sleeping in the same bed, but we might as well be in separate countries. Our gap makes the Mississippi River look like a babbling brook. He's hurt. When he's awake, his face is pulled into a permanent grimace. Even as we pretended everything was perfect for our families on Christmas day, his forehead was drawn in a scowl. He laughed, but it was forced. His eyes are frosty when he does look at me, which isn't often.

The only time I've witnessed any happiness is when he plays with Ainsley. He's barely let her sleep in her bed since we arrived back in Dallas just in time to celebrate Christmas. He bathes, feeds, gets her up in the morning, and tucks her in at night. Colin is trying to clinch the Daddy of the Year award, making up for lost time, and trying to prove a point to me that he can meet all of her needs. Trust me when I say that I've gotten the message, loud and clear.

We managed to get through Christmas faking it, but it didn't hold a candle to last Christmas day. Then I was pregnant, and we were both so happy. He couldn't go five minutes without caressing my swollen abdomen. We celebrated Pancho's first birthday—well, first year with us— with a little doggy party. Both sides of our family just indulged our nonsense. Our laughs were not forced, and after everyone went to bed, Colin unwrapped me like a present and made love to me under the Christmas tree. He said that the best gifts he'd ever been given were lying under him. His wife and his baby.

What a difference a year makes.

I've tried to reason with Colin that my dad's medical practice needs me. Yes, I've hired another doctor, but no one has the knowledge about the medical practices that I have. Sure, Carmen can keep the books going, and the doors open, but she doesn't know the medical protocols that my father had established. She doesn't know how to manage the young doctors working for us because frankly, she isn't a doctor.

My father's medical practice thriving is my way of ensuring his immortality. Yes, Doctor Collins is no longer with us, but what he spent his whole life creating is still making people's lives better. When Ainsley is old enough, I want to be able to bring her to his practice, and show her what her grandfather built. I want her to feel the same pride that I felt as a kid in what my dad did for a living.

I can't make Colin understand this. To him, the world is black and white as it's always been; there are no greys. He doesn't understand that I'm not playing doctor in Houston, having a gay old time. Okay, I am having a bit of fun, but I'm not leaving him. Brad isn't trying to take his daughter away from him.

Brad and I are a well-oiled machine. We can interpret each other's body language. He knows how I like things done, and is also a huge help with Ainsley. Without him, I wouldn't get to go for my morning runs, which are my lifeline to sanity. Brad pitches in with her when I'm too tired to move, which, lately, has been most days.

I'm miserable. This whole situation is miserable. Colin's playing for a wildcard spot in the playoffs tomorrow, so I lie very still trying not to wake him when all I want to do is cross the great divide and snuggle into his side.

It's pathetic to admit, but I want, no, I *need* my husband to want me again. This Siberian prison that he's put me in is the worst form of torture. When I try to lay my hands on him he jerks back as if my touch burns.

That hurts the most. We've spent the last twelve nights together after being a part for almost a month, and the only kiss that I've received was a chaste one at midnight on New Year's Eve. And I'm sure that I only got it because Aiden and Amy were celebrating with us.

Part of me feels like I should be the angry one. He's the one who got drunk and had a bar fight. He's the one who was helped home by a beautiful, busty, blonde who's about ten years my junior. He's the one who fanned the media's flames surrounding our relationship. We made the cover of every entertainment magazine at the grocery-store checkout line. Nothing makes them happier than proof of the fabricated stories.

But I'm not angry with him. I know why he poisoned himself. I know why he did what he did. The hurt was so deep that he didn't know how else to deal with it.

That breaks my heart.

Our bedroom is cast in a green glow from Ainsley's baby monitor. I roll onto my side and watch Colin's naked chest rise and fall, ensuring that he's asleep. Only then do I slide against him, pressing my clothed chest against his ribcage. His forehead is relaxed, and I'm pretty certain that my bold move didn't awaken him. I carefully pick up my hand and place it over his heart, longing to feel his pulse under my palm.

It only rests there for two beats before he removes my hand and places it on my hip. He doesn't say anything as he turns onto his side, breaking our contact and presenting me with his back. He doesn't have to. His rejection speaks volumes, making our bedroom air thick with unsaid angst.

I scoot away from him and cling to the edge of the mattress. Tears slide down my cheeks and collect on my pillow, dampening the area around my face. That's how I eventually fall asleep the second to last night in Camp McKinney Penitentiary.

****

I attend Colin's game and pretend that everything is perfect between us. Seriously, I deserve an Oscar for my performance. Last night's rejection was the nail in the coffin. Something has got to change.

Dallas easily clenches the wildcard spot and advances to round one of the playoffs. It was hard watching him on the sidelines. I saw his face full of joy. Colin was laughing and smiling. It was so genuine unlike our fakeness around our family. I even allowed myself to pretend that it was me who made him that happy. That I was the one that he was laughing with instead of Ty.

I dread going home because I know that the happiness will not extend inside the walls of the McMansion. No. Our home is filled with tension, hurt, anger, and sadness.

As we're filing out of the stadium in a large crowd mixed with all the fans, the smell hits me. And it hits me strong. Someone very near me has on Colin's cologne. My stomach takes note, and becomes desperately queasy. Pushing through the densely-packed people, I try to escape the smell while still holding my breath.

Jenny is the only one who notices and follows me to the outer edge of the ramp. "You okay?" she asks as she grabs my arm. She's clearly concerned, which is rather novel.

I carefully let out the breath that I'm holding and open my mouth to inhale. I'm terrified of smelling the cologne again. How humiliating to vomit in a crowd of people. Once I've sampled the air and realized that the offending odor is gone, I reply, "That was so weird. Someone had on Colin's brand of cologne, and it made me sick."

"You're pregnant," is all she says. There's no excitement or apprehension in her voice. She might as well have said, "There's pasta in the refrigerator."

People are pushing around us, but I remain nailed to the cement on the ramps of the Cowboy's stadium. All the crowd noise fades to silence. I can't be pregnant. My husband isn't even speaking to me. Our marriage is hanging on by a thin string as it is. The last thing we need right now is another baby.

I feel my eyes well up with tears, and I beg them to stay at bay. *No point crying about this until I know for sure.*

On the way home, I stop by a drugstore and am perfectly humiliated to be buying pregnancy tests while I'm flanked by Miguel. He's so professional, and pretends to ignore my purchases.

Julie, my other sister, is staying with us, and watched Ainsley while we went to the game. Aiden had asked if Amy could be his date to Colin's game, and it seemed nice that he'd want her there. I love Aiden and Amy together. He's the wild to her calm. She's the support that he needs. They have the same life goals. I'd never have set them up, but those two dating is definitely one of the positives that came out of my father's death.

Julie and Pancho greet me when I walk into the kitchen. I look at Julie and ask her a gigantic favor, using my pleading eyes. "Can you watch Ainsley this evening, and keep both of you upstairs? Colin and I need to have a talk, and it might get pretty loud. If it does, take Ainsley in the movie room and put on something for y'all to watch. I don't want her to hear us fighting."

Julie, of course, agrees. I have the best sisters.

Next, I go into our bedroom and shut the door behind me. I pick up my phone and dial Carmen. I've never been particularly close to my stepmom. Us girls began calling her Aunt Carmen when she was Daddy's nurse ages ago. Then, when Daddy left Mom for Aunt Carmen we realized that one, she wasn't really our aunt and two, she was becoming Stepmom Carmen. In the end, I have two beautiful half-sisters out of their marriage that I adore, and all has been forgiven.

Carmen answers on the third ring, and we spend the next five minutes making small talk. I know her first Christmas without my father was difficult. It was hard on us girls, but then again, he hadn't spent Christmas with us since my half-sister, Sarah, was born, which was more than half my life ago.

Finally, I dive into the heart of the matter. "Carmen, I'm at an impasse. I want to continue working at the practice. The last couple of months, in spite of the circumstances, have been the most fun that I've had since I started practicing medicine. However, Colin is no longer willing to let his wife and daughter reside in another city."

Carmen interjects, "As he shouldn't, sweetie." Her voice breaks. "Life is too short to not spend your nights with the one that you love."

I collapse onto the red college chair and stare out the bay window in our bedroom. Our backyard looks like a resort. Memories of our wedding flood my senses. It was such a happy day. Carmen's right. Life *is* too short to not spend the meaningful moments with the one that you love.

Talk about a knife in the gut. "You're right. That's why I'm hoping that I can come back and work until Colin's next playoff game, which is next week. Then, I'd like to stay with him until the season is over, and we can return to Houston as a family."

"Of course, of course," she reassures me. "We'll make it work."

"I plan on discussing this with Brad, and see if he'll stay in Houston to help you out. He's very capable of doing everything that I do, except for the whole doctoring part."

She laughs and agrees, "Bradley is something else."

I hang up with her, feeling better. I'm hoping that my plan will pacify Colin, and begin the repair work on our marriage.

My next phone call is to Brad, and it takes me a good ten minutes to work up the courage to hit the dial button next to his name. When he answers in his usual upbeat way, I say with a heavy heart, "Brad, I need to have a very frank conversation with you."

Brad exhales. "I've been expecting this chat. Am I fired?" He sounds so pathetic that I swear my soul weeps.

Before I can respond, he continues. "I can understand if Colin doesn't want us working together anymore, but Ainsley is my goddaughter. I'm her guncle. Caroline, I'll never have kids of my own, please don't take Ainsley away from me."

Poor Brad gets choked up, and I feel like a complete ass. Brad's done nothing wrong except doing his job too well. "Calm down. Look, I'm not firing you, or banning you from Ainsley's life. Think of this as a time-out. I need for you to help out Carmen in Houston, and give Colin and me a chance to figure out solutions to our problems." I don't add *because your presence is like pouring salt in a fresh, bloody wound.*

He sniffs. "Promise me I'm not losing my best doctor friend."

"Never," I reply with a smile in my voice. "You know that I can't tie my shoes without you."

"Well, honestly, Caroline, you shouldn't be wearing shoes that tie. They're way too matronly. Legs as gorgeous as yours should only be in heels." He's back to sounding like my Brad, which is such a relief.

We spend another fifteen minutes on the phone, bantering back and forth about nothing in particular.

Colin's feelings toward Brad are justified, so I'm going to have to spend some time setting boundaries for all of us. He's too important to me to not have him in my life, but Colin? Well, he's my heart. Somewhere, there has to be a middle plane where we can all coexist.

I step outside and begin heating the hot tub. Operation Win Back My Husband commences now.

Chapter Seventeen

Colin

If you'd have ever told me that I wouldn't want to come home because my wife is there, I'd have called you a lying bastard. Now, I drive under the speed limit, attempting to avoid the inevitable—being at home.

I pull into the driveway and leave Bertha sitting near the road. *Neighbors are going to love her, out front of their pristine neighborhood.*

As I walk towards the backyard, the sound of the hot tub bubbling greets my ears. Honestly, the last thing that I want to do right now is see my wife in a bikini, because my heart and brain remember very clearly why we're so angry. My dick, on the other hand, has no clue, and is quite upset that we've been ignoring her.

Sure enough, she's in the hot tub with the same set up as always. I stand there for a moment, trying to decide what I should do. Getting in the hot tub will result in me naked and unable to keep my hands off of her. Going inside and rejecting her will probably result in her leaving me.

I walk over to the edge of the hot tub and look down seeing her gorgeous tits bobbing up and down in the water. Her hair is piled on her head in a messy knot, and she's got on the fucking white string bikini that should be against the law. My cock notices, and stands up to get a look for itself.

LAYNE HARPER

"I appreciate the gesture, but I'm not sure if it's a good idea for me to join you." I rub my sweaty palms on my athletic shorts, aching for her to see through my tough-guy act and invite me in.

"I'm leaving for Houston tomorrow. Please, don't let me back out of our driveway without at least talking to me." Her words register in my brain, but the look on her face speaks to my heart. She looks so fucking lost.

Without replying, I strip off my clothes and ease myself into the hot water opposite from her. She stays in her spot, and I'm not sure that I wanted her to do so.

After a very long silence of me watching her fidget, I can't take it anymore and drop my chin to my chest, closing my eyes. It's too damn painful to watch.

She finally speaks. "Look, I know you need to *be* after games, but there are a few things that I have to say. Let me know when you're ready to listen." She doesn't sound like my Charlie. My Charlie is a balls-to-the-wall kind of chick. Tough is her middle name. This version of her is pathetic; almost exactly how I feel.

I raise my head and open my eyes to look at her. She's so damn timid, like a little mouse. "I'll listen to whatever you have to say, but I will not sit here and endure your excuses. What's happened has happened. You can't give me back the time that I've lost with my daughter. I'm not willing to relive the past. I'm only focused on the future." It comes out harsher than I'd intended, but the words ring true. I silently add, *And I hope you aren't leaving me, because I will spend every dime I have to gain full custody of my princess.*

She nods and begins, "I called Carmen today, and told her that this would be my last week at the practice until your season is over. Then, I'm hoping that we can move to Houston for the offseason so I can continue practicing medicine." As she speaks, she begins to regain some of her confidence.

She pauses, letting her words sink in. I'm not sure how I feel about this. I can tell this is her attempt at offering me an olive branch. Logistically it

194

will work for a few months, but then I'll have to be back in Dallas full-time. What then? Are we just delaying the inevitable? Seems like it to me. We're going to be in the same damn boat in April, and that's not okay.

"Brad is going to be there in my place, helping with all the behind the scenes stuff that I do. That also means that he will not be in Dallas, which should make you happy. I hope you see this as me finding us some grey area in our relationship." She sits up straighter, which brings her perfect boobs just out of the water. Dear God, I want to suck and bite them while she screams my name. "I know that these past months have been hard on us, but I have to say, Colin, that they've been my happiest months professionally."

My heart plunges to my stomach at the confirmation that my feelings have been correct. "What I'm doing is mentally challenging, and physically very difficult. I don't have enough experience to be head of a practice, but I love it. For the first time in a very long time, I feel like I'm me again. I'm not just Ainsley's mom, and the mega-athlete's wife. I'm Caroline Jane Collins-McKinney, business owner, doctor, healer, wife, and mother. Can you understand that?" As she speaks, I watch her face glow in excitement. It's clear, even in the moonlight, she's doing what she loves.

I ignore her question and ask one of my own. "So if you had to make a choice right now, me or your dad's practice, what would you choose?" It's such a dick question. Cruel, really. I wouldn't be surprised if she stormed inside and never spoke to me again, but it doesn't matter. I want to hear her response.

Her face clouds with anger. Without missing a beat, she replies, "Both. I want both, and I can have both if you'll give a little and work with me."

I sit up tall, far surpassing her height, and respond, "Oh, really? So we're going to be married, but have joint custody of our daughter. She spends one week in Dallas, and one week in Houston? That sounds very healthy and stable for her. I mean, she won't be confused at all." My tone is sarcastic and biting. It's the hurt inside seeping out, and I'm not apologizing for it.

She spits back with pure venom. "Colin, you're an ass. You know that, right?" Her eyes narrow to slits, and she draws back as if she's a snake about to strike.

I lean forward about a foot from her face, locking her eyes with mine. "Because I'm not willing to let you take Ainsley away from me? I think that there are a lot of people who'd think that was pretty damn admirable. I didn't have a child to not raise her. She's just as much mine as she is yours." Then I realize that I need to use Charlie's tactic back on her. "How would you like it if I kept Ainsley away from you for months on end? I'd let you see her a weekend here or there, but, every time that you saw her, she had completely changed. You said goodbye to a child who was immobile, and the next time you saw her she was crawling. You missed out on her first movements, her first words, her first trip to see Santa, and no telling how many other firsts that you can't even fathom. Then, the fucking cherry on top, is that she starts calling Jenny *Mama.*" I run my fingers through my matted waves of hair, seething with anger. "I know you, Caroline. I know that you would never stand for that shit, so I don't know why you expect for me to roll over and be okay with it."

There. I said it. I don't break eye contact as I move back to the hot tub bench. I stare straight into her lavender eyes, making sure she sees just how deadly serious I am. She wants to talk, we're talking. She just got my diatribe. Hope it tastes as bitter as it was to spit it out.

We don't speak for a long time, and continue our second-grade staring contest.

Finally, I lean my head back on the cool brick and let the hot water boil me in my own misery. I really don't know if there's anything left to say at this point. We're at an impasse, and I don't see any possible way to resolve this.

But, of course, my girl always has something left in her bag of tricks. "I'm pregnant," she says over the bubbling noise of the hot tub.

I sit up bolt straight, and my face twists into a look of panic and horror. "What did you say?" I feel like I just got hit by a truck. *Pregnant?* She can't be pregnant. We can't bring another child into this living nightmare.

"You heard me. I'm pregnant." There's no emotion in her voice or on her face. She's a blank slate.

"How?"

"Well, you see, Colin, when a man is horny ..." She's being a sarcastic brat right now, and that just pisses me off.

I slap the water, and the sound shuts her up. "I fucking know how you got pregnant, but we weren't trying," I respond, sounding completely clueless. This can't be happening. As usual, our timing is for shit.

"We weren't doing anything to prevent it." She shoots back at me, sitting up as straight as I am. We're both preparing for battle. "We had so much trouble conceiving Ainsley that you didn't want me to get back on the pill. We both knew that it was a possibility."

"How far along?" I ask a little more calmly as I run my hand through my hair. I think, *bald by forty*.

"I don't know. I took the test right before you came home."

"Should you be in the hot tub?" I'm now feeling protective of my unborn child. *The child that I'm not sure that I want.*

"Relax, the water is ninety-nine degrees. We aren't going to cook our baby," she says in the demeaning Charlie tone that really pisses me off.

I slump in the water, and let time tick by. All my fight washes out, leaving me feeling like a limp noodle. I think about the eight lonely years without her. I picture my daughter's chubby cheeks, and contemplate what life was like without her. No. I don't want another child right now, but it's too late for that. We're going to be parents again, so we might as well get on the same page and determine how to make a life together work.

Just above a whisper, I ask, "What are we going to do?"

Every bit of my anger and hurt has been dissolved. The only thing left is resolve. Resolve to the do whatever is best for my family. I just hope that Charlie's on the same page.

She moves across the hot tub right next to me with her body pressed up against my side. My every cell has missed her skin against my skin, and begs me to hold her. I wrap my arm around her shoulders and bring her even closer to me, inhaling the scent of her peppermint shampoo.

She leans up and kisses my cheek. I want more intimacy than that, but I know that I have to initiate it. I've pushed her away too many times.

"I haven't got the foggiest clue what we're going to do, but ..." she says, taking my chin in her hand turning my head so I'm looking at her. "... I can tell you what we're not going to do. We aren't giving up on us. Remember what those eight years felt like? Never again, Colin."

I nod in agreement. For now, I let her plan rest. We'll stay in Dallas until my season is over. Then we'll move to Houston so she can practice medicine. In April, well, I guess we'll cross that bridge when we get to it. I make a decision to approach our relationship like football playoffs. It's one week at a time.

Two weeks later, after securing back-to-back trips to the Super Bowl, Charlie and I visit Doctor Starr. To our complete and utter surprise, we're not expecting just one baby. Charlie is pregnant with twins.

Chapter Eighteen

Charlie

I'm lying in the movie room in one of our recliner theater-chairs. My legs are above my cervix, just as Doctor Starr recommended. My mom is changing Ainsley's diaper in her nursery. Brad is downstairs popping popcorn for us, and bringing up everything that we'll need for the next few hours.

I clutch my phone in my hand, willing it to ring. And not just anyone to call. I want to hear Colin's voice.

As if I am able to control the universe, my phone vibrates in my hand.

"Hello," I all but scream into it.

"How ya doing, beautiful girl?" His voice is like velvet to my ears.

I melt into my chair. "Okay," I sigh. "So sad that I'm not there." I'm trying to not sound as pathetic as I feel.

"You're doing something more important. You're keeping our twins safe," he reassures me.

Three days before I was supposed to get on a plane to the Super Bowl, I discovered blood in my urine. After an emergency trip to Doctor Starr's office, she told me the news. Twins are a high-risk pregnancy. I'm on bedrest until I'm out of the first trimester, and that meant no Super Bowl. I'm relegated to this chair, and one bathroom break an hour.

Colin was understandably disappointed that I couldn't be there, but his worrying has reached over-the-top levels. He suggested hiring a private nurse. I reminded him that I'm a doctor and Brad's a nurse, which is still a touchy subject. Reluctantly, he agreed that Brad could stay with me until he returned home.

It has been almost three weeks since Brad and I saw each other. We've been like preteen girls getting caught up after a long stay at summer camp. Nothing will soothe the ache in my stomach that I can't be with my husband today, but having Brad around is a nice distraction. He's also made a point to get lost when Colin's around, or at least fade into the woodwork. I'll give him credit. He's doing an excellent job of toning himself down.

"Any more bleeding?" Colin asks.

"No. And you'll be happy to know that my mom and Brad are not letting me lift a finger."

"Good. That's exactly what they're supposed to be doing." The stadium noise behind him is so deafening that's hard to understand him.

"Don't you have a game to win?" I use the same tone I would for, "Can you pick up something from the grocery story?"

"Yeah. Yeah baby, I do." He chuckles. "I just needed to hear your voice one more time."

We both get very quiet. The only sound is the chaos surrounding Colin. Not all has been forgiven and forgotten. My unexpected pregnancy, plus the complications with the twins have essentially given Colin exactly what he wanted—Ainsley and I at home in Dallas, and me unable to practice medicine at all. I know that it's a hollow victory for him. He's been almost back to his old self, but this is not the way he wanted to win. He's shifted from irate and brooding to worrying himself sick about the twins, Ainsley, and me.

"Bring me home a souvenir," I pause for effect, "like another MVP trophy."

"You got it. Give Ainsley a big kiss for me."

INFINITY.

That's how we end our phone call before my husband plays for another championship.

Chapter Nineteen

Colin

"Colin, are you fucking crazy?" Aiden asks, leaning over my desk as if he wants to punch me.

"Decision is made. We have a meeting with the team scheduled in thirty minutes." I'm the calmest that I think that I've been in ages.

We're sitting in my office at CharCol Inc.

"Your daughter's first birthday party is in four hours. Can't this wait until tomorrow?" I know that he wants me to think this over. Aiden believes that I'm making a rash decision. I'm not. As soon as I saw two heartbeats on the ultrasound screen, I knew what I was going to do, regardless of the outcome of the game that I played a week ago today.

"This is Ainsley's birthday gift. I'm giving her my undivided attention. We're doing it today." I cross my arms and lean back in my chair, cool as a motherfucking cucumber.

"Have you discussed this with Caroline?" There's a pleading edge to his voice as I watch his eyes grow wide with hope.

"There's nothing to discuss. If I was on the fence, I'd talk to Charlie. My mind is made up, Aiden. You either support me as my agent—more importantly, as my best friend—or I go to the meeting alone. Your choice." I check my watch that matches Charlie's. "I'm leaving in five."

His body deflates as all the fight leaves him. Aiden has known me long enough to know that when I'm like this, there's no reasoning with me. It's part of the reason that I've been so successful in my career. I don't doubt myself—well, at least not professionally.

"You realize that no one has ever done this before. Healthy players don't walk away from the game. I mean, sure, you have the leg injury, but it's not keeping you from playing ball." Aiden rubs his hands on his khaki slacks while his face twists in angst. "Look, man, no one is going to understand this decision. Players play until they can't any longer. No one just walks away at the top of his or her career. Are you hearing me?"

"Add what the rest of the world does to my 'I don't give a fuck' list." My lips curl up in a smirk. "Decision. Is. Final."

"Can you at least explain why?" Aiden asks finally sounding resolved in my decision. He flops back dramatically in the chair across from my desk.

I settle back in my plush leather chair getting comfortable. He wants a reason? I'll give him a reason. "On my wedding night, my wife told me a story, and I'm going to share it with you." I don't bother letting him respond before I continue. "Prince Edward was heir to the British throne. He began dating an American woman who was also twice divorced. When his father died, he became the King of England." I pause and look at Aiden, whose face is clearly reflecting his thoughts. He thinks I've lost my mind.

"I'm answering your question, ass wipe. Follow along," I instruct.

He salutes me, and I continue. "Parliament went ape-shit. The king couldn't be associating with a commoner and an American. Instead of his reign being marred in controversy, he abdicated the throne to his little brother, choosing the girl over the kingdom. They ran away to France to avoid the hounding press, and lived the rest of their lives together."

"And," Aiden says, motioning for me to continue.

"After listening to that story on our wedding night, I told Charlie that I understood why King Edward gave up everything: his birthright. I couldn't live without her. None of this would mean shit," I reply, motioning to all my sports memorabilia in my office. "What I've come to realize is this. All the gold rings and titles in the world don't mean anything if I don't have my wedding ring." I pick up my hand, pointing to the ring that Charlie made for me after she proposed. "And the title of husband and father are my everything. And for me to keep those I have to bid my mistress farewell."

"But Charlie's not going back to Houston. She's on bed-rest, growing your twin spawn. You can play one more year. Maybe even two or three more. You're only thirty-four. You could play until you're forty." Aiden tries reasoning with me. "She's now a full-time stay-at-home mom."

I don't miss a beat. "That might be true. I might physically keep Charlie in Dallas, but my mistress demands too much of me. I have so many regrets about the first year of Ainsley's life. I wasn't there when Charlie went into labor. I didn't see my daughter crawl or take her first steps. Hell, she called another man *Da Da*. I'm done beating myself over the things that I wish I'd done and said. These twins will know their father. I won't miss a second of their lives. Not one single second."

My best friend stands and I walk around my desk, joining him. He pulls me into tight hug. "Thanks for letting me take this ride with you. Who knew when I punched you in your face in fourth grade that it would lead us to this point? I love you."

I give him much more than a bro-hug back. "You're the brother that I always wanted."

It's just Bertha and I on my drive to meet with the team executives. Aiden insisted on taking his rental car. I'm sure he's hoping that this alone time will give me some sort of clarity that he thinks I need. I don't. Since I was around thirteen years' old and showed a talent for playing football, my life has been owned by others. Sure, my parents were great and supported me by nurturing my talent. I never chose to play ball though. It was just expected of me. God gives you a gift; you use it. Universities started recruiting me heavily during my sophomore year in high school. Not once did anyone ask me if I wanted to play college football. Once again, it was expected that of course, I would take the scholarship to Texas A&M.

In college, it was all about playing professional ball. Every time I turned around, someone was whispering about the prestige, or money, or girls, or whatever they could think of to sell me on the NFL. Don't get me wrong. This is not a *poor me* story. I could've at any point said, "I don't want to play football," and my parents would have supported me. They probably would have tried to talk me out of it, but they would have stood by me if that was my decision.

I kept playing professional ball even after Charlie and I broke up because I love the sport. There's nothing like the smell of the fresh-cut grass, the cheers of the crowd, the friendships that I created with the guys, or the feel of doing the impossible and making the play happen. It's the PFM, Pure Fucking Magic that happens every Sunday.

The downside is I've never owned my life. I've never been able to walk through a mall without being recognized. I signed a contract that says that I can't skydive, ride a motorcycle, snow-ski, or put myself in harm's way. Nine months out of the year, my existence is owned by the football franchise. There's no vacation time or holidays. I've never gotten to call in sick to work and play hooky.

Hell, there are guys on the team who don't see their families more than once or twice a season. They watch their kids grow up via Skype.

Football has added lots of dollars to my bank account, as well as the endorsement deals that have come along with it. I've made enough money through my wise investments that my children's children couldn't spend it all.

So why keep playing?

It's never been about the money. The money has been a nice perk. I've won two Super Bowls. I've hoisted the MVP trophy over my head twice. I've done all I can do in my sport. What I haven't achieved is the title of the Best Dad or Husband. And as long as I'm playing football, I'll always spend the season being spread too thin.

No, my whole life so far has been focused on my mistress, football. I'm ready for the second part of my life to begin. The one where I'm a full-time father and husband.

Will it pay as much? Not even close. In fact, the amount of money I'm giving up is staggering. Will it be as rewarding? I'm counting on it.

Walking away from football is the first career move that I've ever made without a team of advisors. Since I was thirteen, every time I turned around someone was whispering in my ear about football. *The first decision that I've ever made on my own.*

My mind starts frantically trying to come up with a major decision that I've made by myself. Going to Texas A&M. No. That's not one. They were the best school that recruited me. I'd wanted to go to Baylor University, but they didn't offer me a scholarship. Certainly not playing for Dallas. They drafted me. I had no say in what team picked me up. Oh my God! I didn't even decide to marry Charlie. She proposed to me. Choosing to walk away from the game of football is my own. This is one hundred percent my own doing, with no outside influences. The nosey media vultures have no clue why they're being summoned in on an off-season Sunday. I'm doing this my way. *I feel the need to turn on a little Frank Sinatra.*

The only reason I told Aiden was because he has to work on the details of releasing me from my contract.

Will Charlie be upset that I didn't ask her opinion on my retirement? Probably not. I hope she sees this as my way of solidifying our future. This is me fighting for us. Here's the proof of my commitment to our family— to her.

I can look back and say that I've gotten everything that I ever wanted so far out of this life. I got the girl, the career, the championships, the kids, and now I'm getting the time to enjoy it all.

****

"Turn on the TV, Charlie," I instruct her when she answers the phone.

"Colin it's so loud here, I'm sure that I can't hear it even if it's on." She argues. Figures. She can't make anything easy on me.

"Look, take everyone in the house up to the movie room and turn on ESPN. I wouldn't ask you to do this if it wasn't important."

"Fine," she sighs. "Don't forget that we have Ainsley's party in an hour. And Amy and I think that it's rude that you and Aiden aren't here helping."

"We'll be there." I pause swallowing the lump in my throat. "And hey, I love you. Infinity."

"Infinity," she responds.

I hang up with her and turn to my coach, general manager, team president, and team owner. "I'm ready."

Aiden fist bumps me and slips out from behind the curtain to take a seat in the audience with all the reporters that have gathered on the Sunday after the Super Bowl. I'm the first to walk out on the stage and stand behind the podium, followed by the team. It's the same Cowboys backdrop that I stand in front of after every home game. This is the same podium that I've been leaning on, answering questions from for the last twelve seasons. It feels like any other press conference, but this one is far from it.

I take a moment to look at the audience. The room is swollen with reporters. My impromptu press conference is filled with the who's who of sports media. There's also some mainstream news agencies that I recognize. Did the Entertainment channel send a reporter? Bizarre.

I'm wearing a faded pair of dark jeans that Charlie thinks make my butt look hot. I decided to wear my Super Bowl winner T-shirt as a positive message to my fans, and I have a Dallas Cowboys baseball hat on. I know that this press conference is going to be played ad nauseam on ESPN and all the other sports channels. And now, apparently the mainstream news and gossip rags. At least if I have to watch it hundreds of times, I'm happy with how I look.

I tap the mic ensuring that it's on, take a deep breath, and let it out slowly before I begin speaking. "Thanks so much for y'all coming in on a Sunday. I know you thought you were getting your weekends back now that football season is over."

There's a collective group of chuckles that fill the room.

Pausing for a second, I clear my throat before I continue. "I've thought about how to say this and have decided that there is no good or bad way, so I'm going to cut to the chase. I've asked you all here to announce my retirement from the game of football."

There are gasps that fall across the reporters gathered. It's not too often that they don't know what's going to happen in a press conference, hence why I wanted it announced today. No spoilers or leaks. I have to leave the game my way—not on the media's terms. I feel like my whole adult life has played out in the press. I want to own this moment. This is my farewell speech. My swan song. I've got to exit on my terms. *I did it my way …*

And it feels so damn good.

"It's been my honor to play quarterback for the Dallas Cowboys organization. I have loved every second that you've allowed me to throw the football. My proudest accomplishments are bringing home not one, but two Super Bowl Championships to this franchise, to the great city of Dallas, and to the state of Texas. I'm honored to have played with some of the finest men in the sport that I also call my friends."

I notice that one of the male sports reporters who's covered my whole career is crying. Like, a grown man has red-rimmed eyes. In that moment, I realize that my announcement is so much bigger than just me, my family, my team. Me leaving the game of football in my rearview mirror also affects the reporters who I see after every game. A lot of them are the good guys of the media. They never asked me about my personal life, and always directed pointed, fair, questions my way. Their criticisms of my play were usually dead on. I respect these guys so much, and feel myself getting a bit choked up. I clear my throat again.

"I'm sure you want to know why. The best answer that I know how to give is that I want to go out at the top of my career. And two-time Super Bowl-winning, two-time MVP is about as top as I can get.

"Now, I'm ready to begin a new chapter in my life. I'm not sure what that entails yet. I'm going to spend at least a week doing nothing." I laugh. Doing nothing but making sure my wife, carrying our twins, is healthy and my daughter is happy sounds like bliss right about now. "But, I do know that it includes the jobs of being a husband and father.

"I don't wish to take any questions at this time. However, I'd like to say thank you to the Cowboys organization and the city of Dallas for your faith and support in me. And to Texas A&M … Gig'em."

The flash of bulbs is almost blinding, and the clicks from cameras fill the air. Then there is the blanket of whispers, gasps, and sharp intakes of breath. I think I pulled off the impossible. I shocked the media. That makes my half-smile break across my face.

I turn around and exit off the stage slipping behind the curtain, leaving the cacophony of noises behind. Fortunately, there is a chair close by, and I all but sink into it. It's over with. Done. Finished. My football career is in the books, left for the media and fans to scrutinize. History will make the final judgment on my career. Aiden says that I'm being selfish, but at this moment, I just don't care what anyone thinks.

I sigh and close my eyes, ignoring the phone buzzing like crazy in my pocket. None of the messages are from Charlie, and she's the only person that I want right now.

Aiden joins me claiming the seat next to mine. We sit in silence, listening to the different members of the Cowboys' organization talk about the team's future. They drone on and on, assuring everyone that there's a plan in place for my replacement, and that this is why we have an off-season and a draft. The Cowboys are going to be just fine.

Aiden is the first one to speak. He leans forward and turns, facing me with a smirk on his lips. "Hey jizz stain. I think that was the equivalent to a mic drop."

I chuckle. "You think?"

It's amazing how great I feel. For the first time in memory, my chest is relaxed and able to expand freely. *God, what an incredible feeling.*

"You know every news station is going to lead with George singing, 'The Cowboy Rides Away,'" he quips.

"My heart is sinking like a setting sun," I speak with a rueful laugh as a smile cracks across my face.

Aiden adds, *"Setting on all the things I wish I'd done."*

So, of course, I have to chime in as I tap my foot to the imaginary beat. *"It's time to say goodbye to yesterday."*

Then the two of us smile and give each other the look. It's the look all boys have before they have to meet with the principal over something bad they've done. We're mischievous fourth-graders again. Together we sing, *"This is where the cowboy rides away."*

And that was the last time that the media heard from me for more than five years …

Year One Post-Retirement

… *"Who in hell does McKinney think he is? You don't walk away from the game of football. It chews you up and spits you out. The game decides when you part ways. It's not the other way around. He's let his team down, the city of Dallas, all his fans, and most of all he's disrespected the game. History will not remember his fantastic plays in both Super Bowls or his MVP trophies. His name is going to become synonymous with selfishness, just like Benedict Arnold stands for traitor. No one, and let me repeat this, no one has ever walked away from football at the top of his career."*

… *"Let's pretend for a moment that Colin is really retiring to spend more time with his family. I know, I know. It's the oldest excuse in the book. Every CEO that's fired says the same thing. But, for the sake of my argument, let's pretend that it's his real motivation. I mean, the guy did walk out of the ESPY Awards when the comedian was poking fun at his girl. So if McKinney is retiring to spend more time with his family, shouldn't we all applaud the guy? I mean, we're the first to call out professional athletes who have a ton of kids and don't pay child support. Shouldn't we reward the athletes who put their kids first?"*

… *"Well, football fans, more bad news. Apparently, Colin McKinney's retirement was not just from football. Aiden Montgomery, McKinney's agent, has confirmed that he's also terminating all of his endorsement deals. Women and advertisers alike are weeping at the news."*

... *"For the first time since Colin McKinney announced his controversial retirement from football four months ago, CharCol has been spotted out and about in Dallas, and she seems to be sporting a baby bump. The couple was dining at a local restaurant, and appeared very happy. Witnesses reported that Colin was overly affectionate, and stroked Charlie's hand frequently throughout their lunch. He pulled the chair out for her and assisted her as she stood up. Next, the couple was photographed walking out of a building that houses an OBGYN's office. Their daughter was not with them."*

... *"We're getting reports that CharCol are parents again. Our sources have confirmed that Colin McKinney and Charlie Collins have welcomed twins. No word on the sex of the babies or names. The twins join their older daughter, Ainsley, who's one. Congratulations to the happy family."*

... *"Controversial former Dallas quarterback Colin McKinney and his wife have sold their Dallas-area home. Sources close to the sale report this was the most expensive residential real-estate transaction of the year in Dallas. No word yet on if the couple is remaining in Dallas."*

Year Two Post-Retirement

... *"The game of football misses number-eight Colin McKinney. The NFL reports that for the first time, their viewership numbers decreased instead of increasing as they've done every single year since the NFL has been televised. We've reached out to McKinney's agent, Aiden Montgomery, hoping to get his reaction, but as of publication we've received nothing from the former football star."*

Year Three Post-Retirement

... *"Is former Dallas quarterback and model Colin McKinney a recluse? Sources are reporting that McKinney suffers from severe a severe mental disorder that prevents him from leaving his home. We're told that his paranoia is so acute that he demands that all of his food be tested for poison, and he refuses to trim his hair or nails. His children are not allowed to socialize with others, and are also not permitted outside of his home unless they're under armed guard. We're told his wife, Charlie, has taken a job at Texas A&M University to escape the demanding needs of Colin's disease. How the mighty have fallen."*

Year Four Post-Retirement

... *"Former Dallas quarterback and spokesman for Ford, Colin McKinney, has been spotted for the first time in public in four years. McKinney was photographed, along with his dog, putting gas in his famous truck that he calls Bertha. If you remember, this truck made an appearance at both Super Bowls that Dallas won and was considered the team's unofficial mascot. As you can see from the photograph above, McKinney looks healthy, and witnesses report he was walking without a limp. This is contrary to earlier news stories that he had been seen walking with the aid of a cane."*

Year Five Post-Retirement

... *"McKinney in the Hall of Fame? You've got to be kidding me. The most selfish player to ever toss a ball doesn't deserve to have his bust displayed amongst football's greatest in Canton, Ohio. Maybe he could be in the Hall of Fame of the most despicable players. He can stand next to OJ Simpson. I question what the nominating committee was thinking. Yes, I'll grant you, the guy put up Hall of Fame numbers, and was a two-time Super Bowl winner and awarded the MVP trophy twice, but he let his team down. What about his character off the field? McKinney should still be playing, not have taken five years off to drive car pool. What kind of numbers has Dallas put up without him? The big zero. The most selfish player to ever toss the football does not deserve to be in the Hall of Fame."*

... "I'll grant you that character is an important quality for Hall of Fame consideration, however, McKinney didn't kill anybody. He's never been accused of a crime, except maybe prescription pain-pill abuse, but even that was just speculation. There was never a shred of evidence to validate the claims. Did the guy retire from football at the top of his career? Sure. Did he leave his team high and dry? Yes. Should that keep him out of the hall? In my opinion, no it shouldn't. You put up the numbers. You don't have a criminal record. Then, you should be a Hall of Fame candidate."

... "Colin McKinney has been elected into the Football Hall of Fame in Canton, Ohio, although his selection has not come without its share of controversy. We've been told by sources that fans have decided to organize a jersey burning protest outside of the Hall of Fame facilities to let the selection committee know just how upset they are with their choice. McKinney did the impossible. He retired from the sport of football at the top of his career. Five years later, and fans still seem to be just as upset at McKinney's decision."

Chapter Twenty

Colin

I toss the football up in the air with my left hand. Once. Twice. Thrice. I catch it each time and toss it again. I repeat this motion for an undefined period of time. Thoughts Ping-Pong around my brain, yet there's nothing distinguishable that I can cling to. How's this possible? Who knows?

The only sound is the pigskin slapping against my hand every time I catch it. I'm kicked back in my maroon leather desk-chair staring at the lake, *our* lake, through my wall of windows. I'll never tire of watching the moonlight dance across the gentle waves of the water. This is the most beautiful and tranquil place on earth. I designed my office space—separate from the main house—to look out on our lake. We've affectionately named it Lake CharCol.

The dark wood floors in my office are buffed with enough shine to reflect a sliver of the moonlight bathing my office in shades of grey. It never occurred to me turn on the desk lamp when I came to my office to take Aiden's phone call.

I'm sure a casual observer would wonder how it's possible to toss a football up in the air and catch it every time without watching it fall. Most people have to see what they're catching. The casual observer wouldn't realize that I'm Colin McKinney, two-time Super Bowl-winning MVP quarterback for the Dallas Cowboys. Or I was.

The casual observer would note the greying hair around my temples, and the dust of scruff on my face, as well as the lines that etch my eyes from years of playing football in the hot Texas sun. The casual observer better also note that I'm in good shape for a man in my late thirties. Hell! I'm in damn good shape for a man in my twenties. I've kept my player physique, which sold a metric ton of underwear, sports clothes, trucks, and cologne for various companies. The Brad Pitt of football ... or I was.

I could color the grey away, but why? I've earned every single one of those hairs. They're a rite a passage for me—a badge of honor—almost.

I toss the football up in the air and catch it, speaking for the first time in minutes? Hours? I'm lost in my own thoughts, and right now, they're not a pretty place to be. You'd think that a first ballot induction to the Football Hall of Fame would be a good thing. It's amazing for apparently every football player but me.

Aiden had called earlier in the evening. I'd answered the phone, expecting our usual banter, and just assumed he was calling about our trip. But when I said hello, he referred to me as Colin, instead of any of the plethora of names we normally sling at each other. Quickly, I cut him off and explained that I was in the house, and would head to my office. I excused myself from my family, giving Charlie a kiss on the cheek as I walked out the front door. Panic flooded my gut. This was bad.

As soon as the front door was closed, I asked, "Amy, Collette, the baby?" My heart attempted to pound its way out of my chest.

"No, no. They're all fine. In fact, Collette is so excited to see her cousins that she's already packed her suitcase," Aiden said with a chuckle at his three-year-old daughter's antics. "No, this is unfortunately about the Hall of Fame. Have you turned on the TV?"

I wiped my feet on the doormat as I entered into my office, sinking into my desk chair. "You know I don't watch TV, especially in the off-season. What are they saying?"

My first round ballot into the Football Hall of Fame stirred up every bit of the controversy surrounding my retirement that I'd assumed had been laid to rest. Phrases like "most selfish player to ever step foot on the field" and "narcissist" are being batted around by the football so-called experts. They make me cringe. My kids are old enough to hear this shit.

"Fuck, I'm dreading this trip," I say in a hoarse voice to no one in particular. I keep looking out at Lake CharCol hoping for inspiration.

I find no words of wisdom. I strain my ears, hoping that the crickets rubbing their legs together in a mating call, the birds tweeting to each other, the bullfrogs croaking to their mates will have an answer, but all those bastards do is let me down. I'm met with nothing but their silence.

I turn around in my chair, still not missing the ball as I toss it in the air, and take in my office. I don't think that there's a more beautiful workspace. It's rectangular shaped. The large, wooden desk is made from old ship wood, and faces a wall of windows that look toward the bend of the lake and the dense, virgin woods. The back of my desk also faces a wall of windows that look toward the modest four-bedroom house that Charlie and I designed with the help of an architect. To the right of my desk is a third wall of windows, and French doors that lead to a balcony built over the lake, complete with four Adirondack cedar chairs. I only have one wall without windows, and it's to my left. I have built-ins that surround the door that leads into Jenny's office, filled with mementos from my playing career.

I spend a lot of time in my office on Lake CharCol. Charlie might say that I'm escaping, but I'm really not. Since I hung up my jock strap, I've stayed busy with my many financial investments that Aiden made on my behalf. Hell! I'm twenty percent owner in an island, for God's sake. The official headquarters for CharCol Inc. are in an office building in College Station. That's where the majority of the souvenirs from my former life are housed. I think of that office space as my reception area. It's where I meet with business executives pitching me to invest in their companies, young quarterbacks who need mentoring, and anyone else who isn't family. No one but family is allowed here in Somerville, in what Charlie calls The Compound. She has a name for everything.

The press says that I've been in virtual seclusion for more than five years. They've even called me a hermit, and speculated that I have a mental disease like agoraphobia. They've said that I was driven to seclusion because I can no longer walk without a cane. What the media doesn't report is that I leave the compound frequently. I've just made it a point to not draw attention to myself.

When I walked away from the bright stadium lights, I went completely radio silent. As Charlie says, I only see the world in black and white. There are no grey areas. That meant no more endorsement deals. No memorabilia singing events. No sideline appearances at football games. No guest commentary on ESPN. No red-carpet appearances at charity events. No waving at paparazzi while I take one of the kids running in the jogging stroller. I turned down every broadcast deal. I've done nothing to place myself in the spotlight. Nothing. Nada. *Zilch*.

I went from the biggest name in the sporting world to nothing in twenty-four hours. Well, that's not entirely true. I was once again the number-one trending story on Twitter and most Googled person for about two weeks, but then it's like the world got distracted by a squirrel and everyone forgot who Colin Fucking McKinney is/was/is.

Speculation and rumors swirled about why I walked away from football. Theories included that I couldn't take the pressure of trying to repeat a championship season for the third time, and had a mental breakdown. I did indeed have an addiction to prescription pain-pills and was afraid of getting busted. Charlie demanded that I quit playing football if I wanted to stay married. I was being blackmailed and was forced to retire. The hardest rumor was that Ainsley wasn't healthy, and I was stepping down to focus on her medical care.

No one seemed to be able to comprehend that my decision was simply to leave the game while I was on top, and to finally be the husband and father that my family deserved to have. Then again, I turned down every interview request where I could have explained all of that to the public.

Why? Because it was no one's business. The world had heard enough from me. Hell, I was sick of myself. I couldn't turn on the TV or read a magazine without seeing me pimping a product. Yes, it was time to leave the bright spotlight.

Sure, I was aware of the horrible things being said about me. The media can always dig up the disgruntled ex-teammate who thought I was an asshole. Aiden and Mark kept hounding me to speak out, to grant an interview, explaining my reasons. Frankly, I was tired of justifying myself to anyone, and most of all the press. So I flat out refused, and spent my time focused on my wife, who struggled every damn day with her pregnancy.

Maybe I should have done one little interview.

I toss the ball up in my hand and catch it for the hundredth/thousandth/millionth time. My life is so good right now. I mean, my life is as close to perfect as it can be while not playing football, but do I want to expose my kids to the media? As far as I know there are no pictures of the twins at all, and Ainsley's pics are from when she was a baby. I cringe at the thought of some asshole reporter asking me questions in front of my kids that would make them think less of me.

I stop tossing the ball, catching it one last time, and lean my head back against the leather desk chair, looking up at the shadowed grey ceiling. I can't protect them forever, but I'd damn sure like to try.

I grab my phone and text Charlie.

Me: *You in bed yet?*

When she doesn't respond immediately, I assume that she's already asleep, and now I've probably disturbed her. Just when I look away from my phone, I hear the trill indicating that I have a text.

Charlie: *A had a bad dream. She begged to sleep with us, but I got her back in her bed. I figured that we didn't need another distraction to keep you up. Coming to bed soon?*

Me: *Let Pancho out. I'll be there in a few.*

I push off from behind my desk, finally letting the football rest, and grab my phone with my right hand. Slipping it into my shorts pocket and walking to the built-ins, I place the football back in its glass box. It's the football that I threw for the game-winning touchdown in the Super Bowl. I made the pass with two seconds left in the game, and we were down by six. *What a feeling ...* electricity surges through my body, and it makes my left hand vibrate. I might even smile at the memory. It was the last pass that I ever threw as a professional athlete.

Next to the glass case that stores my football is a framed picture of Charlie, right before she went to the hospital to deliver Ainsley. We found the pictures when we were cleaning out the McMansion before our move to Somerville. Charlie thinks that Brad took it, but she can't remember. She's in the hotel that she watched the victory parade from. I love the picture. In fact, it's one of my most cherished items. It's her in jeans and a rose-colored sweater. Her stomach is so pronounced that the picture almost looks doctored. She's doing maybe a shimmy or some sort of dance move. Her arms are above her head, and her fingers are positioned as if she's snapping. Charlie's face is radiant. She's glowing with happiness. Her huge, toothy smile matches her eyes. *And to think that about twelve hours later we met our daughter.*

Picking up the picture, I carry it to the closest windows so I can see it better in the moonlight. It makes me smile. I wasn't there when Charlie went into labor, or for most of the drama leading up to Ainsley's birth, but this picture makes me believe that Charlie was okay and happy. I feel more a part of that special time when I look at it. My lips curl into a smile as I set it back on the shelf next to my other treasured possessions.

I step through my door and into Jenny's office—when she's gracing me with her presence—and onto the front porch of CharCol Inc. It's a gorgeous August night. I take a deep breath and smell the comforting scent of pine. An overwhelming feeling of blessings rolls through me. Because of football and wise business decisions, my family is able to have all of this. For the first time tonight, I feel like maybe I deserve it. I'm a man who worked my ass off since I was twelve years' old, when I became serious about football, to give my family this beautiful piece of property to live on.

I walk the fifty yards to the house, listening to the leaves crunch under my feet. When I'm just about to the wrap-around porch, I'm almost taken down by our psychotic love monster, Pancho the Destructicon. My dog and I are as thick as thieves, but when the rest of the family is in the house he doesn't leave his post. We've chatted. We're boys. He watches out for the gang while I'm gone.

Pancho and I have a late-night ritual that Charlie doesn't know about. Us boys like to pee against one of our favorite trees. It's an old oak tree that is not close enough to the lake to house a rope swing over the water, but it's a damn fine tree. In fact, I've thought about building a playhouse around it for the kids. Pancho hikes his leg, and I drop my shorts enough to get my dick out.

About midstream, I hear in her know-it-all voice, "I've always wondered why you don't go to the bathroom before you come to bed."

I look down at Pancho and whisper, "Busted."

She continues, "Is this why I can't get the boys to use our indoor plumbing? Because I don't approve if it is. Nature is not your toilet. In fact, we have five bathrooms inside that you can choose from. It's unsanitary …"

"I got it. You don't want me pissing outside. Noted." I look down at Pancho, and he looks up at me with these huge brown eyes, clearly expressing the regret he feels for the situation that I've gotten us in to.

I fix my shorts, and Pancho and I walk up to the porch, stepping up to where my lovely wife stands in one of my old T-shirts that hits her about mid-thigh, her caramel-colored hair twisted into a half ponytail, face clean of all makeup, and a smirk that says that I'm never going to live this down.

"You look deliciously fuckable," I coo into her ear, hoping that I can use her body as a distraction from my anxiety. I wrap her into my arms and kiss her hair. "I love you, even when you're being an uptight, condescending shrew."

She drops her chin and even in the dark of the night, only lit by moonlight and stars, I can see her mind spinning. She looks up at me and bats her eyelashes. "I love you, even when you're being a disgusting male pig."

I pull back and slap her ass. And then I quote one of our favorite movies that we recently watched. "Take me to bed, or lose me forever."

She throws her head back and laughs. "Show me the way home, honey."

With that, I take her hand, pulling her into a dance position. She giggles. "It's rude to just assume that a lady wants to dance with you."

I nibble on the shell of her ear. "Mrs. McKinney will you do me the honor of dancing with me?"

I don't wait for her response and begin singing "Bless the Broken Road" as I two-step us to the French doors that lead to our bedroom. Pancho runs along ahead as if he's making sure there's nothing keeping me from getting her right where I want her. She's laughing like a teenage girl on prom night as I spin her around and dip her back in my arms for a soul-searing kiss. I fucking love that we've been together this long and still make each other happy.

Once I've waltzed her to our large bed, I dip her again, letting her back rest on the mattress. My T-shirt rides up to her waist revealing her long, lean, beautiful legs and white cotton panties. That's all it takes. My cock makes note of just how much we love being inside those panties.

I shut the French doors behind me and shoo Pancho out of our bedroom, closing and locking the door. All we need is for a little face to appear next to our bed asking why Daddy is making Mommy scream. I then activate our high-tech, top of the line, cost-as-much-as –the-house security system, and then focus my full attention on Doctor Caroline Jane Collins-McKinney, who is the most perfect girl for me.

I stalk toward her, doing a pathetic attempt at a striptease that makes her lavender eyes dance with mirth as she grazes over my physique. I throw my green T-shirt on the floor and run my hand over my abs, and then strike a muscle-man pose.

She scoots further back on the bed and pushes up against the cerulean-blue padded headboard. She hits the bed as if inviting me up. *Hell no! I'm having fun.*

I turn around and face my back to her while I tease, removing my black athletic shorts. I take them halfway down and bring them right back up as I hear her laugh. "You want the full package, baby? I need to hear you."

She lets out a whoop and holler that make me smile like a big dopey idiot. I drop my shorts again, showing her my half-moon and wait for more excitement from my girl.

"Colin, bring that fine behind and unwiped dick to me right this instant." She laughs.

I turn my head over my right shoulder and flash her my half-smile that she fucking loves. "I haven't heard the word please slip out of those beautiful lips of yours."

She brings her knees up to her chest and taps her feet repeatedly on the bed while she shakes her head. "Colin Fucking McKinney, I am crazy in love with you. Come see me. I can't take any more of your pathetic attempts at a striptease."

I mean, I'm a guy after all, so I drop trou, do a 180-spin move that would make an Olympic ice-skater proud, and dive on the bed. She rips off my old-ass faded T-shirt that she's wearing and shows me her still perfect tits, even after breastfeeding our children.

I can't stop myself. I take God's most perfect creations in my hands, giving them equal attention. Licking, sucking, biting, and everything else I can think to do. She positions herself in between my legs so I'm now straddling her. Once she's settled, she reaches up and grabs my very hard dick, and I let out a moan of pleasure that I can feel in my toes. I mean, who could blame me? I'm the luckiest son-of-a-bitch alive.

She holds on to my cock with the force that she knows drives me crazy. There's a certain comfort in being with the same person long enough that they know exactly what you like. *And God, does she know exactly what I like.* She pumps my dick with five long, hard strokes before she stops, and collects the wetness off my tip.

I'd like to say that I'm all cool and immune to her after all these years, but I'm still fucking pathetic. I'd come right now, if she wouldn't give me shit about it for the next forty years. I let out an audible sigh as she massages my wetness around the tip of my dick.

When I can't take it any longer, I dive back for her tits, determined that I'm going to make her come by just sucking and massaging them. I can do it. They've become even more sensitive since the twins. I hiss in her ear, "You're going to scream my name without me even feeding you my cock."

She drops her head back against the ridiculously expensive bed pillows that she bought in Paris and made me haul back to the States. "I'd like to see you try, big boy. My tits are so numb after breastfeeding your three spawn. I can barely feel your mouth right now."

I know that's not true. And oh yeah … Dear Lord, challenge accepted.

I spend the next fifteen minutes—I know, because I watched the clock for future arguments—making this woman scream my name as she attempts to shove my very hard cock inside of her and almost pulls out every hair on my head. She's the one who's going to make me bald by forty.

I want to high-five myself, but I don't because she'd never let me live it down either. When I finally relent my torturous assault on her breasts, I slip my rock-hard dick inside of her and she pulls me in deeper. This is where I want to be. Balls-deep inside of my girl.

I start sliding in and out of her, finding the rhythm that she likes so much. Then she opens her big mouth, "Quit obsessing over things that you can't change."

She does this on purpose.

What I want to do is pull out of her, leaving her longing for me, but I know that she'll just get herself off. Then I'll just have watched her masturbate, and be left with the hardest dick in the Brazos Valley. I punish her just a little by picking up my rhythm and ensuring I hit the spot inside that makes her eyes roll back in her head.

"You think the kids are ready to be introduced to the vultures?" I say, while I continue to slide in out of her hot wetness. *Jesus Christ, this feels awesome.* Apparently she agrees, because her eyes roll momentarily to the back of her head.

"Don't see that we have a choice," she says as she reaches up and begins to twist my nipples in some sort of way that makes my dick pulse.

"I don't know," I groan sounding like a pathetic fuck to my own ears.

Before I know it, she flips me and I'm on my back, staring at her crazed sex-hair that is messy enough that I want to beat on my chest and scream,

"I make this gorgeous woman look like this." Her eyes that pierce my soul meet mine as she brings her full lips into a soft smile. She begins to move up and down on me in a dance that is all her own. *God, I love this woman.* "It's not hard, lover boy." She smirks.

"Oh really, Mrs. McKinney?" I grab her hips and try to direct her movements. "It feels pretty hard to me." My distraction technique is a total fail on my part. I don't know why I bother. She owns me. The eight years that we took off were just so we could build to this point in our life.

She looks down, meeting my eyes, and her perfect tits bounce as she rides me. I feel her clit rubbing against my pubic bone. "They'll have to find out at some point that your retirement was controversial. Kids will eventually tell them on the playground."

"Why are we discussing this while I'm fucking your brains out?" I ask as I slap her ass and then reach up and pinch her very taut nipples.

She lets a moan escape that I'm surprised doesn't bring the house down around us.

She spins away from my hands and begins riding me with her back to me. I fucking can't stand it when I can't see her. She knows this. This is some sort of mind game that she's playing with me and I don't approve. I grab her hips and pull her off of me. "If I can't watch your face and see your boobs bounce, then I don't want to have sex with you."

Charlie rolls off of me and flops back against the bed. She smiles giving me her know-it-all grin. "Then I'll just fuck myself. It's your call," she says as she inserts three fingers inside of herself.

She could make the pope say fuck. I fall on top of her and slide back inside. We pick up right where we left off. "I love you." She smiles underneath me.

"I love you, too. Now kiss me like you mean it."

She leans forward, and I meet her halfway. She takes my mouth with her tongue while I groan, feeling her kiss all the way in my toes. I'll never become immune to her. Her kiss still shoots electricity through my soul as much as it did when we began dating in college.

I grab her hips and roll us so she's back on top without ever breaking our kiss. It's only when I feel her pulsing around my cock that I let go and enjoy my orgasm, feeling completely swept away in the moment.

At some point, she scoots off my chest and cuddles into my side. "You're a good man, Colin. Whatever the media calls you, we know the truth. All the rumors were a lie. You walked away from football to be their dad. That's what we tell them," she says in a dreamy voice.

Her words hit the spot; they're what I needed to hear. I bend my neck and kiss her head. "Wise words, Doctor Collins. But it's not you who has been called the most selfish player ever."

She sits up, apparently now wide awake, and pulls the white bed sheet over her bare bottom. "You didn't murder anyone, Colin, for God's sake. Or any of the other horrible things that other players have done. You just happen to be the most famous player to leave at the top of your career. You weren't like the other guys, who had to be tapped on the shoulder and asked to retire. I get that this is a sports-driven, crazy country. It just irritates me that everyone assumes the worst instead of just accepting your explanation at face value." She leans forward, totally violating any personal space that I might have considered a safe zone and says, "You did nothing wrong."

"The football league and my sponsors beg to differ with you, Doctor Collins. I read something tonight that said my retirement cost them an estimated two-hundred million dollars, just in the first year." I pull her to me and hold her as if she's my lifeline, letting that tidbit of knowledge sink in.

Her only response is "Oh."

Repeatedly stoking her hair, I sing, "Let It Go." Her lips curl up in a smile against my ribs as I watch her eyes flutter shut succumbing—finally—to her fuck coma.

Charlie on bed-rest for her entire pregnancy gave us lots of time to work through the problems, hurt feelings, and resentments plaguing our relationship. We learned to actually communicate with each other and voice our issues. It was a novel exercise for both of us. Most of all, I learned that to fully forgive someone is also to forget. I finally forgave Charlie for choosing Harvard over me, and I've come to accept that she's put our family ahead of her career. Those months were tough, but we joked that at least we couldn't run away from each other. She was a prisoner to her recliner, and I had the media acting as my warden. This is by far the strongest our marriage has ever been.

If I hadn't walked away from football, I wouldn't have Charlie pressed against me now, or my children upstairs asleep in their beds. That I do believe.

Chapter Twenty-One

Colin

My wife falls asleep in a position that can only be deemed comfortable by nomadic rogues and pirates. I use the remote next to my side of the bed to the turn off the lights, and I pull her more closely to me so her head can rest on my chest.

The dad in me says that I should get up and unlock our bedroom door so if one of the kids needs us they can come in. Instead, I listen to the horny-ass husband that says I'm not disturbing the gorgeous woman woven around my body for all the tea in China.

I slump in the bed, and there's not a chance of me sleeping comfortably like this, but I don't care. Put it on my "I don't give a fuck list." My wife, snuggled around me like climbing ivy and those three precious heartbeats upstairs? This is what life's all about.

I let her head fall against my shoulder while I pull the covers just over the top of us, giving me some warmth, when I hear the door handle jingle. Charlie's mom sixth-sense kicks in, and she rouses for just a second.

"I've got this," I reassure her as she falls toward her pillow, snuggling into a much more comfortable position that is, unfortunately, not on me.

I jump out of bed and throw on my athletic shorts and turn the lock. When I open the door, a set of lavender eyes are looking up at me that melt my heart. "Hi," I coo. "Is everything alright?"

Jax or maybe Liam—I can't tell them apart—is standing there in Batman PJs with tussled white-blonde hair and a sleepy look on his face. "Liam kicked me." So this is Jax. "It made me want Mommy."

Perfectly logical. When I get kicked, I want Charlie also. "Come on, buddy. Let me take you back to bed."

I pick up half of the fearsome twosome and carry him through the large expanse of our open living room and up the wooden stairs. I've been telling Charlie for a couple of weeks that it's time to put the boys in separate beds—they're five after all—but she gets a pained look on her face and stares at the ceiling.

I get it. The fearsome twosome have been together forever. But our identical twin boys are outgrowing their bed. I pick up Jax and place him inside of the bed with rails to prevent them from rolling off and breaking something. "I love you, little man. Go to sleep for me."

"Daddy, am I going to be a football player like you?" my precious son asks me.

I smile and reply, "No, baby boy. You're going to be a train engineer."

His face lights up. "I'll be a super train engineer."

I look at him like the lovesick fool that I am, and kiss his hair. "Yes, you will, Jax. Yes you will."

Instead of going back downstairs and getting into bed with my sated wife, I stop off at Ainsley's room. It's decorated like a princess lives here. Oh wait! She does. I tiptoe to her bedside and kiss her beautiful forehead while I pull her white blanket over her shoulders. She's as gorgeous as her mother, but with my build. This six-year-old, reading, writing, mathematician owns me like I didn't know that I could be owned. All Daddy's need their boys, but dear God, who knew that I needed my daughter so much. She makes me a better man every damn day of my life.

She rolls over and snuggles some pathetic stuffed animal that she's claimed as her everything. I smile down at her, hoping that this ratty dog will chase away whatever bad dreams plagued her earlier. I give her another kiss on her forehead and whisper, "Sweet dreams, beautiful," against her hair.

Pancho, always on guard duty, escorts me down the stairs and back to the bedroom where my girl is taking up the whole bed. I sit down on my side and attempt to reposition her so I've got a little more room. No luck. She rolls onto her stomach, and throws her leg over my hips. I glance over at the three-fourths unused large bed so grateful that after as many years that we've been together, plus all the fights, traveling, three kids, and life-changing events, she still clings to me in her sleep. Who cares if I sleep well? It's not like I have practice tomorrow.

****

Sunlight wakes us every morning. We don't have curtains or blinds, because we live in the middle of nowhere. There's no need to protect our privacy. It's really the best way to wake up. We positioned the house so our bedroom faces north. That way we catch a few more minutes of sleep. As I emerge to wakefulness, I realize that my sleeping partner is gone, and must have been up for some time because the bed is cold.

The telltale signs of morning cartoons and smell of bacon frying in a pan makes my stomach growl. Sounds like the twins won the morning TV battle and chose *Teenage Mutant Ninja Turtles*. We only have one television in our house on purpose. We could eliminate some of the arguments if I'd agree to put one in the kids' playroom, but it's not going to happen. Learning to share is a life skill. It starts with compromising on what shows we watch.

I lean back against the headboard and look down, realizing that I'm still in my athletic shorts with giant morning wood. My options include lying back down and thinking about my fifth-grade English teacher that had a mole on her chin with a black hair growing out of it, or I could take a shower and rub one out using Charlie's conditioner. Or I could try to persuade my wife to give me a quick pity-fuck in the closet.

I go with the third option. "Charrrrleeee ..." I call. "I've got a BIG problem"—And I do emphasize the word big— "in here."

"Ainsley, if you don't want to watch what your brother's are watching then read a book. It's a lovely morning. Go read on the back porch. Or better yet, get ready for swim team. We're leaving in forty-five minutes."

"But Mommy, when is it my turn to choose the show?" she whines.

I decide to help, so I yell, "When you figure out how to compromise with them."

She lets out a huff that's loud enough that I hear it in our bedroom, and stomps across the living room. Then the French doors that lead from the living room to the back porch open and shut with a little too much force. Normally, I'd correct her for slamming doors, but my situation prevents me from getting up.

Charlie comes to the bedroom door and leans against the doorframe with a mug of coffee in her right hand. "What's your big problem?" she asks, looking at the tented bed sheet that I've made with my hard cock. She shakes her head, and says, "You're awful."

I flash her my half-smile and say, "Up for some closet time?"

"I've got to get ready for work. Can't you take care of it yourself?" She's smirking as she says all of this. I can read her like a book. When she says serious stuff while her lips turn up it means that she wants me to beg for it, which I'm not too proud to do.

"Closet time will distract me from the big, bad media. It's really your way of doing your part." I sound so cocky, which is exactly the angle that I was going for. I add the last bit knowing what her reaction is going to be.

"Fine. You've got about five minutes of *Ninja Turtles* left. Let's see what you can do with it, big boy," she says as she sashays threw the bedroom and into the master bathroom, discarding her coffee mug on the sink vanity. I follow her into our sex closet. It's actually her closet. She had a bench seat built in under the guise of needing a place to sit to put on panty hose and shoes. I know the truth. She wanted it because it makes a great place for her to brace her upper body so I can take her from behind.

I lock the closet door behind us, and watch her slip off her black cotton jogging-pants and remove her pink thong. She gives me a knowing wink before she turns around and assumes the position. I drop my athletic shorts like they're on fire and walk up behind her, palming both of her tits working her nipples into hard points. While continuing to massage the left one, I check to see how ready she is.

My girl is slick, and I love it. She plays hard to get and she's not affected by me, but then I feel how turned on she is. I lean over her back and whisper in her hair, "You're sloppy for me. I fucking love you."

She gasps as I continue to slide my fingers in and out of her, finding the right spot. Over and over I do this. It's a fun game of torture we play. I'm not quite letting her have her orgasm, just keeping her on the brink.

Then I nibble, lick, and bite the spot on her shoulder—just above her collarbone—that makes her crazy.

"Take me. I'm going to come." She pants as she tries to wiggle away from my nimble fingers.

I use my right hand to hold her in place, not letting her reach for my cock.

"Not yet," I reply, checking my watch. "I still have three minutes."

Dropping to my knees, I spread her legs wider apart, staring at her pink, swollen pussy. She's still leaning on the bench, and seeing her in such a vulnerable position makes me even harder. I begin to sample her wetness with my tongue and smell her arousal. Dear God, I love everything about her. Her smell. Her taste. The moans of pleasure that escape her mouth. She is a fucking smorgasbord for my senses.

"Colin," she groans. "I'm almost there."

I chuckle to myself. I don't know why she feels the need to tell me. I know. I feel her swell against my lips and tongue. I can taste her increased arousal. She begins to pulse like a heartbeat against my chin.

Standing up, I slip my cock inside of her as she clamps tightly against me and pulls me the rest of the way in. I feel the rush of fluid and know that she's coming as I slide in and out of her keeping her orgasm going. She throws her head back, and hair falls over her back, and brushes the two dimples at the top of her behind.

My body feels like I've got electricity running through it as my orgasm spills out of me and into her soft folds. I'm a sweaty motherfucker and fall against her back, grabbing her around her small waist as if she's my lifeline.

"Best five-minute sex ever." I pant against her shoulder blade.

She turns around and sits on the bench and I drop to the ground, putting my head on her lap. She runs her long fingers through my damp, matted waves. "Did you sleep last night?" Charlie asks in a soft voice, tinged with concern.

"Not especially," I reply, wrapping my left arm around her calves. She's my damn lifeline. I need her so much.

She smiles again, and runs her hand over my stubbled cheek. "Don't let the press tarnish this honor. You deserve to be in the Hall of Fame."

Chapter Twenty-Two

Colin

"Car's leaving in ... five ... four ..." I yell as the twins race each other to see who can get their tennis shoes on the fastest. Ainsley waits patiently by the front door, and Charlie grabs her purse and work bag. "Three ... two ... one ... Let's go people."

I give Pancho a goodbye pat on his head, and instruct him to watch the house. I swear the dog all but jumps to attention.

My family is walking ahead of me. That's really not accurate. I don't think the twins have the ability to walk anywhere. Run, jump, hop, skip? That's what they do. Walking? Not so much.

The boys are dressed in shorts and T-shirts for gymnastics and are now racing each other to the car. Ainsley is dressed in her bathing suit with a pair of bright pink shorts. She's carrying her blue-sequined swim-team bag, complements of Guncle's Brad and Carter. Charlie's dressed for work, and is attempting to instruct everyone on what we need to pack for Ohio.

Just then, Ainsley must find a hole in the yard, because she trips and falls, tumbling over herself. Panic grips me. Just as I'm about to race over and make sure she's okay, her two little brothers, who heard her cry, stop dead in their tracks, turn around and run back to her.

Ainsley is sitting on her bottom, gripping her knee to her chest. She's trying to be brave, but I watch her bottom lip tremble as she fights to keep the tears at bay. The boys kneel down beside her, so concerned about their big sister. They begin examining her knee and checking for other injuries. Liam, because he's in the orange T-shirt, kisses her scrape, while Jax rubs her arm as if reassuring her that it's going to be okay.

It's such a tender moment that Charlie and I both keep our distance, watching our boys take care of their sister.

Before I know it, the twins help Ainsley to her feet, each offering her a hand. Jax picks up Ainsley's swim bag and carries it the rest of the way to the car. All three are laughing and teasing again, as if nothing happened.

Was leaving football at the top of my career worth it? Yes, if for no other reason than this moment. If I were still playing I'd be at training camp right now, working to get into season-ready shape. Instead, I woke up and made love to my wife. Now, I'm off to take my kids to their activities and then spend the rest of the day playing with them. We'll probably do tricks off the rope swing before dinner. My boys know how to take care of their sister, because I taught them. Not Brad. Not a nanny. Me. I've modeled that behavior for them. And I couldn't be prouder. A smile breaks across my face as my body grows warm with pride for my family. *This moment is PFM.*

Bertha is parked in our garage next to the family car. I give her a good slap on the tailgate, silently reassuring her that I'll take her for a drive soon. Damn truck is still running, and does a fine job of hauling supplies for the compound.

We climb into the minivan, and before the arguing can begin I remind the boys that they watched their show this morning, so it's Ainsley's turn to choose. I also remind her to pick something that all three will enjoy. Fortunately, she chooses an episode of *The Justice League*, so everyone will be happy.

I don't necessarily believe in TVs in cars, however, we live forty-five minutes from just about everything. The TV buys Charlie and I a few minutes of adult conversation.

The way I situated our home on the property was done with security in mind. Our home is across the lake from the entrance to the land, off of the main road. Once you're on our property, it's almost a mile drive to our front door. The road is curved with switch backs. Aiden teases that there's no way anyone could drive it drunk. It's not that bad, but it's a challenge the first time someone new visits us, which isn't all that often.

We pass by one of the lake cottages that we built for guests. We have three on the property. Each one can sleep up to eight people. This particular one is where I put the double-wide trailer that I bought for us to live in after the twins were born.

As soon as I retired from football, Charlie and I finally got serious about building our vacation home, which has become our permanent residence. Before the twins were born, I had the land cleared for a road and utilities run.

We stayed in Dallas just long enough, so Charlie could be close to Doctor Starr. Once the twins were healthy enough to come home from the hospital, I hammered a *For Sale* sign in the front yard of the McMansion inside of the gilded cage, and we got the hell out of Dodge.

Strangely enough, it was purchased by the hotshot first-round draft pick that the Cowboys took. What does a twenty-one-year-old kid need with that much house? Probably the same things that I wanted it for when I was first drafted. Fortunately, Charlie and my parents talked me into a condo instead.

The five of us lived in a three-bedroom, two-bathroom mobile home while we built our dream house. Looking back on it, I don't know how we did it. We could have fit eight of our trailers in the McMansion, but I'll say this: it was a relationship solidifying two years. Charlie and I were just focused on each other and our family.

"I talked to Brad yesterday," Charlie says while she's turning up the volume on the kid's show.

"Oh yeah," I state, not taking my eyes off the road.

"They're excited about the trip to Ohio, and asked if they could take the kids for a couple of hours. Maybe get lunch or find a park. I think they're missing them." Then she reminds me that is has been almost four months since we last had Brad and Carter for a visit.

"I'm sure that will be fine. But suggest they stay in the hotel. It's got the security that Jenny says is trustworthy." I inwardly cringe, and it has nothing to do with Brad. I make a mental note to check with her about security for my family when we leave the hotel.

Once I retired from football, Brad helped out Carmen in Houston for about six months, and then he and Carter moved in together full-time. Charlie no longer needed an assistant, so he's remained our kids Guncle that we share all holidays with. He's just Charlie's friend now, and we're cool. Will Brad and I ever be fishing buddies? No, but I appreciate how much our kids mean to him and Carter, and feel blessed that they're a part of our lives.

I reach over and grab Charlie's hand, giving it a squeeze. Her skin is so soft compared to my calluses. I can't get enough of our contact. "Speaking of the hotel, have you talked to Rachael?"

Charlie drops my hand and cocks her head, raising an eyebrow. "Seriously, you've got to play nice. Don't be an asshole."

"What?" I ask, acting very innocent. "Jenny just needs to know if Rachael requires a crib for her room?" I can't keep my shit-eating grin off of my face.

She gives my arm a gentle punch, and I grab my bicep and gasp dramatically in pain. "Colin, lots of women date much younger men."

"He's what, twenty-four? That's much, much younger, babe. Like, she-could-be-his-mother young."

"Thanks for reminding me," she says with a pout while she crosses her arms over her chest. "You know he plays for the Yankees, right? That means he can throw much harder than you."

She didn't just question my throwing abilities ... "Is that a challenge? Tell Rach to bring her child over one day to play." I do emphasize the word "child." "We'll just see who has the stronger arm."

Charlie rolls her eyes at my pissing contest, and grabs my hand.

We arrive at Charlie's building just as the kid's show is ending. She gets curbside service. Only the best for my girl. I put the car in park while she grabs her purse and work bag. She checks and double checks to make sure that she has everything that she needs. I've known her almost twenty years and she's still just as beautiful as the day that she walked into Jack's office.

Her caramel-colored hair is a bit shorter now, and she highlights it to cover her grey. Apparently, she doesn't think grey hair makes her look more distinguished. Her skin is still clear with a touch of light olive. She complains about the smile lines around her mouth, but I love them, because I like to think they're proof of the great life that I've given her.

Charlie's eyes are the same eyes that locked with mine so many years ago. When I look into those eyes, I see our past and the years we spent not talking. I remember looking into them again when the elevator doors opened at the hotel in Los Angeles. They're the eyes that locked with mine when she walked down our makeshift aisle to marry me by our swimming pool. Those eyes pleaded with me to be her partner when Ainsley was born. The same lavender eyes filled with terror and fear when the twins were being born via C-section way too early. However, my favorite emotion in her gorgeous eyes is love. Love for me. Love for our kids and dog. Love for our family. Love for the life that we've made together.

"Why are you looking at me so strangely?" she asks as she cocks her eyebrow up. Charlie leans over to give me a goodbye kiss.

I grab her face with both of my hands and pull her to me, giving her much more than the usual peck on the lips. We're mugging down over the armrest in the minivan. *Oh! How the times have changed.*

The kids start making gross out, gagging sounds, but I could care less. This is my girl. She's always been my girl, and will always be my girl. I hope that before I die, her gorgeous lavender eyes are the last thing that I see. Then I'd die a happy man.

She breaks our kiss, and gives me a reassuring rub on my arm. Staring into my eyes, she says, "It's going to be okay, Colin. Quit stressing. In two days, we leave for the festivities in Ohio. I want you to enjoy this huge honor. You deserve it, sweetheart."

I flash her my panty-dropping half-smile. "No worries, Professor McKinney. I love you to infinity."

She reaches up and touches her necklace and smiles. "Infinity."

I watch her walk into her building on Texas A&M's campus where she's a Biomedical Engineering Professor. She only teaches one class, because she's pioneering research on how to better construct the rods used to stabilize bones after compound fractures. I have no idea how she got interested in it.

Does she love her job as much as she did practicing medicine? No, but she often reassures me that it's very fulfilling, and she adores working with her students.

She's wearing a lavender dress today. I choose to believe that she picked it out on purpose. Charlie complains about the last five pounds of baby weight that she needs to lose, but her ass has never looked better. I watch it sway from side to side as she makes her way to the building's entrance. Her long, toned legs look even sexier in the black heels that she's wearing. I start fantasizing about having her legs wrapped around my waist while those heels dig in my ass. Tonight. The heels are staying on tonight.

"We need to go, Dad. We're going to be late," Ainsley pipes up from the third row, sounding just like her mother, deflating my cock.

"Then we'll be late. It's rude to leave before you make sure that the person that you're dropping off makes it inside safely," I explain to the crew. If the truth be told, I'm hoping for a look back and a beautiful smile.

Wait for it …

Wait for it …

There it is. My gorgeous girl looks back over her shoulder with her face glowing. As she raises her hand to wave, her wedding band catches the sun.

The double doors close behind her, and I feel a sudden pang of loneliness. If I didn't have a car full of kids, I'd chase after her and plant one more kiss on her cherry-red lips.

God, I'm just one boy, loved infinitely by one girl. Luckiest son of a bitch alive.

~ The End ~

Fifteen years later …

"Hi, baby girl. How's everything?" I ask, leaning back in my office chair and propping my feet on the desk. Lake CharCol is so smooth that it looks like glass today.

"It's good." Then there's a long pause. "But Daddy, there's something that I need to talk to you about," Ainsley says in a tone that indicates that she's a tad scared to discuss this with me. I know what she has to tell me. She's already talked to Charlie, who was kind enough to prepare me last night for this call.

It went something like, "Remember, Ainsley is twenty-one years' old. I was nineteen when we began dating. She loves you so much, and wants your approval. Just go easy on her." Charlie was smart enough to tell me this while I held her after making her come multiple times. She can play me like a fiddle.

I grab a bottle of water off of my desk, and twist open the lid. "You can talk to me about anything. You have my undivided attention." I pat myself on the back for sounding like such an awesome parent.

She begins to say something, but changes her mind. I'm not going to make this too easy on her, so I let her stammer for a couple of seconds.

"It's easier if you just spit it out," I coax.

I hear her taking in a deep breath and letting it out. "I've met a boy."

No. I'm not going to make it too easy on her at all. "That's great, sweetie. I just assumed that you met boys every day. You do go to a co-ed school."

She lets out a frustrated sigh, and I can imagine her rolling her lavender eyes just like her mother does. "This isn't just any boy. This is a guy that I really think I like."

I stare at the framed picture of Ainsley on my desk. It's her graduation-from-high-school picture. Dear God, she's gorgeous. Charlie's caramel-blonde hair with waves and lavender eyes. My tall, athletic frame and olive complexion. Yes, our daughter is a knockout, and fortunately, she's stayed away from boys—apparently until now.

"Does this guy have a name?" I ask. Charlie didn't tell me who the boy was, just that Ainsley had been seeing someone for a few months.

"He does have a name …" she replies, obviously not wanting me to know what it is. I can hear the trepidation in her voice.

"Well, do I have to tickle torture you to tell me, or are you going to spit it out?" I coax, motioning for her to continue.

"His name is Royce," Ainsley is clearly terrified to say his name out loud, and I detect a slight tremble in her voice.

I scan my brain as to where I've heard that name. Royce. Do we know any Royces? Friend's kids? No. Guys from church? Doesn't ring a bell. The twin's friends? Nothing. The only Royce that comes to mind is Dallas's new hotshot quarterback, Royce Barber.

Battery acid floods my stomach as the realization punches me in the gut. I reach my hands up, running my fingers through my still very thick hair.

My baby girl is dating Royce Barber, NFL quarterback. Doctor Jack Collins is laughing his ass off in heaven right now. Fuck my life. History repeats itself again.

Dear Reader,

Well, this completes Colin and Charlie's journey. I hope you've enjoyed being a voyeur in their lives. It has been my pleasure to share their story with you. Thank you so much for buying my books, leaving reviews, emailing me, and writing messages on social media. You're support has been overwhelming and changed my life in so many ways.
I'll miss Charlie and Colin terribly, but there are some fun projects that I've been working on.

Here's one of them … Rachael's story will be available this summer. It's a standalone book, meaning that you don't necessarily need the Infinity Series backstory to enjoy it. You've only seen her through Charlie and Aiden's eyes. I think you'll love being inside of her head as much as I do. So as an added treat, keep reading. Here's the prologue to her book *The World: According to Rachael.* It will be available Summer 2014.

Oh! One more thing. As always, I love hearing from you. Please email me at Layne@LayneHarper.com. Find me on Facebook at Layne_Harper_Author, or Twitter at @Layne_Harper. My website is www.LayneHarper.com. Indie authors live and die by your reviews. Please leave a comment on Amazon.

Without further ado… Here's the prologue for The World: According to Rachael.

Hugs,
Layne Harper

The World: According to Rachael

By: Layne Harper

Prologue

I shouldn't have had that last beer. Hell. If I'm honest with myself, I shouldn't have had the last pitcher. I knew how important today was before I agreed to meet my frat brothers who invaded D.C. for a visit.

If I had the least bit of intelligence, I'd have said, "Sorry guys. Big day at work tomorrow. Hit ya up tomorrow night." There are probably twenty-three-year-old guys who exist in this world who'd have done that. They are the responsible ones that my dad preaches about. The men, he calls them, who know exactly what they want out of life: God, family, and a job.

I'm not one of those men. I'm an escaped Texas refugee who fled to Virginia on a lacrosse scholarship. I love the green hills of Virginia. I love being half a continent away from my mother, father, and overbearing big sister more.

The guys and I closed down the bar last night. It's one of my favorite haunts here in the metropolis of Washington D.C. It's casual, unpretentious, and full of Irishmen—just my kind of scene. The three of us kept girls off the radar last night. It was a bros night. Max didn't discuss his almost-fiancée, Marissa. Jake and I threw away the girl's numbers we received. No, last night, seemed like a finale of sorts. It was like we were all tiptoeing around the giant, pink elephant in the room: we're growing up. We relived the glory days of college, told and retold our favorite stories, and discussed important world events. You know, things like *Is boxing a dead sport now that MMA is so popular?*

We'd all graduated in December. Max and Marissa had moved to Atlanta, and were just starting their careers in finance. They shared a playing card-sized one-bedroom apartment, and hand-me-down furniture and kitchen gadgets. Jake was in New York, trying his hand at working at his dad's real estate company, and looking to score with anything that had long legs and said she was a model. Me? Well, I'm using the nine months between the end of college and the beginning of law school to "experience the real world." My dad got me this job as a campaign aid for Senator Jones, the next president of the United States of America.

Am I a republican? Not necessarily. Personally, I'd like to keep the money I make in my checking account, but I also can't pass a homeless guy on the street without stuffing at least a buck in his cup. I haven't figured myself out enough to even come close to knowing if Langford Jones will make a decent President.

My dad said my job title of Campaign Aid will look great on future resumes. I'm sure he's right. In fact, the man is rarely wrong. Doesn't mean that this job doesn't suck gigantic sweaty balls.

I'm one of the lucky few who are actually paid to staff this office hellhole. What am I paid to do? Any shit job my boss asks. Sometimes I use my double major in political science and finance to do very difficult tasks, like stapling information packets on our candidate's talking points. Other mental exercises include making coffee, scheduling appointments, grabbing lunch from the corner deli, and answering the phone.

Nowhere in any college brochure I read, did it say that if you graduated with an almost perfect GPA and a double major, you'd start out your career placing and picking up sandwich orders.

Bitter? Maybe. I knew I wasn't ready for the real world yet, so I decided to escape to even more higher education at George Washington Law. What am I going to do with a law degree? Who knows? What I am NOT going to do is stay in politics. I can guaran-damn-tee you that. What this job working in the campaign headquarters has taught me is to stay far, far away from the gory world of our country's political system.

"Want a donut?"

I look up from my menial task of filing—there are no stray papers lying around, because the dragon lady is visiting today—and see Lucas leaning against one of the old, grey, dented metal filing cabinets. Lucas is one of the reasons that this job sucks so much. He's maybe five-feet five-inches in heels, and as round as he is tall. I mention his appearance only because, well, I think of him as the slime a snail leaves behind. He's Steve, my boss's assistant.

Lucas gets off on making me, who he calls "pretty boy," do all the crap tasks in the office. I could overlook his SHORTcomings if he hadn't of asked me on my first week, and in front of the other staffers and volunteers, if I were gay. Because apparently men who do things like wear matching clothes, brush their teeth twice a day, comb their hair and put some product in it are gay. My mouth had gaped open. First of all, it's none of his business. Secondly, who does that? I mean have some tact—manners, for God's sake. That's like asking a woman what she weighs, or if the curtains match the drapes. Rudeness is the biggest turn-off for me. Call me a southern gentleman. Call me a ladies' man. Whatever, but poor manners are the surest way to get on my bad side.

Lucas waves a donut under my nose as if he's taunting me with it. I shake my head. The dude has a sugar glaze that surrounds his lips with flakes of sugar dotting his poorly-groomed beard.

My top lip rises in disgust. "No thanks."

"What? Pretty boy doesn't want to ruin his perfect abs?" he says using some sophomoric voice from grade school.

My hands ball into tight fists and I mentally count to ten before I tell him to go fuck himself. My body relaxes as I pretend to shuffle through the papers I'm supposed to be filing. "Something like that," I reply as I attempt to hide my disdain.

He shrugs his shoulders and says, "More for me," as he shoves another jelly-filled bit of fried dough into his pie hole.

I look down at my stack of paper, hoping that Lucas will move on to harassing someone else. I sort through the *H* file folders, looking for the name Darrius Howard. Whoever had this job before me must've failed Alphabetizing 101. These filing cabinets look like a frat house after an all-weekend party.

Apparently, Lucas hadn't left. "Don't forget Rachael Early, the next President's Chief of Staff, is stopping by today. We're all supposed to be on our best behavior." This is all said through an open mouth, revealing the mushed contents of the red jam and light-tan dough.

I ignore Lucas, and all but let an *F* bomb fly at the realization that once again, these files are so out of order. Darrius Howard's file is nowhere even remotely near the other "Ho" file folders.

The dull headache from too much beer the night before flares into a migraine. I'm sure it's somehow Lucas's fault. I reach up and use my thumb to press where the pain is the most intense.

Normal people would interpret this as me not feeling well, and leave me alone. Not Lucas. He goes full speed ahead.

"Steve told me to tell you to order a couple of sandwich trays, that carrot and raisin salad, and …"

I look up from what I am doing and turn to Lucas with a caustic grin on my face. "Let me guess … and a large tub of mayonnaise potato salad." My stomach flips at just the thought. I swear to God, when this job is over I will never, and I do mean ever, eat, look at, or be in the same room as a jar of mayo. How Steve and Lucas can consume it every single day is really beyond me.

Lucas nods and says, "Yeah. Exactly."

When he finally leaves, I reach into my pants' pocket and pull out the aspirin I was smart enough to grab this morning on my way out the door. I pop two tablets into my mouth and dry-swallow. It's one of my many talents.

Next, I check my watch. I'll need to place the deli order in thirty minutes so I have enough time to pick it up and have it arranged as Steve likes it before our "war meeting" with Rachael.

I haven't met the infamous Rachael before. Rumor has it she's a mega bitch. Like, she eats people that cross her for breakfast. Just her name makes Steve tremble in his wing-tipped shoes.

I picture her looking like the female version of Attila the Hun. The facial hair is still present, and she carries a sword for chopping off the heads of campaign staffers who fail in their tasks.

My first day on the job, I was told to avoid Rachael if I ever met her, and never look her directly in the eye. She can apparently sense weakness, and likes to make young campaign staffers cry.

One of my coworkers likes to tell the story of Rachael bringing two well-known senators from different sides of the aisle to a Kumbaya kind of moment simply by threatening to intervene in their negotiations. Trust me, I'm about as excited for this war meeting as I am ordering mayonnaise potato salad.

We've been preparing the office for this momentous occasion all week. I kid you not. Lucas handed me a bottle of spray bleach and had me scrub the wood around the bottom of the walls. I'm sure this was by far the best use of my double degree.

Maybe I should be like Max and Jacob, and go ahead and face the real world. What am I going to do with a law degree anyway? It's not like I want to actually practice law.

I set my stack of papers that need to be filed to the side and make my way to my desk. *Desk* is really a misnomer. It's a folding table for my personal laptop to rest on. My desk chair? It's a metal folding thing, probably picked up at the Salvation Army. I seriously don't wear the nice slacks, my mom insisted on buying for me, to work because I'm convinced they'll be stained from the rust. Plus, the tags are still on them, so if I need beer money I can take them back to Brooks Brothers.

I bring up the web page of the deli that's bookmarked in my Internet browser and grab one of the millions of phones on the folding table. Campaign offices may not have desks, but we've got probably two hundred landline phones for dialing for dollars.

"Hi, this is Graham, at future President Jones's campaign office." My eyes roll so far in my head, I swear I see my brain. We've been trained to spew that nonsense each time we speak to anyone. Something about if you say it enough times it'll come true, or some kind of bullshit like that. "I'd like to place an order ..."

I drone on, essentially placing the same order I call in every day, except this time it's in larger quantities. My shoulders slump forward. Another pet peeve of mine. Good posture is supremely important. Nothing says unsure-of-oneself like a rounded back. Right now, I don't care. I've got twelve weeks, three days, and five more hours of this horrible job until I can quit for law school. I might have to solicit the help of my perfect, beautiful, and very intelligent four-year-old niece in making a countdown chart. This has got to be the worst job ever!

Then, as if the universe decided to further piss on my parade, I hear a few bars of my school fight-song play, alerting me I have a text. Before I look, I know exactly who it's from. Max and Jacob are crashing at my apartment. Begrudgingly, I extract my phone from my pocket.

Max: *Just waking up. How come there's only one beer in the fridge? Your place sucks.*

I mumble to my phone, "How about some mayo potato salad?"

The phone goes back in my pocket without a response because I just can't take my friends' snide comments at the moment.

If there were any justice in this world, I'd be just waking up at my apartment. Max, Jacob and I would hit the local hotdog stand on the corner and head to the park to toss the football. Then, when it started getting dark, we'd go back to my place for showers. A night of sheer debauchery would follow: girls, booze, and everything red-blooded American men hold dear.

Instead, I look around at the sparse office space future President Jones' campaign office occupies. The walls are painted a dull, pale yellow. Yard signs are stapled along their surface. We have piles more of them in the large room we use as a storage closet. The place is damn depressing.

I assumed my first job out of college would have mahogany-wood walls, and rich leather chairs. My secretary would be named Sylvia, and be a former model with waist-long blonde hair that she keeps up in a tight bun. Maybe some glasses? She could rock the sexy librarian vibe.

Instead, I'm the secretary in a drab office space where I share a small room and "desk" space with twenty other staffers just like me. The only difference is Lucas has decided every shit job is mine.

Pushing my metal chair back, I come to the conclusion that it's better to wait for the food at the deli than sit here watching Lucas shove more donuts in his mouth while Steve barks orders at anyone who'll listen to "clean this place up."

As I make my way toward the door, one of the other staffers grabs my arms, and says with a look of panic etching her otherwise very nice features, "Rachael will be here in one hour!"

The look on her face reminds me of some bad B-movie horror flick. She could be clutching my arm and screaming, "The aliens will be here any minute to suck our brains out of our skulls," while she brings the back of her hand up to her forehead in a dramatic faint.

Touching her arms, I attempt to reassure her that it'll be okay. "I'm off to get the food," I say as if I'm talking to my niece. "It'll be okay."

"Good," she says, pushing a stray piece of auburn hair out of her eyes. "Good thinking. Maybe food will keep her from firing all of us."

Fireworks go off in my head. There are ringing bells, and a choir of angels sings "Hallelujah." Fired? That doesn't sound half bad. There's not enough time before law school starts to get another job. I could spend the last couple of months hanging with my friends. Drinking beer. Sleeping in. SOLD. *Dear God, please let us be fired.*

Before I have a chance to respond, Steve is yelling at her about some figures that need to be prepared.

I continue my quest to escape and push open the bathroom door, slipping inside, grateful it isn't occupied. Standing in front of the mirror, I actually look at my reflection. I've been avoiding this since before graduation because I know my image is not the man I want to be. I look like me. My dark brown hair is fixed in the rumbled style popular now because of Sawyer on *Lost*. Thank God for Visine, because my blue eyes are no longer bloodshot from one-too-many beers. I did shave this morning, and put on a pair of plain blank pants and a white dress-shirt, tucked in with a thin black belt. Of course, I didn't forget to pin "Jones for President," complete with the waving flag on my shirt pocket. My build is still as muscular as it was when I was playing lacrosse. Now, though, I just play on a local weekend-warrior kind of team. Most of the guys are trying to recapture their college years. Thank God I'm not part of that group.

I stare at my reflection, pondering how in the hell I ended up so wishy-washy about my future. Mr. Most Likely to Succeed now looks more like Mr. Most Likely To Follow In His Father's Footsteps. Why? Because what better option do I have. I'm grown up, according to society, and have no clue what I want to do with the rest of the seventy years I hopefully have on this earth. Two degrees and law school at least delays moving back to Texas and being a junior partner in my dad's accounting firm for a couple of more years.

I slap the marble bathroom counter and hope for the best. "Come on, Rachael. Live up to your reputation and fire us," I speak to myself in the mirror before I make my way to the deli.

The aspirin has done the trick. My headache is back to a dull throb, and my stomach doesn't revolt when the smell of salty French fries floods my nose. I slip onto the barstool at the counter, and am greeted by the blonde waitress who I flirt with every day.

"Hi Graham," she says, leaning forward on the counter to show me her more than ample cleavage. "Your order will be ready in about fifteen minutes. You guys must have something big going on. That's a lot of food."

"Big boss is paying us a visit today. Steve decided to be nice and buy the office lunch." I grab one of the discarded, grease-stained *Washington Post*s lying nearby. *Catch the hint. I don't want to talk to anyone today.* The top story is something about the Middle East. I scan the article, but don't really read it.

"What DO I care about?" I ask myself instead of reading. The whole office is in a panic because they're worried about getting fired. What's wrong with me that I'm hoping to hear those words? A smile forms on my lips. The idea of being fired is the first time that I've smiled when I've thought about my future. Pathetic.

Mentally, I bang my head against a wall. There's got to be something wrong with me. I picture being destitute and living on the streets to induce the feeling of stress. I picture having to call my dad and tell him that I lost my law school opportunity because I was fired by the she-devil, Rachael.

Nothing. I feel no sense of panic. I can't even get my breathing to pick up speed.

I really am an apathetic loser.

"Peace in the Middle East. What an elusive idea," says a lyrical voice next to me.

"Yeah." I half-heartedly chuckle, attempting to ignore the voice by burying my nose deeper in the newspaper. This is one of the things I liked about ditching Texas. No one strikes up random conversations here. You look forward, and mind your own damn business.

"I'd like a Diet Coke to go please," the voice says to the flirty blonde waitress. "Have you gotten to page four yet? There's a great article on future President Jones."

I mean, I'm clearly holding the newspaper and perusing the second page. *No, I haven't gotten to page four yet, and hopefully the waitress will hurry my order up so I never have to read it.* "No, I just started reading the second page." I'm giving off the biggest don't-talk-to-me-lady vibe I can. Just let me stew in my apathy.

"Would you mind turning to the page, and reading the article?" the voice asks. My Texas radar goes off, and I detect a faint hint of southern accent. Should have known. Talking to a stranger. Asking for absurd favors. Only someone from the south.

I put down my newspaper, expecting to turn and give her a quick lesson on how DC works. We all ignore each other; that's some free advice to make her stay here more pleasant.

Then my heart begins to race. Not in panic, like I was trying to induce earlier. No. This is because this girl literally steals the oxygen from my lungs.

The voice belongs to Tinker Bell. Not the sorority girls dressed in slutty Halloween costumes that showed up every year at our Halloween frat-party version of the fairy. No. She's the Tinker Bell that Walt Disney drew that my niece is obsessed with. The woman is stunning, with light-blonde hair pulled tightly away from her heart-shaped face. Soft white bangs sweep across her forehead. Her eyes are captivating. They're way too large for her face, but they're the bluest blue I've ever seen. Her nose is a pixie nose, tiny and cute, and just the tip points to the ceiling. I find myself longing to touch my lips to the tip.

But it's her mouth that makes my dick take notice. Her lips are so deeply red that they look burgundy. She's captivating, sitting on the barstool next to me in a green business suit. Her body is tiny, like a pixie, and her legs, Jesus Christ. I let my eyes travel down to admire her bare, alabaster-toned legs. As if just to torture me, one of her green heels is dangling off her big toe, revealing her red, perfectly manicured toes. Feet are a big deal. They have to be well cared for. Huge, flat toes that look like rocks are major turn-offs.

The top of her head only meets my shoulder.

I'm staring. I know I am, but I can't help myself. This woman isn't close to my type. I normally like very tall women. There's nothing sexier than a woman who almost reaches my six-foot one-inch height. I also like long, brown hair. But my type flies out the window as I check out the fairy next to me.

She smiles, revealing gorgeous, straight, white teeth. I long to run my tongue over those teeth, exploring the smooth porcelain before I nibble on her maroon lips. *God, I need those lips.*

What's wrong with me? I'm Graham Jackson. I don't chase girls. Girls come after me.

"Your order is ready." Tinker Bell tilts her small head and nods to the pile of food in front of me.

"What?" I ask, clearly forgetting where I am, and what I'm doing in this cramped deli at noon on a Thursday.

She picks up a white Styrofoam cup and purses her lips around the tip of the straw. My dick takes notice, and all but begs those lips to move further south.

"Isn't that your food?" she asks again. Her dark brown arching brows meet together in confusion.

Food. Yes. The reason I'm in a deli. Yes. Rachael, A.K.A. Attila the Hun will be at our office in just a few minutes. "Yeah. Sorry," I mumble as stand up, and grab the mound of stacked sandwich platters and white bag filled with the salads.

I balance the four plastic trays on my arms and put the bag on top, making my way for the door.

Desperately, I long to turn around and take in one more sight of Tink before I enter my personal hell, but I don't dare. I can't afford to do anything that throws off the balance of the trays. *Yay! I was fired for dropping Attila's food.*

"Let me get the door for you," the polite southern voice calls from behind me.

My heart falls in relief. I can see her one more time. "Thanks. That would be awesome of you."

When she rushes past me to push open the glass door, I notice just how petite she is. *She really is a pixie.* I don't think she's even adult height, but she's so in proportion, almost as if an adult, athletic female had been left too long in the dryer.

I scoot past her, turning on my southern charm. "Isn't it my job to hold the door for you?" Is there a worse pick-up line? No. I don't think so. FAIL.

"Well, the way I was raised, you help out your fellow man." She pauses, and adds, "Or woman whenever they're in need." She doesn't say it catty or mean-spirited, like a lot of girls I know would have. It's said in a very matter-of-fact, self-assured tone. I like that. And she's not making me feel like an idiot for dropping such a lame line.

Next, she's opening the double doors of my office building. *How'd she know where I was going?* Who cares? She's apparently coming upstairs with me.

"Second floor?"

"Yes. Thanks for your help. My boss's boss is visiting today, so the whole office is freaking out. He'd kill me if these," I nod toward the pile of food, "didn't arrive in pristine condition."

"Planned visit?" she asks as she leans against the elevator railing, crossing her arms over her chest. I've yet to see if she has nice tits, but for once, I don't think I care.

I find myself not wanting the elevator ride to be over.

"Arrives any minute. Apparently it's been scheduled for a couple of days, because all we've done is prepare. Like, a work stoppage." I roll my eyes so she knows just exactly how I feel about this.

"What's your boss's boss like?" she asks conspiratorially.

"Never met her. Word in the office is she's a real ball-breaker." Fuck! I just said the words "ball-breaker" to Tinker Bell.

"Really?" Tink asks. I carefully examine her face to see if I've offended her. Fortunately, she seems okay.

The elevator doors open, and she walks ahead of me, pushing the campaign office's doors away from her. As soon as she does, I hear the roar of greetings from inside.

My stupid, beer-soaked brain from last night actually ponders for a moment why she's getting such a nice greeting. I mean, she just hit buttons and opened doors for me. Then, the light bulb turns on inside my head. *Oh, shit! Tink is Attila the Hun.* But where is her facial hair?

If I could kick my own ass, I would.

I just told her—the enemy—our secrets. Reviewing the conversation in my mind makes it even worse. My chin falls to my chest, and I pretend to carefully watch what I'm doing as I begin to arrange the trays across our conference room table.

There's no need for me to find a mirror. I know my face is bright red.

The infamous Rachael Early is being fawned over by Steve. He's offering to give her a tour of the office. Then Lucas inserts himself in the conversation, shoving some report he did under her upturned nose that I wanted to kiss moments ago. Out of my peripheral vision, I watch the bastard hand her his plastic-covered report. His red, glistening palm touches the exposed white skin of her wrist that her jacket has revealed. I long to nibble on that wrist and feel her pulse against my tongue.

Then, I rage. How dare the snail-trail Lucas touch her? Shoving his head in the toilet and flushing it for touching my Tink sounds like a brilliant idea.

What's wrong with me? Jealous? That's not my style.

I walk to the window, watching the cars pass along the street. Thousands of people are rushing to their small jobs. Each one is a cog in the system that keeps this democracy running.

I've got to get myself under control.

"Graham Jackson does not fawn over girls," I whisper to myself. He's the one who has his pick of the girls at the end of the night. There is a little voice in the back of my head that says, "That was the Graham Jackson, star lacrosse-player, president of his frat, and college big man. Maybe this Graham Jackson, out in the real world, has to chase girls."

A yellow taxicab aims for a red SUV inserting itself into traffic. For a second, I hope against hope for a T-bone accident. Maybe it would cancel this meeting, and I could just go home. No luck. The SUV lets the cab safely into the next lane.

This is ridiculous. She's a world-class ball-buster. Everyone knows that. She's not Tinker Bell. In fact, she's more like Captain Hook. Makes staffers cry. Fuck. Now, I'm an adult man thinking about Peter Fucking Pan.

Steve asks everyone to take a seat, shaking me out of my own head, which is probably a very good thing. I plop down in a chair at the end of the table and fiddle with the yellow legal tablet and pen in front of me. It must have been placed there by one of the staffers so we can take "notes" on all the important things Rachael has to regale us with.

The guy to my left suggests I make a plate. It actually takes me a few second to figure out how in the hell one makes a plate. My face must betray my thoughts, because he motions toward the food. My stomach is in knots, and it isn't from the beer last night. I finally have the moment I've heard about when you experience lust at first sight, and it has to be with her.

I'm confused, and my head and body are at war with each other. *She was nice. Nothing like what the rumors said about her. Would she be interested in a guy like me?* Does she care I'm probably seven years younger than she is?

She travels the country being future President Jones' right-hand woman. The last thing she wants is to date a much younger college graduate who doesn't know what he wants to be when he grows up. Hell! If I asked her on a date, my dad's credit card would pay. Pathetic.

No. I need to forget Tinker Bell/Attila the Hun ever existed. *She doesn't have facial hair. In fact, she has the sexiest blue eyes ...*

Stop it!

Once everyone gets settled with their heaping plates of food, Steve stands up and makes the obvious introduction. "Room of pathetic individuals, this is the fairy, Rachael. Rachael, meet the scabs of the earth."

Rachael stands and takes a sip of the Diet Coke she ordered in the deli. "Hello everyone. It's a pleasure to meet you. Steve talks so highly of the efforts you're putting forth to share future President Jones' message. I've come today to meet you in person, and thank you for your on-the-street efforts, and to make sure that this campaign is a positive experience for everyone."

She might as well have been speaking Spanish. I didn't hear a word she said, only listened to how her voice sounded like a song. *Is that her fuck-voice? When her petite legs are wrapped around my waist, is that the voice she'll use to scream out "Graham?"*

I've resolved myself to the fact that my dick will stand firmly at attention until she leaves. Let's hope I don't have to write on the dry-erase board, or war board, as Steve calls it.

The next thing I know, Lucas is talking. I usually just tune him out until I hear my name exit his nasty mouth. "He really doesn't seem to have his heart in the campaign. It's like he's just here to collect a paycheck." His voice sounds like he's my niece, tattling on me for something horrible I said, like "shut up."

Did that bastard just rat me out? I'm in shock. Are we an office of seven-year-olds? Okay. It's partially true. But, I mean, seriously. Why call me out in front of everyone? My weeks are numbered here … twelve weeks, to be exact.

Rachael's voice cuts through the fog of immaturity. "I'm not here to play referee, Lucas. That is your name, correct?" She drips honey, and I love it. She's cutting and authoritative without being snippy. "Let me tell you why I believe Langford Jones should be the next President of the United States of America."

She's so confident, and her presence alone commands our attention. Maybe the rumors about her were wrong …

I lean back in my chair and prepare to listen. I've read the talking points of the campaign hundreds of times while stapling them together. Frankly, if there were a pop quiz, I'd make a one hundred. Maybe if I can record Rachael reading them to me, the job will be less mentally numbing.

"Langford is my friend," she begins as she stands up straight at the head of the conference room table. "I was hired to work in his office when he first earned his senate seat. I was fresh out of graduate school, and didn't know what I didn't know." Jesus, I could relate to that. "I interviewed with him, not one of his assistants. He told me his goals; his dreams for the future of our county. I was captivated by him, and his vision. And after that meeting, I was inspired enough to turn down a job offer from Trump International, making a lot more money. Ready to take on the world, he hired me. I was prepared to campaign and march into battle with him."

Her mouth twists into a little smile. "Then, I was handed a ream of paper and told to go make copies. When I was done, I sorted and stapled everything I'd copied. Not a glamorous job."

Was this lady speaking my language, or what? That was me right now. I'm half tempted to raise my hand and ask how she got herself out of copy-room hell.

Rachael pauses and places a fork full of mayo potato salad into her mouth. Potato salad has never looked so damn appetizing.

"I put a smile on my face, and made copies every single day. Two months later, I received a promotion to errand girl. You get the idea. My idealized job was far beneath what I thought a Wharton School of Business graduate should be doing. Every day, I wished that I'd accepted the offer of working for Donald Trump. I reasoned that he wouldn't have made me make copies."

She pauses while she licks some stray mayo off her burgundy lips. Her tongue darting out and swiping over the offending glob of whiteness. "Oh God!" I groan as my eyes drop to my cock.

"One day, I'd had enough. I put on my power suit, newest heels, and marched into the Senator's personal office without an appointment."

She smirks. "Apparently, no one did that." Her musical laugh fills our dreary conference room making it feel more cheery. "Like I said. I didn't know what I didn't know."

Her face lights up at the memory, and she's the most mesmerizing thing I've ever seen. "I told him that I believed in everything he stood for, and I was being underutilized, stuck as messenger girl in his office. I reiterated for him my schooling, GPA, and I threw in the turned-down Trump job offer. Then, because I wanted to really hammer my point home, I repeated my accomplishments in all the different languages I speak."

The room chuckles, and I notice Rachael has everyone's attention. Pens are resting on the yellow legal pads, and all eyes are captivated by my own little fairy.

"Instead of responding and telling me I was a snot-nosed brat, he stood up, and grabbed his suit jacket. Then, the spun on his heels and invited me to his home for dinner. I was dumbfounded, and muttered something like a thank you.

"When we arrived at his townhome, dinner was on the table. The boys, who were very young at the time, minded their table manners. His wife, Shelby, was lovely to me. She asked about my childhood and college. This was the most normal family meal I'd been a part of.

"After dinner, we all went into the backyard and played catch. Shelby put the kids to bed, while Langford sat me down for a fatherly chat. He said we all have to start at the bottom and pay our dues. All a college degree does is prove you can complete something. He told me to keep working hard, and eventually I'd get to be on the battle lines, fighting alongside him for our country. He thanked me for taking the job, and reassured me he appreciated all the things that I did every day, no matter how small they seemed. He reminded me I was the face of his office. I was the staffer who interfaced with the other senator's offices. I was the one who the other employees based their assumptions upon."

Her lips wrap around the Diet Coke straw, and I barely notice. Rachael is speaking to me. My dad has essentially given me the same lecture probably one thousand times about paying my dues. For some reason, coming from Tink's mouth, the words penetrate my thick skull so I actually hear the meaning.

"That day, I learned that future President Jones was still paying off his student loans. He'd married Shelby, who was the only person to ever beat him in the school spelling bee. He fathered a baby with her when they were only sixteen. They gave the baby up for adoption and consider it the hardest, but best decision they've made. I saw Senator Jones as a human being for the first time, and not this political force to be reckoned with."

Oh my God, he's a real guy. Made mistakes in his past and still got elected to the senate? Is that even possible? I was liking the guy Rachael spoke about more and more with each passing second.

She looks at us conspiratorially, and then does this exaggerated move where she looks over both shoulders. In a fake whisper, she says, "Most importantly, he shared with me that he hates that the political system holds words you spoke or views you expressed at a younger time against you. He said, 'Rachael, I didn't know I wanted to be president when I was kid, so I've certainly not lived my life like someone who's running for office. I think being impulsive and fearless is a sign of youthful exuberance. I'll forgive you bursting into my office this afternoon if you promise to work your tail off to earn the right to demand to be listened to.'"

Rachael spent the next hour driving home future President Jones' speaking points. She reviewed the pillars of his campaign with us. No-nonsense is a good and appropriate description of her personality. Her charisma and enthusiasm was contagious, and by the end of the war meeting, I didn't even want to pour salt on the snail, Lucas. Instead of counting down the days until I could bid farewell to this tedious job, I actually found myself wondering if I could still volunteer for future President Jones' campaign while attending law school.

Also, I realized at some point while Rachael was speaking, I forgot that she was gorgeous and sexy. I quit thinking about her being my pixie. Names like Attila the Hun and Ball Buster flew out the window. Instead, I saw her for who she really was: a smart woman who, in her early thirties, has earned the trust of future President Jones, and become his right-hand woman. She believes in him, and she inspired me. She's tough, because she's proud of what they've built together and wants to protect it. That was obvious. Rachael is a force to be reckoned with. I want to be a force also.

Clarity. They say when you get it it's better than sex. I'm not so sure about that, but for the first time since graduation I don't feel as lost. It's like the haze clinging to my brain has been burned off. I know I don't want to be a Junior CPA in my dad's firm.

No, that's not quite what I mean. I will not SETTLE for being a Junior CPA in my dad's firm. I want to get my law degree, and work for the good legislators who are making the country a better place. Like future President Jones. The ones who, like me, haven't spent their lives knowing who they were.

My eyes have been opened. Drape peace beads around my neck and call me a hippie, I think I just found my calling. I want to be the next Rachael Early when I grow up.

... Want more of Graham and Rachael's story? It will be available Summer 2014

About Layne Harper

Layne Harper taught Tom Brady how to throw a football, and she's E.L. James' red room consultant. In her spare time, she travels the world with Angelina Jolie helping orphans. Not really, but it sounds more exciting than her normal life. She's mastered the art of takeout dining, turning down the volume right before the singer says a bad word, and disguising wine in a thermos for evening soccer games. She can make a snow cone that rivals the best in the world. Layne writes constantly in her head, on napkins, her kids' homework, or whatever is close by. If you want to know more about Layne, check out her website at

www.LayneHarper.com.

www.ingramcontent.com/pod-product-compliance
Lightning Source LLC
Chambersburg PA
CBHW050020180626
46810CB00002B/503